Nothing Left To Lose

Nothing Left To Lose

A NOVEL BY

Allan G. Johnson

Plain View Press

ISBN: 978-1-935514-94-7
Library of Congress Control Number: 2011930987

Cover art: "Red Clouds," pastel by Karen Jones
Cover design by Pam Knight

Acknowledgements
Recognition and thanks for use of the following:
"For What It's Worth," by Stephen Sills, Alfred Music Publishing,
by permission of the publisher; Part I, lines 1-2, 15-17; Part II, lines
4-7, 11-14, 16-18 from "Howl," from *Collected Poems, 1947-1980*, by
Allen Ginsberg. Copyright © 1955 by Allen Ginsberg. Reprinted by
permission of HarperCollins Publishers.

Plain View Press
P.O. 42255
Austin, TX 78704

plainviewpress.net
pk@plainviewpress.net
512-441-2452

For Susan Bright

Also by Allan G. Johnson

Fiction
The First Thing and The Last

Nonfiction
The Forest and the Trees
The Gender Knot
Privilege, Power, and Difference

*In peace, sons bury their fathers; but in war,
fathers bury their sons.*

Croseus of Lydia

One

1

Anne stood on the steps of the dormitory and watched the boys, many of them her husband's students, on their way to class. It was cold, the middle of January, with fresh snow on the ground. A chill went through her, the blouse offering no protection, and a youthful face going by looked at her, curious, as if wondering why she'd be out without a coat. She cupped her elbows in her hands and thought of her own boys, so much like these before they went away.

She lifted her head and closed her eyes against the sun bright in the sky, and summoned into her mind the simple, hopeful device she had invented to calm the ever-present fear of losing Joshua, now in the midst of war, and Andrew, soon to graduate from college and follow the path laid down by his father and then his brother. She felt the warmth of the sun on her face and calculated it was tomorrow in Vietnam. She imagined herself drifting in the air just above where Joshua threaded his way through the jungle, the air thick and hot, or across some grassy highland or beneath a dark and starlit sky, the strap from his helmet swinging gently back and forth as he walked and hummed a little tune. Tomorrow, she thought. The miracle of the International Date Line. It comforted her as she played in her mind with the idea that if it was always tomorrow there and yesterday here, then somehow they were both protected from today, where everything happens, the present held at bay somewhere in between where it could do them no harm.

She went inside to finish the breakfast dishes. She stood at the sink, looking out the window as she had so many times before, and her mind wandered back to the spring evening in 1966, almost two years ago, the shattering of glass and her body sinking down, her heart pressing on everything below.

There was no snow outside the window then, open a crack to admit a breeze coming from the west across the great lawn that fronts the school that had been her home since the end of the World War II. She was doing the dishes while Joshua and Andrew sat at the table behind her and talked with their father, their voices easy and light. The air moved the curtains as she looked out at the sky streaked with pink, her face smooth and full of thought, her hands occupied, her mind free to roam and wonder.

And then something happened.

There was William clearing his throat and saying, "So, you went ahead, then?" and Joshua's chair creaking beneath his shifting weight and his voice, soft, "yes," speaking down into the table, "I did."

There was something about the tone of it, the hesitation wrapped inside a tightness in his throat, the strained little beat after each word, that combined to still her hands in the air, the glass held lightly in her fingers. She had missed what went before and didn't know the context for the rest. For an instant she imagined he'd changed his mind as he'd done so many times before that they took his announcements with a grain of salt, yet another girlfriend, or changing his major just one more time, so it wouldn't surprise her if he'd decided against going to law school and was set instead on politics or medicine or teaching like his father.

But as the silence took on depth and weight she knew it was something more.

Joshua spoke, his voice earnest and low, and she missed all but the opening "I" and then heard the word that made her forget what she was doing.

"What?" she said over her shoulder, and then he told her he'd joined the Marines and that was when she dropped the glass. She looked down and saw it fall before it left her soapy fingers. She knew what was about to happen and yet did nothing, as if she were suspended above herself, watching herself watch it slip away from her and shatter against the hairline crazing in the old sink.

There was a long silence after Andrew jumped up to ask if she was all right and William chimed in wanting to know if she was hurt. But she said nothing, noting how Joshua's silence rose up to meet her own.

"What about law school?" she said at last, still looking down at the broken glass.

Joshua cleared his throat. "It can wait." He looked at his father and then down at the table, pressing the tines of his fork into the place mat.

"For what?" she said, turning to lean back against the sink. "Why can't *this* wait? You can be a lawyer in the Marines. They do have lawyers, don't they?"

"It's what I have to do."

"I figured something like that," she said. "But why, for God's sake?"

"Anne," said William, "go easy."

"Easy?" she said. "You want me to go easy? My son announces he's going to Vietnam and you want *me* to go easy?"

"Mom," said Joshua, "I'd probably get drafted anyway."

"It's true," said Andrew.

She shot him a hard look and his face darkened as he looked down.

"You don't know that," she said, turning back at Joshua. "The draft board isn't going to yank you out of Yale law school."

Joshua stared at the table and pressed harder with the fork.

"How long have you been thinking about this?" she said.

"A couple of months," said Joshua, glancing at his father without lifting his head.

She looked at William who sat calm and self-contained, his lips parted as if to say something, but silent as he returned her look. She tried to imagine what he was feeling, but couldn't tell, his face so smooth, as always, and the light over the table reflecting off his glasses, obscuring his eyes. She felt suddenly nauseous and laid a hand across her stomach.

"Did you know about this?"

"He mentioned it."

"And you didn't tell me."

"I asked him not to," said Joshua. "I wasn't sure and I thought you'd worry."

Anne glared at her husband, her eyes hard and full of light. She sighed as she turned to Joshua.

"And you didn't think it would worry your father."

A stillness filled the room, edgy with risk.

"I forbid it," she said, shaking her head and looking down at the floor.

"Mom."

"Anne," said William. "It's already done."

"I forbid it," she said, gritting her teeth against the tears filling her eyes.

"Mom, I'll be all right."

"You don't know that," she said, the words catching in her throat. "Tell me, please. How can you know that?"

"Well, you know. You never know. I could get hit by a truck tomorrow—"

"That doesn't mean you lie down in the road and wait for it."

"I'll be careful."

She shook her head. "Joshua," she said, "don't do this."

"I have to."

"That isn't true."

"I took the oath. It's done, Mom. Like Dad said."

She looked at him, but he wouldn't meet her eye.

"Well," she said, stiffening, "no need to talk it over with your mother then, since war is none of my business. That's for the men to decide, isn't it. And since you didn't bother to tell me until now, I won't have to worry, will I. What a relief."

"Mom," he said, but she was already halfway down the hall and into her bedroom, slamming the door behind.

Looking out at the snow, Anne remembered the desolate feeling of the door closing behind after she fled the kitchen. She shook her head as she placed the last dish in the drainer and dried her hands. Then she set about making a batch of cookies to send to Joshua. She'd received the letter a few days before, asking her to send a care package. "You know," he wrote, "like you did when I was at camp." The list was food mostly, with chocolate chip cookies mentioned twice.

She spent the rest of the morning baking and was wrapping twine around the little box when she stopped and shook her head, a look of disbelief spreading across her face, that she was sending cookies to a place where her boy would sit and eat them, perhaps sharing them with friends, when all around, every day, other men would do their very best to kill him, to blow him apart or cut his throat or shoot him through the heart. For several moments she couldn't reconcile the two images in her mind, the lakeside camp in the hills of western Massachusetts and some rice paddy or mountain pass halfway around the world, and she stared at her fingers poised over the package, the string suspended between them, and suddenly felt confused, as if she'd done it all in her sleep and just now woke to find herself standing in the kitchen with no idea of how she got there.

It seemed the rhythm of her life revolved around the arrival of the mail each day, and whenever there was a letter from Vietnam, the decision of whether to share her feelings about it with William. She'd come to know early on that she couldn't be with him and read or feel her way through the letters, or the lack of them, as she needed to.

"Sometimes I think I'd rather have bad news than none at all," she said on a summer evening a few months after Joshua went away.

"There are lots of reasons why he wouldn't write," said William.

"I know. I know them all. You've told me them before. But I can't help it. He's only 22."

"He is a man."

"A *young* man," she said, "who tries to sound older than he is. So damn carefree, on a lark, 'I'll be okay, what a beautiful country'—"

"It keeps his spirits up."

"Of course it does. He can't help it. It's what he does when he's scared, going on and on, like pedaling a bike to keep from falling over. It's like him going to summer camp and writing to say what a great time he was having and would we come and get him right away. I would've, too, if you hadn't made such a thing of it."

"What do you have against him growing up?"

"Nothing."

She had looked at him, his face turned away from her, the expression nearly blank as if he was waiting for her to wind down.

"And when he's not whistling in the dark," she said, "he's telling more than I want to know. What do I need with mines and booby traps . . . all those wires and bits of string they can't see and trip over and get . . . " her eyes filling with tears, " . . . blown up," fluttering her fingers before her face like wings beating the air.

"I don't know what to do," she said. "I don't know how to feel. Sometimes I wonder if I'm losing my mind. I keep thinking I've got to get him out of there. But I know I can't. There's not a damn thing I can do. And they're going to kill him. I can feel it. They're going to keep him there until they've killed him one way or another and then they'll send him home. In a box if he's lucky.

"And if not that, then breathing and walking and looking just like he's alive." She looked at him. "Only he won't be."

He said nothing, his eyes watching her face before turning away.

"War changes everything, doesn't it, Will. And now it's changing Josh, having its way with him, day by day, night by night. Eating his heart." Her voice dropped to just above a whisper.

"And I will never see him again."

And then she began to cry and he reached out and gave her a tissue and stood and went into the kitchen.

That evening she sat on the couch and enacted her solitary ritual of watching the news and its fresh installment of the war. She stared at the black and white images playing out across the screen—generals and politicians explaining strategy and predicting victory, helicopters and jets landing and taking off behind reporters holding microphones, hair blowing about their heads. Clouds of fire billowing up from the jungle floor. Casualties on stretchers or lying in fields in strange, contorted poses. Young GIs, shirts off in the sun, leaning against sand bags and smoking cigarettes and smiling and waving or flashing the two-fingered sign of peace to the camera, their eyes hidden behind dark glasses. Then scenes of anti-war protesters, students and some veterans of the war parading in front of the White House as they chanted, "Hell, no, we won't go!" and "LBJ, LBJ, how many kids did you kill today?"

The back door opened and closed and she heard William's footsteps down the hall, stopping at the doorway as he watched her watching television.

"I don't know why you subject yourself to that," he said.

"You never know. We might get a glimpse of him."

"Jesus, Anne, do you know how many are over there? Half a million? You think you're going to see him in all that?"

"I know," she said, waving him away.

She could feel him standing behind her, shaking his head and watching her until Walter Cronkite appeared on the screen, pages of text in his hands, looking earnestly into their living room. Then she heard William turn and go down the hall and out the door. She imagined him crossing the stone patio and sitting on the top step and lighting a cigarette and watching boys go to and from the library across the way, their voices sharp and young in the evening shadows.

He never smoked inside the house, out of consideration for her distaste for the odor that lingered. Sometimes, though, she would go out and sit with him while he smoked, positioning herself downwind to catch the scent of a freshly lit cigarette which, oddly enough to him, she enjoyed. But it wasn't for this that she came and sat beside him in the evening air, rather to witness the change that seemed to come over him, a sinking down in his body, a softening she saw at no other time, except for unguarded moments when they were making love and she looked into his face and felt the man she used to know emerge, separate and whole, the two men sharing the single body, but one held inside the other, silent and invisible until an opening appeared. Later, he would watch *Gunsmoke* or some other show he liked while she sat down the hall, reading in bed, and then he'd come to her and they might make love and she would look into his face above her in the dark and think how smooth and hard the muscles were, rarely broken by a smile anymore, until the moment he let down and the orgasm swept through him, his head dropping toward his chest as if in prayer, and she'd think he was going to cry or dissolve, the tenderness of being held inside her more than he could bear. It was a mystery to her, this power that seemed to reside in her woman's body, this sacred portal that drew inside a soul yearning after itself and calling it love.

And then he would lie against her, his eyes closed and the breathing slow and deep with little shudders, and she'd feel him separate as he returned to the man he had built for himself to inhabit, and he'd open his eyes and there might be a little smile that met her own as he leaned forward to kiss her and tell her that he loved her.

She sat back, propping an elbow on the arm of the couch, the fingertips of one hand across her lips as she watched the news. The back door opened and closed and she heard his footsteps down the hall, drawing near until he reached over her shoulder and held out a letter.

"I read it on the way home," he said.

She unfolded it on her lap.

Dear Mom and Dad,

I keep writing this and throwing it away. We'll see if this one makes it out. I don't want to say these things to you, especially you, Dad, but I have to tell someone and there's no one I can talk to here. I've never been so scared in my whole life. It's like it's all the way in my bones. Anyone over here knows you have to be crazy not to be scared sometimes, but for me it's all the time. Guys are getting killed every day right next to me, guys I know. I see arms and legs and heads blown off so close I can touch them and now I can't get it out of my mind when I'm awake and when I go to sleep it's in my dreams. Sometimes it just comes into my head like when you're not even thinking about something that happened a long time ago and then you remember how it tasted or smelled. I can't stop thinking it's going to happen to me. There's no safe place over here. I feel like the whole world's booby-trapped. We just got back from getting jumped by VC who pinned us down in a field all night and all the next day. It was boiling hot and we didn't have any water or any way to help the guys who'd been hit. We were lying there all day waiting for someone to get us out. All we could do was listen to guys dying, saying our names, begging us for help, talking to people who weren't even there. One guy was talking to his girl and then his mother all morning and I remember thinking he must have died when he went quiet. Some units are going into villages and wasting everything, burning huts and food and killing animals and then people, even old people and kids. The worst thing is that when I first heard about it I couldn't believe it, but then I understood. We're so frustrated and scared and mad all the time it's amazing we don't blow the whole place to bits just to get it over with. I don't know why I'm here. None of it makes any sense. I know I can't and it's stupid but all I want is to come home. I just want to get out of here. Now I've said it. I'm sorry. I'll be all right. Don't worry. Really. I'm sorry.

Love, Josh

For a long time they were quiet, her looking down at the piece of paper, him staring out the window.

"There must be a way," she said, wiping her nose.

"A way to what?"

"To get him out of there."

"That isn't possible."

"Why not?"

"Anne. You're not thinking."

"Maybe not. Maybe it's not the time for that." She sighed. "I wish," she said, her voice low, "for once you'd join me in feeling something instead of going right to the logic of it. As if I didn't know it's impossible."

"Then what are you saying?"

"I want him home."

"So do I. But there are right ways and wrong ways."

"Such as?"

"Without his tail between his legs."

She looked at him, her gaze unwavering, staring him down, her eyes not leaving his face even as he turned his head away.

"What," he said, looking back at her.

She said nothing, some buttress of support giving way inside of her, unable to resist any longer beneath the weight of the last twenty-three years bearing down on her, twenty-three years of nightmares and denial and silence and living in the presence of a frozen heart guarded by a mind that never slept.

"What is it?" he said, his voice louder and sharper.

She opened her mouth as if to speak but then her eyes widened as a shudder went through her and she looked down at the floor.

"Would you rather he came home the way you did?"

He looked quickly at her and then away, his hands held loosely in the air in front of him, the thumb and forefinger of one softly grasping each finger of the other over and over like working a rosary. And then she watched her words sink in and the feeling drain from his face as he turned to leave, then stopped in the doorway and spoke into the hall, his back to her.

"This isn't summer camp," he said. "He's a soldier. More than that, he's a Marine. And we're at war. You don't come home from a war just because you're afraid. Everyone's afraid. It's part of the deal."

"Deal?" she said, standing up. "What deal?"

He turned and looked at her.

"He took an oath. He has a duty to his country and to himself. He has to see it through."

Even at a distance she could see the muscles work along his jaw.

"What's the other side?" she said.

"What do you mean?"

"What's in it for him?"

"He gets to hold his head up when he comes home," he said through his teeth, turning away, "and know he wasn't a coward."

"Don't you have a problem with sending boys to such a hell?" she said.

"He's a *man*. It's his turn, Anne"

"His turn for what?"

"To go."

"You're talking in code. Go to what?" she said to his back receding down the hall, "go to *what?*" calling after him as he went out the door, the last word catching in her throat, the door already closing behind him.

She sat down, tears running down her face as silence enveloped the room. And then a boy somewhere upstairs put on a Janis Joplin record and she picked up the letter, *I'm sorry*, staring down at the words, then a nod and a whisper, "But not to me."

William crossed the snow-covered ground between the dorm and the library and went in through the main door, waving to the librarian without looking at her perched behind the circulation desk. He passed into the dimly lit stacks, his pace quickening as the books and their familiar dusty smell surrounded and took him in. He climbed the stairs two at a time to the top floor, circled around to the far corner and stepped into an empty carrel, closing the door softly behind. He sat in the dark, eyes shut, and listened for a sound, but there was only silence save for the groan of a radiator muffled by the thousands of books just beyond the door. And then he began to tremble, first in his hands and the muscles of his face and then spreading through his arms and legs as a gasp escaped his throat and he gripped the chair as if it was the only way to keep himself from flying apart into the air.

Anne heard William come home just after 11:00 and she lay in bed listening to the footsteps down the hall, hesitating outside the door to their bedroom before going on, then the silence and the soft pop of the cap coming off a bottle of beer.

She lay in the darkness and waited for him, dread pooling inside her. And then he was in the room, crossing to the closet, taking off his clothes, pulling on pajamas, climbing into bed. He lay on his back, hands behind his head.

"You awake?" he said, his voice soft.

She murmured as if looking back from the far edge of sleep.

"I'm sorry," he said.

She turned her head halfway toward him. "Why is that?"

"I don't mean it to be like this."

"Tell me how you'd like it to be."

There was a long silence.

"Will?"

"What?"

"I asked how you'd like it to be."

"I don't know."

She sighs. "I think you do."

"No, I don't. If I did, I'd say so."

"No, you wouldn't."

"I think I know my own mind."

"Your mind's not what I'm talking about."

"Then what?"

"I never know how you feel."

"I tell you what I think all the time."

"I know," she said. "That's the point."

"Anne, you're not making any sense."

"Not your sort."

"And what is that?" he said, folding his arms over his chest.

She felt his academic mind begin to circle like a lawyer around a hostile witness.

"What do you want from me?" he said.

She lay in the dark, trying to decide whether it was a real question or a veiled accusation, and then realized it was both.

"I want to feel like I'm not alone."

"But you're not."

"Yes, I am."

"You don't mean that."

Deep inside her, anger wrapped around the dread to make a hard and empty space.

"If you say so," she said, a familiar weariness coming over her. "I'm going to sleep."

She lay awake, seeing Joshua's face against the crescent moon barely visible through the trees. And then suddenly she saw in herself a woman whose husband was missing in action, leaving her to hold out and hold on, unable to let go, and yet knowing the time would come when either he must return to her or she would have to decide that he was dead and move on to live alone in her grief or search out in another man what she had loved so much in him.

William stared at her form outlined against the window and sensed a shift he could not name, feeling her separate and far away, farther than ever before. And just beneath lay a deep pool of fear, ancient and menacing and alive, as if waiting to grab hold and drag him under and down.

For several weeks Anne managed to give herself over to the familiar hard edged purity of the New England winter. An ice storm coated the trees and etched the sky in fine crystal that glistened in the sun, only to melt and fall and skitter across the crusted snow. While others complained about the weather, she bore a secret appreciation for its clarity and the revelation of the inner life of trees that took on an entirely different shape and character once freed of their mantle of leaves. She sat on the steps in front of the dorm and followed with her eyes the trunks of tall elms reaching toward the sky, then bowed her head beneath the weight of her own yearning for some sign of grace, of tenderness or mercy. And then she imagined spring, when Joshua would be only a few months from coming home. She looked at the trees silhouetted against the sky, picturing in her mind the green buds at the tips of branches. Coming into their leaving, she thought, smiling at the play on words.

On a cloudy morning, the air dense with the promise of snow, Anne had just sat down at the piano when the doorbell rang. She got up and opened the door to find Jack Heath, the headmaster, standing in the hall, his eyes cast down.

"There's a telegram," he said, his voice flat and low. She noticed he was in shirt-sleeves in spite of the cold and felt herself slowly filling with dread that she kept at bay, if only for a few seconds, by noticing his bow tie askew and lifting her hand as if to set it straight, then coming into her mind once again, the irresistible weight of dread, and finishing the motion of her hand by using her fingers to comb the hair away from her face.

"Who from?"

"The Department of Defense." He held it out to her, his face dark and ashen, and she took it from him without a word.

"Let me know if there's anything I can do," he said. She nodded as she closed the door.

She went down the hall, moving slowly, not looking down at what she carried in her hand as she sat at the kitchen table. She slit open the envelope with her finger and pulled out the single type-written page, her eyes blurring over the words, *we regret to inform*, but gritting her teeth, forcing herself to read the rest, sure that he was dead.

And then stunned that he was not.

She stared, uncomprehending, at the words, *missing in action*, and felt herself suddenly suspended somewhere in the awful barren space bounded by grief on the one side and hope on the other.

She stuffed the telegram in the pocket of her dress and leapt up, the chair falling backwards with a clatter on the floor as she bolted down the hall. She was halfway to the door, pushing an arm through the sleeve of her coat, when the door opened and William stepped inside, stamping his feet on the mat and pulling off his gloves.

"Let me see it."

She thrust the crumpled piece of paper into the air between them and for a moment he didn't move, looking down at the telegram and then at her and back again. The muscles along his jaw slowly tightened and his face smoothed as he took it from her hand and straightened out the wrinkles, slowly and methodically, then put on his glasses and bent his head to read.

Anne slid slowly down against the wall until she came to rest on the floor, her face buried in her hands. The paper shifted and crinkled above her, followed by a soft clearing of his throat, and then the rustle of the page as he dropped his arms and it brushed past the fabric of his trousers. She heard him take off his coat, the closet door swing open, the hanger come off the bar, the muted clunk as it returned bearing the weight of the coat. Every sound came to her slowed and magnified and strangely isolated from the rest—the fine winter grit beneath his shoes as he approached her, the movement of his clothes, the single sniff as he bent down to take her arm.

"Come on," he said. "Don't sit on the floor." When she didn't move, he squared himself in front of her and took her beneath the arms and lifted her up, holding her against him until he felt her legs bear up beneath her weight. He stepped back and removed her coat as she stood there, small and vulnerable, and took her hand and led her to the living room.

"What does it mean?" she said, sitting on the couch.

He sighed. "It means they can't account for him. They don't know where he is."

"Another way of saying he's dead."

"No," he said, leaning down to look up into her face. He looked at her until she met his eyes and made a little nod and then he sat back on the couch.

"It's a good bet that he's hurt. Otherwise he would have stayed with them or made his way back."

"Or he's a prisoner."

"Yes, it could be that."

"Either way, he's lost."

He covered her hand with his.

"He just has to find his way back."

Her voice softened to a whisper. "He can do that." She looked up into his face, tears coming into her eyes. "He *can*, can't he?"

And then, without a sound, a shudder moved through her, releasing the tears that rolled down from her eyes, dripping off her jaw and spotting the blouse. She felt his hand on her back and heard the calm, soothing voice he could do so well in moments of great feeling when he, himself, seemed to feel barely anything at all, not cold, but so thoroughly contained she couldn't see beyond the smooth exterior.

"It'll be all right," he said.

She looked at him, searching for a sign of the man she had married long ago, open and unguarded. But his warm and caring eyes revealed almost nothing of the inner man she'd known, and as she sank into his arms it was as if falling into a deep well of loneliness.

She called Andrew to tell him the news of Joshua. She waited while the boy who answered the phone went to find him in his room, trying to prepare herself by picturing him in the phone booth in the hall of the dormitory, his hip cocked to one side in the jaunty way he had.

But the boy came back on the line to tell her he wasn't there. She asked him to leave a note to call his mother.

She waited all afternoon for the phone to ring and when it finally did early in the evening, she ran down the hall, past the kitchen where William looked up from the table as she went by, and picked up the phone and stood there for a moment listening to the sound of Andrew's voice, trying to slow herself down, not wanting to sound alarmed.

It's my son, she wanted to say into the phone, *my son who is missing and lost and unaccounted for*, but she did not.

"It's your brother."

She could see William listening from the kitchen, a cup of coffee in his hands. She turned away, pressing herself into the corner of the couch as she spoke into the phone, one hand laid against her belly like a compress on a wound.

When she was done, she sat in the dusky light and looked out the window as the sounds of boys filtered down from the floors overhead.

"Is he all right?" he said.

"I don't think so. I thought he might come home."

"There's no point."

"Maybe not. But he needs to know he can if—"

"He's better off there, keeping busy, not sitting around here waiting."

"He's alone," she said. "It'll be hard on him."

"He can handle it."

She looked at him watching her as if waiting for a nod that would not come. Then he set the cup in the sink and went down the hall and stepped into his study and softly closed the door behind.

Late in the night, they lay in darkness, wide wake, silent.

"How are we ever going to do this?" she said, turning her head to look at him, unable to see if his eyes were open and yet certain he was awake, sensing the presence that separates consciousness from sleep, just as the living give off a palpable sense of being whose absence makes a room containing the dead seem more than empty, a negative space drawn inward on itself. Against the lamppost light coming through the window, his eyelids drifted slowly down, then up again.

"We just wait."

"I don't think I can."

"You have to."

A thud came from overhead. Anne pictured a boy in bed, a book or shoe left on top of the covers along with yesterday's clothes, who slept and dreamed as he migrated across the bed, following or fleeing whatever it was he dreamt of, his foot nudging the book or shoe until finally it fell to the floor and he woke, startled, perhaps even a little afraid, not knowing what it was.

Now she turned and looked at William, his head against the pillow, the steady rise and fall of his chest, and wiped the corner of her eye with the edge of the sheet as she rolled over to face the window.

At some time during the night, she would not remember when, she finally fell asleep, only to be woken by a muffled scream that shook her awake and pulled her from the bed.

She found William standing in the hallway, his forehead rocking back and forth against the wall, his feet lifting and falling, stepping in the air. She spoke his name, softly, and then rested her hand on his shoulder.

"Come on," she said, gently turning him toward the living room. "Come and sit down."

He looked at her and then from side to side and toward the ceiling, his breath coming fast and shallow as she led him down the hall. They sat on the couch and he rested his head in his hands. She stroked his hair, matted with sweat, and laid her hand on his back just behind his heart.

"The dream," she said.

He nodded into his hands.

"Can you remember it?"

As he had for more than twenty years, he answered with a slow shake of his head, and she did not press him further. At first, years ago, Anne had kept her distance because she was reluctant to touch what seemed an open wound. But then it became something else, a forbidden territory, a suffering she was forced to witness over and over but with her hands tied and her mouth taped shut. And so she felt them enter what became an arid, empty space of silence where she had once felt hopeful and alive but where her heart was now like a sponge that was hard in your hand, old and small and so dry it couldn't take up water unless you plunged it deep and gave it a good squeeze to stir the memory of what it was and what it was for.

She sighed and looked at the long wet patch down the back of his pajamas.

"Come on," she said. "Take a shower. And back to bed."

They went together down the hall to the bathroom. He looked at her and then away like a boy who'd wet his bed. He went inside and when she heard the water flowing in the shower she went to the bedroom, laid out fresh pajamas, and climbed beneath the covers. Then the faucet groaned and there was a silence until the bathroom door opened and he padded down the hall, a towel around his waist.

He stood by the bed and dressed himself, his chin dropped down toward his chest in a way that made her think again of a boy.

She lay back and looked at his head against the pillow. He had never screamed before that she could remember. Cried out many times, but never this. She tried to recall the sound of it, the pitch and tone, and all she could think of was an animal caught in some great agony, eating through itself in a frantic effort to be free.

Anne woke in the early hours to find herself alone in the bed, as she had so many times since the end of the war. She looked across the abandoned terrain of covers, low and rumpled in the pale light coming through the window. She smoothed her hand across the cool sheet and speculated he'd been up for quite awhile.

She listened for sounds of him, a cup set down on the kitchen table, the refrigerator door closing, a sigh. But all was quiet.

She lifted her eyes to the window and the close grey sky pressing down on the elms. The light was coming up and a small patch of blue showed on the western horizon. From overhead came the sound of footsteps, boys stirring from their beds, soon to come pounding down the stairs, still dressing as they ran, fastening buttons, adjusting ties, voices loud and boisterous, *far-fucking-out, man*, on the way out the door and across the quad to the dining hall.

She often woke this way, alone, in the middle of the night or just before dawn. Sometimes she found him sleepwalking. Or he might be awake and sitting outside on the granite stairs cut into the slope of grass that rolled down to the great lawn, his place marked by the glow of a cigarette that drew her to the window where she watched it rise and flare as he drew on it, descending in a gentle arc as his arm swung down to rest on his knee.

The weight of his absence pressed down on her, and then was joined by thoughts of Joshua, like a finger laid against a bruise, just enough to keep her from falling back to sleep. She got out of bed and walked across the hall toward the bathroom. An alarm clock rang from somewhere on the floors above and was quickly silenced.

After eating breakfast she walked down the road to Adams Hall to collect the mail. In the lobby she waved to the receptionist who waved back from behind a wall of homesick boys gathered like hungry piglets around their mother. How unnatural, she thought, sending boys away from home so young, these children of the upper classes, come to learn the rules and meet the right people before assuming their legacy of privilege. Even at their most cocky, perhaps especially then, she saw only frightened boys, desperate lest anybody know, including themselves, just how young and frightened they really were.

At the far end of the hall was the headmaster's office, and just before that an outer office that served as a faculty lounge and mailroom. Jack waved through the open door, his other hand holding a phone to his ear. He had served in Europe from D-Day until he was wounded and sent home with a steel plate in his forehead, which, at parties, after a few drinks and especially on the losing end of an argument, he was fond of thumping with his knuckles while popping his tongue against the roof of his mouth and saying, "If I only had a brain!"

She rifled through the handful of mail, looking for the familiar APO return address, then felt a weakness in her legs as she realized there wasn't any point.

"I heard," said Jack from the doorway, hands in his pockets, leaning against the jamb. "I'm so sorry," pausing at the sight of her eyes cast down, and then, "He'll be fine, Anne. Really. He will. Marines are the best there is."

"That's what everyone's been saying all along," she said.

She took a step toward him as she felt something turn inside her.

"Tell me, Jack, why does that give me so little comfort?"

He looked away and then back at her. "Probably because you're his mother."

"Well," she said.

He took his hands from his pockets, "I didn't mean—"

"You know," she said, walking up to him, her voice so low only he could hear, "you're always talking about that steel plate of yours. You act like it's something funny. Why is that?"

He looked at her, a startled look on his face.

"I know it's not," he said.

"Then why?"

"Because it's not. It helps . . . you know."

She sighed. "I don't want my boys coming home with steel plates in their heads they have to joke about the rest of their lives."

"No one wants that, Anne."

"If they come home at all," she said. "How come no one talks about that? They're shipping body bags home every day. I see it on the news. How come we don't talk about that before it's too late?"

He shook his head, looking down at the floor, color rising in his face.

"I don't know."

"Sure you do," she said, leaning in toward him.

She stepped toward the hall, then turned to him again. "Jack, how did you get that anyway? What happened exactly?"

"I'd rather not say."

"No," she said.

He nodded, pain showing in his eyes, then turned and went into his office.

She walked quickly down the hall and out the door into the cold and stood on the steps and looked up to what had become a blue sky, streaked with long thin clouds splayed out like horses' tails in the wind. She looked down at the mail in her hand, then turned and went back inside.

"I'm sorry," she said, standing in the doorway of Jack's office. "You didn't deserve that."

"I know. He'll be all right. You have to believe that."

She stood for a moment looking down at the pattern in the carpet. The sound of boys' voices drifted down the hall.

"No," she said, shaking her head. "That's just it. I don't. Not anymore."

2

Anne poked a fork at her lunch as she stared at the unopened mail beside her plate. She stayed in the apartment all afternoon. For awhile she stood at the window and looked out across the lawn, the sky blue above the snow bright in the slanting light coming from the west, the elms casting long shadows. The walkways were full of boys, the younger ones pushing and tugging at one another, jockeying for position, throwing snowballs, ducking, laughing, books balanced on their knees while they packed the snow in their hands. The older ones, seniors in particular, walked with a greater sense of ease and purpose, as if they knew where they were going and had no worries about what they'd find when they got there.

She turned away and went to the kitchen and cleaned the counters and the sink and then scrubbed down the bathroom and did laundry. After tucking the folded clothes into the bureau drawers, she took out a stack of Joshua's letters and spread them on the bed to read them one by one.

Toward evening she sat in the bathtub, steam rising from the water flowing through the spigot. She recalled her boys in the bath, clouds of bubbles clinging to their hair, small voices in the room as she sat and watched. It was so easy then, she thought, keeping them safe, but she knew now what an illusion that was and felt a fool for believing it.

As she walked into the living room, her bathrobe wrapped around her, it was beginning to snow outside. She turned on the television.

She almost didn't heard William come in the back door, so engrossed was she in the news. She was only vaguely aware of him going into the kitchen and then standing in the doorway, one hand in his pocket, in the other a bottle of beer. He began to say something, but she lifted her hand to silence him.

"You'll want to see this."

"I doubt it."

"No," she said. "I really mean it."

Together, in silence, they watched the pale image of Walter Cronkite lean toward the camera as if trying to get closer than usual to relate the stunning unfolding of what would be known as the Tet Offensive, the sudden and massive enemy assault launched across the length and breadth of South Vietnam, including Saigon where the enemy briefly occupied the U.S. embassy.

"I didn't think it was possible," she said, her voice trailing off as the screen shifted from one battle scene to another.

They watched the rest of the news in stony silence, William sitting on the arm of the couch by now, sipping the beer, holding the bottle loosely by the neck. A quiz show came on, *Truth or Consequences.* They sat and stared for awhile and then he walked over to the television and turned it off.

"I thought we were winning," she said.

"It depends on what you mean," he said. "Winning isn't something that happens as you go along. You're either there or you're not. The rest is just . . . " He drank from the bottle. "I don't know. My teams have been winning games right up to the point where they lost. It's no different with war. You think they're winning right up until they get buried alive."

She looked up to see him staring at the blank screen and waited for him to say more, knowing he wouldn't, that this was as close as he would come to speaking of it, the great impenetrable thing he brought home with him in 1945. Still, after all these years, he'd have her believe he'd left it behind and meant them both to leave it there. And yet here it was, in all the signs she'd come to recognize—the nightmares and walking in his sleep, lying awake at all hours of the night or wandering in the dark, and that faraway, vacant look she saw before her now, a look so removed she thought she could run a needle through his finger without him feeling it at all.

Later they lay beside each other in bed, their voices drifting in the dark.

"He'll be all right," he said.

"That's what Jack said."

"He's right."

"He said I had to believe it."

"You do."

"But I don't."

They lay in silence and then she rolled over to the far edge of the bed.

"Goodnight," she said.

He turned and looked at her, then reached out and laid a hand on her hip.

"Goodnight," he said and turned away.

She looked out the window, still feeling the weight of his hand, like a phantom, and felt the protective boundary separating today from yesterday and tomorrow coming apart, today everywhere at once and making no distinction.

William waited for the cadence of her breathing to drop into something slow and soft, then got up and went down the hall to the kitchen. He sat at the table in the dark and thought about Joshua, waking up not knowing where he was, as soldiers often do, returning to the world with a moment of panic that sets the tone for whatever follows.

He got up and wandered about the darkened apartment, first to his study and then to the bathroom and then he went outside for a smoke in the softly falling snow. He looked up at the dark brick dormitory wall with its rows of white framed windows running upward for three stories to the roof, and imagined it breathed and slept and dreamed as a being whose care was his responsibility. And it occurred to him, as it had before, how this school had saved his life, this tight little world, bounded in every way, by geography and tradition and role, that might hold together from the outside a life that had come apart from within.

He looked up at the western sky and wondered, as he often did, what Joshua was doing at this moment and if he was still alive. He considered that he was not, more seriously than he ever had before, but still he could not make it more real than a thought in his mind, a possibility, too remote to discern the details.

He went inside and lay on the couch, covering himself with an afghan. He thought of General Sherman leading his army across Georgia to the sea, William Tecumseh Sherman for whom he was named by his father. "War is all hell," Sherman wrote, "and there is no point in trying to reform it." And then he thought that's where his son had gone, to take his turn in hell, soon to be followed by his brother. It was, he believed, what every man had to do if it came to that, and if they turned away, and there where men he knew who had, it left them with something missing in their character and in its place a softness, a vulnerability he could not imagine for himself.

He wondered how he came to name his boys in the same way that he'd been named, Anne making no objection he could recall. It seemed he could do whatever he wanted when it came to naming sons. Perhaps she thought the daughters would be up to her, except that, as it turned out, she never got the chance.

First came Joshua Lawrence Chamberlain, hero of Gettysburg who led his men in a desperate charge down the wooded slope of Little Round Top to save the day from otherwise certain disaster. A professor of rhetoric and language at Bowdoin College, he was a gentle man with soft eyes who somehow knew exactly what to do in his moment of greatest peril and had the courage to see it through.

Then came Andrew Jackson, "Old Hickory," hero of the War of 1812, Indian fighter, and seventh president of the United States.

His mind wandered to the gentle slopes of Arlington National Cemetery, row upon row of gravestones stretching out through the trees as far as he could see. There were, he knew, many such places in Europe. He had never gone to see them, knowing them to be full of men no different from himself save for some small accident of timing or geography that so easily separates the living from the dead.

He watched a funeral march make its way among the gentle slopes, a soft breeze lifting branches on the trees above a caisson drawn by four white horses, a knot of mourners following close behind, and then the silence in the air pressed down upon him, thick and warm until he could resist no longer and closed his eyes and dropped into sleep and dreamed the dream

inside a heartbeat buried in darkness urgent and clutching at the blood rushing by, a laboring breath squeezing soft cries from the throat, and all around a low sound distant a first but then so close the air gives way to let it pass, a dry and vengeful whine darting and fast like a rage of hornets

footsteps, running, pausing, scraping the ground before stumbling on

straining to hear through darkness that swirls and thins like a lifting fog

only to realize he is listening to himself

running down the middle of a street strewn with rubble and bodies and dense with smoke

tripping and falling on the bloated corpse of an old woman, their faces coming together, a stench of rot rising through her broken teeth

crying out and rolling away, scrambling to his feet

in a panic as he runs

and runs, until a flash of light from a doorway down the street catches his eye and the dry and angry whine smashes into his helmet, spinning him around as he falls

his mind still turning inside his skull even as his body comes to rest and then the panic pushing him to his feet, pain throbbing in his head, turning to run the other way, his helmet in one hand, his rifle in the other, running past burnt out shops, a truck turned on its side spewing smoke, the smell of burning rubber

a flash from down the street and another to the side and still more from the rooftops and the hornets biting into his ear, burning the

inside of his thigh, severing the finger from his hand
reaching up to the pain, the blood flowing warm down his hand to
the little stump of finger
falling to his knees amidst hornets dancing all around, kicking up bits
of cobblestone, tattering his clothes, biting his flesh, fear crowding
out the pain to fill him with a terror that lifts him to his feet to send
him careening down the street again, screaming and shooting at
anything that moves, seeming almost to fly, legs so light his feet
barely skim the ground past shadows stepping from doorways,
leaning around a corner
his rifle hot in his hands as if dispensing fire
arms flung outward as bodies crumple in little clouds of dust
one and then another,
blinded by tears, a sound, a blur of motion, his arm held out to the
side, the stump of finger cooling in the air, numbing the pain
until he sees the building in front of him, the red shutters and the
blue door hanging open at the top of the stairs, down into the cellar
and the dank and fetid air rising up to meet him as he leaps from the
bottom stair into the darkness, stumbling through a narrow passage
ragged and smelling of earth like a tunnel dug by hand, until at last
an open space and a flight of stairs that he climbs and climbs, his
lungs aching and the blood pounding in his ears all the way to the
top where he plunges on to the corner at the far end of the hall and
turns and almost sees for the first time what he already knows is
there, a gasp taking him by the throat

William woke with a start, bolt upright on the couch, his breath coming hard and shallow.

The same, every time, waking before rounding to the corner's other side. He lay in the dark, his body stiff and slow, his head heavy with pain. He went to the bedroom and dressed in the dusky light, then stood and looked at Anne as she slept, her face smooth against the pillow, a hand turned upward, holding nothing but the air, her body outlined by the gently rolling typography of sheets and covers. Her lips made a little motion, like the surface ripple of a deeper conversation, and a furrow appeared between her eyes and he felt an impulse to reach down and smooth it out, but did not.

One by one, alarm clocks sounded from the floors above and the building stirred, floors creaking as boys turned themselves out for another day. Toilets flushed, water ran down through the pipes in the walls, closet doors opened and closed. Then came the voices, like an aviary waking up, a bellow here and a chirp and a screech there, a high-pitched laugh dropping suddenly to something deeper and more mellow and then cracking upward again. He poured a cup of coffee and brought it to his lips as his eyes rolled toward the rumblings of this restless and temporary depot in a nebulous land of in-between, whose inhabitants, no longer children and still not men, would nonetheless soon come of age for war.

He scrambled eggs and ate his breakfast, the fork against the plate making a hollow and lonely sound. He washed the dishes and then collected his books from the study and walked softly down the hall to the bedroom. She did not stir when he leaned down to kiss her.

He joined the boys streaming toward the chapel for the service that marked the beginning of the day. They nodded when they met his eye, calling out to him with 'Sir' or 'Mr.,' a moving sea of hatless boys, winter coats hanging open over jackets, narrow ties, rumpled chinos, and down below, scraping over the ground, brown penny loafers, some worn to falling apart only to be strapped together with white athletic tape. Peter Hay streaked by, shoes scuffling and necktie flying out over his shoulder as he ran, gasping out, "Morning, Mr. Carson," and William noted the stocky build and yet how quickly he moved as he weaved among the other boys. In his mind he aligned the boy's frame with the dimensions of a lacrosse goal and felt encouraged by the fit, all that was wanting, he thought, being to break him of a few bad habits.

William went to chapel primarily because he was expected to take attendance. From the balcony he looked down at row upon row of shoulders beneath closely cropped hair. Some boys sat ramrod straight, others slouched down so far they could only be asleep. He held the seat map in his lap and scanned the rows, marking the name assigned to each empty seat. When he had finished, he didn't listen to the sermon, but instead looked out at the sunlight coming through the high windows, the gray trees laced with snow against the soft morning sky.

Suddenly the organ sprang to life and the students stood to file down the aisles, led by the seniors in the front rows, pouring outside and down the broad steps and across the road and up the path that cut across the great lawn to the classroom buildings. He watched the last of them leave and then fell in behind, like a dog tending stragglers and strays.

His first class was U.S. History. By the end of the fall, he had laid the groundwork for the Civil War—Southern fears of Northern domination, the presumption that blacks were mere property and slavery their natural condition, all resulting in a widening gulf poisoned by a long history of animosity and distrust.

And so the world unfolded and unraveled in his corner classroom on the second floor of Butler Hall as he tried to move young minds to feel the enormity of what was at stake in their own country not so long ago and the calamity that came of it. But every year there came a point when he saw how little they knew of true calamity. He looked across the rows of heads bent low over desks, hands tight fisted around ball-point pens that scribbled some version of what he was saying, and he felt their youth and their waiting, itching for the good part, the point of it all, the battles and diagrams they'd heard about from previous generations taking the required course in U.S. History. They were waiting to study the disposition of opposing forces, shifting lines of defense and attack laid out in red and blue and green and yellow chalk, and to argue the merits of one strategy or another, the what if, the if only, and the but for this or that.

And he realized, each year, in the weeks just after Christmas, that he was waiting, too.

He was barely in the room when the agitation rose to meet him, filling the air like water flowing over rocks, *Tet* and VC bubbling to the surface, voices edged with amazement and disbelief. They didn't quiet down as they usually did when he positioned himself behind his desk and arranged his books and papers. Except for a studious few, they looked at one another and not at him. He cleared his throat and waited until one by one they turned their attention to the front of the room, Peter Hay among the last.

William's eyes lingered on the boy as if to steady and help him hold himself together. Throughout the fall he'd watched him drift, barely passing his exams, staring out the window, whispering to other boys, once even nodding off. And this morning he seemed incapable of sitting still, bordering on frenzy. Slowly, in the place of William's dissolving patience there arose something closer to ruthlessness, like an alpha wolf who grabs a pup by the soft skin beneath the neck and drags it down and rolls it on its back to stand over it, shoulders hunched down to close the distance, eye to eye, lips pulled back to show the teeth, the throat emitting a growl that sinks in deep around the bones.

William looked about the room, lingering for a moment on the trees outside the windows, then cleared his throat again, more loudly than before, Peter Hay looking up in his direction.

"Today is Bull Run Day," William began, "or for those with a Southern point of view, First Manassas."

Today was the day they'd been waiting for, when the study of 'why' gave way to 'how,' to armies and the men who led them. The colored chalk was neatly laid in the tray beneath the board, the rubber-tipped pointer hung on a hook to the side, and the map stand had been brought forward from its place in the corner.

"We're going to spend the next several weeks looking at some of the major battles through which the Civil War was fought, and before we do, I want to say something about why." He paused and waited for a certain feeling—familiar by now after so many years of teaching—a settling of young minds in the stillness coming into the room.

"In the history of warfare, the Civil War is important because it marked the invention of total war." He looked about the room, at chins resting on hands, heads bowed low over moving pens, except for Peter Hay sitting back in his chair, looking straight at him, on his face no feeling at all.

"By 'total war' I mean armies hurling themselves at each other relentlessly, marching across open fields against artillery and well-entrenched sharpshooters and with horrendous numbers of killed and wounded in a matter of days or even hours, entire regiments simply disappearing in a few minutes, the dead lying in piles or strewn about so thickly on the battlefield you could walk from one side to the other without ever touching the ground."

He leaned back against the chalk tray and looked about the room. Boys laid down their pens and lifted their heads. Peter Hay leaned forward and rested his arms on his desk, his right foot balanced on the ball and the leg jiggling up and down.

"At Antietam, the number of casualties was four times those on the first day of the D-Day landing in World War II, and without the benefit of machine guns and tanks. At Gettysburg, 150,000 men fought, and some 50,000—" he paused, "*fifty . . . thousand . . .* were killed or wounded in just two days."

He looked at their faces and wondered what he was seeing, if they were impressed or appalled. Or merely fascinated.

"The Civil War also introduced trench warfare and making war against civilians and war that seemed endless, two sides slugging away at each other until both could barely stand. They were like boxers who just keep at it, hoping and praying the other will fall so they can be done with it. It was war as move and countermove, gaining ground only to give it up again, battles that settle nothing, advance nothing, achieve nothing but slaughter and misery."

Feeling their attention fully on him now, he turned to the board and began to draw the disposition of forces on July 16, 1861, as the Union Army marched westward from Washington toward the Confederates waiting for them on the far side of Bull Run Creek running past tiny Manassas Junction. Students went back to taking notes with a subdued rustling of paper, but there was something else, as well, a continued agitation from the back of the room. He turned to see Peter Hay leaning into the aisle and gesturing with his hands as he talked to the student next to him.

"Is there a problem, Mr. Hay?"

"No, sir."

"Good," he said, returning to the blue line running from north to south. How easy it is, he thought as he drew, to reduce twenty thousand men to a line and then erase it with a stroke.

He looked over his shoulder as Peter Hay's whisper again cut through the air just above the scraping of the chalk. Their eyes met and the boy looked quickly about, reaching up to push a shock of hair from this forehead as he picked up his pen and looked down at his notebook.

Once more William drew and spoke, the boys leaning toward the sound of his voice as if to pull the story from him with their eyes, and him marveling at how spellbound they were, year after year. And then into his ear came once again the barely audible sound from the back of the room, and without hesitation he reached down and took the eraser in his hand and in a motion so swift and smooth that no one saw it coming, he turned and hurled it through the air in a low unerring arc leading straight to Peter Hay and landing squarely on his chest with a thud that raised a small pastel cloud of dust before his face. The eraser fell to the floor and a stillness filled the room as the color rose in the boy's face turned downward toward the eraser lying just beyond his foot.

"Now that I have your attention, Mr. Hay, gather up your things and get out. You will come to my office after class."

For a moment everyone looked at the boy staring at the eraser on the floor.

"I have another class then," he said, not looking up.

"I guess you'll have to miss it."

"I don't have any more cuts this term."

"That certainly puts you between a rock and hard place."

The boy nodded.

"Mr. Hay."

"Yes, sir."

"Goodbye. I'll see you in my office."

The boy stood and took his books in one hand and his coat in the other and walked quickly across the back of the room and out the door.

William watched the door close and then turned to the class.

"If anyone else thinks the greatest calamity in the history of the United States isn't worth his full attention, he'd best leave now."

There was not a movement or a sound.

When the bell sounded at the end of class William waited until the boys had left before gathering up his notes and going back to his office where he found Peter Hay sitting on the maple bench just outside the door, leaning forward, head down, feet drawn in close beneath the seat, his hands loosely clasped between his knees. Even at a distance he could see the residue of colored chalk on the pocket of the boy's jacket just over his heart, and it occurred to him that students would for years tell the story of the day when Mr. Carson, instructor in history and varsity lacrosse coach, displayed the kind of dazzling control he wished upon his attack men who might thread the ball just above the goalie's shoulder, tuck it neatly into an unguarded corner to make the netting quiver and the crowd rise to its feet.

William brought himself erect and stiffened his stride to a soldier's marching in review, his footsteps falling on the marble floor with a clarity that echoed down the hall and slowly lifted and turned the boy's head in his direction. He opened the door and stepped inside, the boy close behind.

"Have a seat."

Peter Hay sat in a chair by William's desk, looking down at the books in his lap as the silence lengthened.

"What?" the boy said at last, his voice tentative and soft.

"You tell me. What's all the commotion?"

"Nothing."

"Bull, nothing."

The boy released a breath and sank down in the chair. "We were talking about what's happening."

"Happening where?"

"In the war."

"Which war?"

A puzzled look came over the boy's face. "Vietnam. Tet."

"Not in my class," said William, arching his eyebrows, "not unless I say so."

"My brother's—"

"I don't care."

William paused to watch the words sink in.

"You're worried about your brother."

The boy nodded.

"Well, that's good," he said, and then, bearing down on the words, "but not in my class. You understand? You have a job to do in there, and I expect you to do it." He leaned forward. "If you're in my class and your pants catch on fire, you keep it to yourself unless you find a way to make it fit the topic."

The boy lowered his head to hide a little smile.

"You think I'm kidding, but I'm not."

The smile went away.

William looked at him for a moment.

"You have ability, Peter. Not a lot, but enough. More than many. But you lack discipline, and a man's got to have that. You have to know your duty and do what it requires. That means doing things you don't want to do. And when you screw up, you take your punishment and you don't complain about it. It's sink or swim out there, and you'd better make up your mind which it's going to be for you, because believe me, nobody's going to pull you out when you're going down. You'd better be ready to do that for yourself."

He sat back and looked at Peter Hay as two boys passed by in the hall, their voices echoing off the marble floors and then fading as they turned the corner and climbed the stairs.

"What do you think about what I'm saying to you?"

"I don't know, sir."

"I suggest you make it your business to know."

William took in a long breath and blew it out on a sigh.

"Are you going out for lacrosse in the spring?"

The boy looked at him, surprised. "I thought I might."

"Varsity?"

"Maybe. I'm not sure I'm good enough."

"I've seen you play. You could be good enough. Do you know what I mean?"

The boy looked at him and then down at the floor as a nervous smile moved quickly across his face.

"I think so."

"See you in class."

That night William dreamed the dream, and again the night after and the night after that, and each time, Anne rose to bring him back to bed. But on the third night, as she stood in doorway of the bedroom and stared down the length of the hall to where he stood leaning against the wall, his familiar outline suddenly turned in her mind into the young and slender form of her older boy.

"I want you to tell me about it," she said as he settled beneath the covers.

"About what?"

"The dream."

There was a long silence.

"I can't."

"Why not?"

"You know why not. I don't remember."

"I don't believe you," she said. "I don't believe you've had nightmares for twenty years and never remembered them. It isn't possible."

"You think I'm lying."

She sighed. "Call it what you want," she said, "but I think you do know."

"Why would I do that?" he said, and she felt the shift in his position as the interrogation began.

"I don't know," she said. "And I don't really care. I just want to know about it. I've waited long enough—"

"You've waited—"

"Yes. I have. And now I want to know."

"I've told you all I can."

She turned her back to him.

"What do you want from me?" he said.

"I just told you."

"Well," he said, his voice quiet, "since I can't give what I don't have, is there anything else?"

"I want to know what happened to you."

"It was a long time ago."

"No," she said, "it wasn't. It was just a few minutes ago. And last night and the night before that."

"I'm sorry."

"I don't need you to be sorry. I need you to talk to me."

"There's no point—"

"There's every point," she said. "Because you have *feelings* about it. More than I've seen you feel about anything. Even me."

He looked away.

She rolled onto her side and looked into his face. "Tell me what you feel about something. Anything. Andrew. Josh."

He worked the muscles in his jaw.

"And don't say you don't know."

"You know how I feel—"

"No, I don't," she said. "You have to tell me."

They stared at each other across the small distance between them. She waited for him to blink or show some tiny fissure in the smooth composure of his face, but if there was one, she couldn't make it out.

"I worry about him," he said.

"What about? What are you afraid will happen?"

"What exactly do you want to know?" he said, his voice rising on an edge of impatience. "About war? What it's like?"

"Yes."

"You're better off not knowing."

"No," she said. "I'm not. Not any more. You may think you're better off not telling, which I doubt, but I know I'm not."

She looked at his face, his eyes fixed on the wall.

"I need to know," she said, the words catching in her throat, "and I need to hear it from you."

He shook his head.

"Jesus Christ, Will, war is what's got him. Our son is lost in it halfway around the world. And you're telling me I'm better off not knowing?"

Still he didn't move or shift his gaze until he looked down and cleared his throat.

"I wouldn't know where to begin."

The words came to her like the slightest turn of an ancient knob on a door she'd been watching for a hundred years. She climbed out from under the covers and sat cross-legged, pulling her nightgown over her knees and the comforter to wrap around her.

"I really mean it," he said. "I don't know where to begin."

"What's in your mind right now?" she said. "What do you see?"

He paused and then nodded.

"What?" she said.

"Just a road."

"Tell me where."

"In France."

"Describe it to me."

He sighed. "It's in the country. There are fields on either side. It's raining. We walk down the road. Every once in a while a truck goes by. Or a tank. A jeep. Something."

He stopped and she leaned forward.

"And then?"

"I don't know," he said, shaking his head. "You asked me what I saw." But in his mind there was more playing out before his eyes, which he kept fixed on the wall so she wouldn't sense what was going on behind them—the German 88s coming in, huge shells landing all around, shattering the air as they tear up the earth and men who dive into ditches only to be sniffed out there as well.

The clock ticked on the bedside table.

"I'm going to sit right here until you tell me," she said.

The silence filled William like wet cement, rising through his body until his jaw felt immovable in his face. He wanted to break the silence now, as he'd wanted to for more than twenty years, but he could not move the thick inertia that lay curled inside him, old and nearly dead. If he could have moved, he'd have looked at her and seen something in her eyes that might have pulled him from the bottom of the deep hole he inhabited. He would have cried if he remembered how. But all of this was mere possibility as he watched from a distance the rescuers passing by, too far to see the waving of his arms.

As her eyes searched his face, a fury gathered inside her, her breath coming shallow and fast. She could feel him leaving, disappearing behind the mask. Almost frantic, she rose up onto her knees, hesitated, and then swung her arm and slapped him hard across the face. He barely moved, eyes suddenly wild, but when she went to slap him again, he caught her wrist and held it in the air until she wrenched herself free and sprang off the bed and ran from the room.

She was sitting on the couch, her face in her hands, when he came down the hall and stood in the doorway. For a moment there was nothing but silence and waiting and then his voice entering the room, the words heavy and flat.

"You want to know," he said. "Okay then, I'll tell you. It's very simple. Everything is about death. All of it. Everything you eat or drink or breathe. Everywhere you look, everything you touch. You smell so much of it you start to think that's just the way the world smells. And then everything smells that way. Flowers. Snow. Your fingers. The rain."

There was a pause.

"And you wait for the moment when it discovers you.

"It is being in hell, except that you're alive. That is what it's like."

She heard him turn and walk back down the hall.

Anne sat in the dark and thought of the William she used to know, the young man who worked in his father's garage and drew pictures in his spare time, and who, when they fell in love the summer following high school graduation, sat with her beneath a tree beside a pond off in the woods to the west of town, and drew the landscape, often including images of her. And sometimes he stood outside her window and played his father's ukelele and sang "Yes Sir, That's My Baby" in a voice that could barely carry a tune. But she didn't mind.

On a late August night toward the end of that first summer, they went swimming in the pond, shedding their clothes and bathing naked beneath a full moon.

She asked him to make love to her, but he would not.

"Why?" she said, standing pressed against him, a thin blanket wrapped around them.

She looked up at him, trying to make out his face in the dark. "Don't tell me it's God," she said.

He shook his head.

"Then what?"

He shrugged. "I'd be scared of . . . " he sighed, "you know . . ."

"Getting me pregnant."

"And besides," he said, "when we do that . . . I want the whole world to know. I want people to see us walking down the street, people who came to the wedding and had a good time and who like us together. I want them to look as we go by and see them blush because they know we love each other forever. And they can see it on our faces with nothing to hide or worry about someone finding out. That's what I want with you."

She started to cry and he didn't understand and she said it was all right, he should just let her cry, and so he did and they stood under the moon until she stopped, and then they talked for awhile before getting dressed and going back to town.

Then came the attack on Pearl Harbor on a quiet Sunday morning in early December, 1941, and within a matter of days the country was at war with both Germany and Japan. At first it meant little to them, a matter for politicians and professional soldiers, but then the call went out for volunteers and every young man they knew, it seemed, wasted no time in joining in the rush. They married the day he signed up.

In the weeks before he left she knew for the first time in her life the feeling in her heart of having someone as her own, only to lose him three months later on a dockside in New York. She couldn't see his face to wave goodbye. There were too many of them crowding the decks of the ship, four or five deep along the rails, craning their necks for one last glimpse. She looked up and waved anyway, imagining him looking right at her, his face wide open in a grin, like the one he wore the first time he watched her taking off her clothes, about to have the time of his life and not caring that she knew. Sometimes he laughed out loud when they made love and it startled her at first until she realized it was just the sound of pure delight. And when she climbed on top and moved slowly over him, he spread his arms out wide and arched his back in a look of such unguarded surrender that she was stopped by the sight of it, and when he murmured, "Oh, keep going," she smiled and settled back into the rhythm of her moving against him.

"Oh, Billy," she'd say, trying to leaven the words with an Irish lilt that would float them into the air above him, drifting softly down, "Billy Boy, Billy the Kid, Billy Goat," always Billy in those hurried days before the war took him far away.

It was 1945 before she saw him again and she could tell that he'd left something behind and was no longer a man to be called Billy. He hadn't been wounded seriously—a small piece of shrapnel tore some skin from his arm in North Africa and he lost part of a little finger somewhere in Germany in the closing days of the war. And there was the medal in the small box covered in leather with his name stamped in gold. It was nothing, he told her, everyone got one just for being there. It all didn't seem to amount to much, but still the man who stepped off the train, a duffle bag slung over his shoulder, his head looking left and right and back again for some sight of her in the crowd, was neither intact nor whole. He had a vacant, preoccupied look, as if trying to remember what he'd left behind and where. But he could not, and so in its place was a lingering hesitation wrapped around the vague awareness of something lost that was, from time to time, longed for, but just short of being remembered.

She missed calling him Billy, missed the softness carried on the ending y, the sometimes vowel, and one morning several months after his return she called him Will across the breakfast table. He looked at her and she at him, both a little surprised until he smiled and she asked him if he'd mind that and he said no, it was fine, he'd like it actually.

"Tim used to call me that," he said, and then looked down into the bowl of cereal in front of him, his cheeks gone slack. "Not Willy, though," he said without looking up.

"Okay," she said and remembered the steamy July morning when his father called to tell her about Tim being killed on Iwo Jima along with most of his platoon, and the feeling of something breaking apart inside her, the easy assumption that someone else's son or brother or husband would be the one not to come home.

"We must pray for William," said her father-in-law, and she noted his use of Billy's formal name—he'd always called him Bill—as if to lend the prayer some greater weight.

"I always do," she said.

They stayed in his parents' house after his return, sleeping in his old room. The nightmares began right away, the sleepwalking several months later. He was restless during the day, barely able to sit still for anything, preferring to go out for a walk or a drive. She and his parents hovered loosely around him, as if he were a toddler who'd just found his legs and they wanted to allow him freedom to move while protecting him from the harm that might come of it.

And then he came into the living room one evening and announced he was going to college on the GI Bill to get a teaching degree.

"Teaching what?" his father asked.

"History. U.S. history." And she looked at him standing in the doorway, hands thrust deep in his pockets, eyes squinting as if into a bright light, and felt herself fill with tenderness.

Anne woke curled beneath the afghan, her head on a small pillow at the end of the couch. He was standing next to her, looking down, framed by the early light coming through the window behind him. He'd already shaved and his tie was loose beneath the collar of the blue button-down he always wore to class. His hair was neatly combed and his tweed jacket with the leather patches she sewed onto the elbows lay across his arm.

"I'm sorry I hit you," she said.

"I don't know how to do this."

"It doesn't matter," she said. "Even one scrap a day. Write it on a piece of paper if you have to. It doesn't matter how you do it."

"All right."

Boys along the walkway called out his name. Some he didn't hear, while for others, the words entered his mind a few beats behind, like a conversation with an echo, making it difficult to know when to listen and when to speak. And so he hesitated and noticed the look on their faces, puzzled and amused, in the presence of an adult whose usual command of the situation had suddenly deserted him. He smiled awkwardly and shook his head and muttered, "Good morning," and hurried on to the safety of the faculty lounge.

He stood by the window and sorted through his mail, seeing none of it as he passed each envelope to the bottom of the pile, and suddenly he was aware of a hand laid gently on his shoulder and then a voice, softened by caution, and he turned to see Jack's hand and then his face, eyes narrowed, lips making words.

"What?" he said, dropping a letter on the floor.

"I said, 'How are you?'"

"Not great," bending down to pick up the letter, "but we'll manage."

"He'll be all right, Bill," leaning in close, "he's a Marine, after all."

"Right."

"You let me know if there's anything you need. Anything at all."

"Thanks, Jack," he said, looking down at the mail.

He carried the envelopes in his hand as he walked to class so he'd have a reason to look down and avoid the greetings and the eyes that might look into his and see the turmoil he could not contain. As he neared the classroom, students' animated talk filled the hallway with names of generals and battlefields and opinions about strategy and tactics and failure and blame, all colliding in the air around him.

He walked to the front of the room and pulled a stack of notes from his briefcase, looking for something that felt familiar, but it all seemed strange, the handwriting somehow not his own, and he felt a sense of disbelief and then panic, as if looking up from the bathroom sink and seeing the wrong face in the mirror. He'd been through this sort of thing many times before, but always in his sleep, in the teacher's version of schoolroom nightmares, showing up for the first day of class completely unprepared or not getting to class at all, struggling against one obstacle after another while the clock marks the progress of his undoing.

But he knew that now he was awake, which only deepened the sense of alarm. His mind tried to focus on the words but could not find the beginning of a sentence or connect one fragment with another. The class slowly settled down, faces turning in his direction one by one. He looked down at the pages of notes so as not to feel the eyes upon him. He wondered if they knew, but then he couldn't think of what it was they'd know if in fact they did.

And then a sudden calm came over him and he no longer saw the rows of faces as he fixed his gaze out the window at the bare trees and the cemetery beyond. So still and focused was his presence that the silence in the room took on a pure, suspended quality, the students spellbound and unmoving, until he blinked and looked quickly to one side and then the other and then down as he cleared his throat and turned and picked up a piece of chalk and wrote on the board a single word, Fredericksburg.

3

Andrew lifted his head and stifled a yawn as he put down the pen and stretched his hand to relieve the stiffness in his fingers. All around him in the overheated room he saw row upon row of heads bent over desks, feet and legs splayed across the floor and wrapped around chair legs in every imaginable configuration, little puddles on the floor from snow melting off boots and shoes, hands pressing down to move pens across the page and write the final exam in Topics in U.S. History.

His roommate, Steve, was in the far corner, and Andrew was certain he hadn't taken his eyes off the desk or stopped the movement of the pen since he began, a model of studious concentration, a gangly red-haired juggernaut of well-honed argument that Andrew knew to avoid after sharing a room for the fall term. Unlike Andrew, who had always known he would wind up a ground soldier like his father and his brother, Steve applied for the Intelligence Corps, and Andrew had no doubt he'd get it, strutting about in freshly pressed fatigues, interrogating prisoners, outwitting and wearing them down until they realized there was no escaping the illogic and futility of concealing what they knew. And maps with little colored pins, and estimates of the enemy's order of battle, briefing bird colonels and generals whose fatigues were not only pressed but tailored.

Quite unlike either of them was Andrew's other roommate, Joe, who wouldn't be caught dead in a U.S. History course or any course, for that matter, that required him to string together one paragraph after another. Short and hard with muscle, he only had time for math and science and engineering.

"I just want to know how things work," he'd say, "and if I can't touch it, it's not a thing. Give me short answers any time—how big, how far, and when to blow it up," a sparkle in his eyes, "like, kaboom!" yanking an imaginary lanyard on an imaginary cannon in an imaginary tank.

Andrew leaned back in his chair and stretched his arms over his head to yawn as he considered the doctrine of Manifest Destiny, which he first heard about four years ago in his senior year required U.S. History course, which he took with Mr. Winchendon two doors down the hall from his father's classroom. He didn't think much about it then, it seeming obvious that the U.S. would spread itself and the blessings of liberty wherever it could, but now it seemed more complicated than that, although he wasn't sure why. There was something too certain about it, too pat, too neat, too little room for doubt, and somewhere in the shadows, shot through with fear, like he sometimes thought he saw in his father's eyes when he was trying to defend some idea or rule that everyone around him knew was arbitrary or just plain wrong, but that he seemed bound to stick to no matter what, as if he had to because he'd come apart or die if he did not.

Andrew glanced at the clock and scanned the room until he found Ruth Koszinski sitting next to the far wall. He saw her the first day of class and thought she had an interesting face, her eyes set wide apart and always fixed on something, but it wasn't until the term was nearly over that he came to know her name.

It was just after Thanksgiving when she waved her hand in the air as Professor Hardy, the stout, white-haired chair of the History Department, explored the finer points of the Dredd Scott decision. He was quoting the Chief Justice's opinion that blacks had "no rights a white man was bound to respect" when—

"Excuse me," she said.

He looked over his glasses in the direction of the voice, so many students in the hall, unable to tell just who was interrupting, saying yes as he waved his fingers at no one in particular.

"When do we get to what it was really like?"

"What?' he said, cupping his ear as if he hadn't heard.

"When do we get to what it was really like?"

A pause as he thought it over, not so much the question as why it was asked at all. "For whom?" he said, still trying to pick her out in the crowd.

"Africans. The ones white people kidnapped and turned into slaves."

He found her, his face blank except for a carefully contained downward cast of puzzlement.

"Well," he said with a shrug, "in this class I suppose we don't."

"Why not?"

"Why not? We just . . . don't. There isn't time."

"But we could talk about it now."

"Yes," he said, drawing out the word. "I suppose we could, but we're not, you see. We're talking about Dredd Scott and the Supreme Court."

"Because you think that's more important."

Even from his seat in the back row, Andrew could see Hardy's eyes narrow.

"I'd say that's rather obvious."

"Are there other courses that look at it?"

"None that I know of."

"And why is that?"

"Miss," he said, "if you want to know about this, I suggest you consult the literature. There are slave narratives, for example—"

"I know that," she said. Andrew watched Hardy's lips keep on working as if he hadn't been interrupted, even though her voice was now the only one in the room.

"But what I don't understand," she said, "is why it's not important enough to get into the syllabus. I mean, why is it less important to feel what was really at stake for Dredd Scott, I mean his *life*, than to read the opinion of some racist judge—"

"Miss," he said, drawing himself up behind the podium.

She looked at him.

"I was about to answer your question," he said.

"Good," she said. "Go ahead."

"Thank you," he said with a little sniff.

Andrew leaned forward and watched her in rapt attention along with the rest of the class, thinking she must be crazy, a smile coming over his face as he wondered how it would feel to be just like that, out of your mind, afraid of nothing at all.

"You cannot understand the history of the United States unless you understand the Civil War," Hardy said, the words slow and weighted down by the deep tone of his voice, "and you cannot understand the Civil War unless you understand the workings of government, including the Supreme Court and the Dredd Scott case—"

"I know that—"

"Oh, you do? Well—"

"But why should we *care?*" she said. "I mean, who cares about any of it if we don't know what it *did* to people. I don't get it."

He pressed his lips together and looked down at his notes and then up toward the high windows along the wall. He sighed.

"You see no value in the study of history?" he said, his eyes still on the windows.

"Of course I—"

"Those who cannot learn from history," he said, wagging his finger in the air, "are doomed—"

"Yes, I know," she said, "Santayana," speaking faster now, bearing down on the words, "are doomed to repeat it. I just don't understand what history *is* if you take out what really happened to people. And we do seem to be repeating history a lot in this country even though our leaders must be up on their history, having gone to places like Harvard and all. So, maybe it depends on what you mean by history—"

"What is your name?" he said.

She stopped and looked up at him, her face so calm Andrew couldn't take his eyes off it. Then she sat back, folded her arms across her chest, and closed her eyes.

"Ruth," she said.

"Ruth," he repeated, taking a fountain pen from the breast pocket of his jacket, slowly removing the cap and writing in the margin of his notes. He looked at her over his glasses. "Ruth who?"

"Koszinski," she said, opening her eyes. "Ruth Koszinski." Andrew strained to hear the last name but couldn't make it out except for sounding Russian.

The room was silent as Hardy began to write but then stopped after the first few strokes and stared down at the page, his eyebrows drawn together and the color rising in his face.

"K-o-s-z-i-n-s-k-i," she said, "Koszinski."

He scribbled the name. "Now," he said, tidying his notes, "if we may continue. The Dredd Scott case."

Andrew finished the exam and studied her, his chin resting in his hand, watching her reach up while continuing to write and take a length of hair dangling in front of her face and fold it behind her ear. Even at a distance her blond hair looked a little wild, as if she rarely took a brush to it, or shampoo and water. He wondered about the texture and the smell and the rest of her, the scent of her skin beneath the jeans and the bulky sweater several sizes too large. He closed his eyes and imagined the spot just where the neck meets the collarbone, his lips planting a kiss in the little hollow, and then he opened his eyes to find the chair empty where she'd been just a moment before and he turned to see her disappear through the door as the proctor shuffled her exam among the rest. He grabbed his coat and bolted for the front of the room, holding the pen in his mouth and the exam in one hand while trying to put on his coat with the other.

That day in November as he watched her leave after class, the other students giving way and keeping a certain distance as she moved among them up the aisle, he wondered where she lived and what she'd say in the next class. But she wasn't there or the class after that and then the term was over and his only chance to see her again was at the final exam following Christmas break.

He pushed open the door and stepped into the cold, one arm in his coat and the other out, and saw her walking across the snow covered green, bright beneath the sun at its highest point in the sky. The green was crisscrossed with shoveled walkways filled with students going to and from exams, but she preferred the snow, her body sinking down as the snow gave way beneath her weight. He hurried down the steps and set off after her.

Usually he would take his time and look up at the sky and feel comforted by the buildings all around, sturdy Georgian brick and white clapboard and cupolas and bell towers and six foot sash windows, a sight that could, if the timing was right, the sky a certain way, his mood rising like a hawk on an updraft of air, fill him with the sense that no matter what, some things do endure, things that he could count on, like goodness and truth and the inherent sense of justice that he believed could be found in every living thing. Today could have been such a day, but Ruth Koszinski's pace was uncommonly fast and he barely noticed anything except the back of her purple coat as she crossed the street at the far side of the green, and the flash of sunlight on the glass doors of the student center as she pulled them open and disappeared inside.

He walked quickly through the lobby to the mailroom and knelt down in front of his box. It rarely contained anything, but now there was a letter leaning against the side and he smiled as he made out the return address through the window.

Andrew took the letter to the snack bar and was about to read it when he saw her at a table, a book open in front of her beside a cup of coffee and another book. Crossing to the far side of the room, he scanned the menu on the wall as if making up his mind. But he saw only her, cupped in the periphery of his vision, turning a page or bringing the coffee to her lips. He stepped toward her, threading among the tables until he was next to her, looking down along the smooth angle of her nose to the book beside her hand and the title, *Catch-22*, on the cover. He tried to think of what to say, but everything that came to him seemed lame and stupid.

He turned and walked away to the counter where he stood and watched her until she happened to look up and see him and he quickly turned to the clerk and ordered coffee and a donut. At a table in the far corner he sat and watched her drink and read, lifting her head sometimes and looking out the window as she turned a page. It seemed foolish to want so badly to say something to her, and doubly foolish to not be able to. Sighing and rubbing the bridge of his nose, he felt the weariness from studying for finals catch up with him at last, and then took a sip of coffee and a bite of donut and looked up and saw that she was gone.

It first appeared as a patch of white against the door of Andrew's room, a red thumbtack stuck squarely in the middle. He cleared the last stair and walked over to it, his eye fixed on the penciled script, a single letter 'A.'

Call your mom it said, a lightness in his chest spreading slowly to his belly as he leaned his forehead against the door and looked at the note, something about it, not, *Your mom called,* with the implied invitation to call back, but rather the simple command, the imperative mode, as Miss Mulready would have named it in seventh grade English.

He opened the door and dropped his books on the bed and then went downstairs to the lobby where a pay phone hung in a booth along the wall. He closed the door, spread a pocketful of change on the shelf below the phone, and punched a coin into the slot, the operator's voice coming on the line to ask for the number, which he momentarily forgot.

As it rang and rang, he pictured the empty living room, thinking she must be out, but still he let it ring, imagining the power to seek her out wherever she might be. Then the sharp familiar click and a moment of fumbling before her voice, his mother's voice, "Hello," catching on the word as she paused to clear her throat.

"Mom," he said, and then he felt her let down on the other end of the line and imagined her sinking into the chair beside the phone, her hand held to her mouth, a knuckle laid softly between her lips like a key poised before a lock.

"Oh, honey," she said, and he knew, hearing her call him that, watching through the glass as Steve came in the front door without seeing him, whistling up the stairs.

"What's the matter?"

He felt her holding on in the silence, trying to spare him and yet only making it worse in the waiting.

"It's your brother," she said, and he felt her draw herself together, pulling the air in through her runny nose. "Josh is missing."

"What do you mean?"

"They can't find him."

"Where was he?"

"Someplace . . . " she said and then a pause, the confusion in her mind palpable in the strained background hush of the phone, "I don't know. Kay something—"

"Khesahn."

"Yes, that's it."

"Do they say what happened?"

"They don't seem to know. Your dad called the Pentagon but all they said was that his squad went out on night patrol and had some trouble and when they got back he wasn't with them."

"He can't just disappear."

She blew her nose. "I don't know, Andrew. They said they'll let us know as soon as they find him."

He blinked away the stinging in his eyes, noting the choice of words, not when he got back or showed up, but when he was found. He drew a sleeve across his face.

"He'll make it, Mom."

"Of course he will," she said. "Your father said soldiers come up missing all the time and then just wander in."

He nodded and pictured her nodding with him at the other end of the line.

"Will you be all right up there?" she said.

"Sure. I'm okay."

"You can always come home."

"I know."

"I love you," she said, and he turned his face away from the footsteps coming down the hall.

"I love you, too, Mom," he said, his voice catching and drawing from her a little moan like the sound she made when he was small and feverish and he told her it hurt and she passed a hand across his brow and looked down into his face as if she would give anything to make it go away.

"It'll be all right," she said.

Walking into his room, Andrew was relieved to find he had it to himself. He put a Simon and Garfunkel record on the phonograph and lay down on the bed and opened his brother's letter.

Dear Drew,

I don't write much because I usually don't know what to say. Things are not good over here. I don't remember what I thought this was going to be, but it's definitely not. I don't think anyone knows what the fuck we're doing. They send us out to hunt VC and then they want to know how many we killed and don't care whether we got the right ones. I shot a kid the other day. Do you believe that? I didn't know. He was just some little guy in black pajamas. Gunny yells to get him and I turn and see him down the hill running along a little strip of high ground between rice paddies, not fast, kind of loping along. I gave him a lead and squeezed off a round and his legs went out from under him like somebody cut a string. Margolis whistled behind me and said nice shot and I went down to see. I was still a ways off when I saw how small he was, bare feet, probably eight or nine. All he had was a little bowl of rice spilled on the ground in front of him. There was blood in it and all over his belly and his face looked surprised and I couldn't take my eyes off him until this old woman came out of the trees along the side of the field and started yelling in Vietnamese and I knew right away the boy belonged to her, a grandson maybe, bringing the rice. I walked up the hill but kept turning around because I could feel her sneaking up behind me, but every time I looked, she was sitting on the ground beside him rocking back and forth and making that noise. I couldn't stop shaking. Now I can't sleep. I think something's really wrong. We kill them and they kill us and we take ground and they come right back once we've gone. People don't like us and they're afraid of us, just like we're afraid of them, even though we're here to help, at least I thought we were, but I'm not so sure anymore. I don't know. I don't know a goddamn thing. Except this is some bad shit and you don't want to be over here and if you think being an officer will make it any better, think again. It's worse. They don't know what the fuck they're doing and when they screw up we get killed. So when they get taken out it's a relief. Sometimes guys do it themselves. It's easy enough.

So you watch your ass little brother. Be sure what you're doing. This is the real thing over here and you don't know what real is until you've been in this one for awhile. So far out it's in you know? Whatever it is it's not for you.

Don't show this to Dad, okay? And write to me. It helps me remember who I am.

Semper fi
Josh

Andrew looked up at the ceiling, discolored in various shades of white that looked like high thin clouds.

What did it mean, he thought, to be missing?

He remembered hiding from his parents and the game they played looking for him, all the while knowing just where he was, their voices sounding worried until they suddenly opened the door or pulled back the covers and gave the gift of being sought after and found.

He comforted himself with the thought that missing and lost are not the same. Josh could be out there somewhere taking a little time for himself, missing from them but still knowing right where he was. He did it all the time when he was a boy, and Andrew, being younger, had to track him down if he wanted to be with him. There were places in the bird sanctuary on the edge of campus that were known only to the two of them, or so they thought, at first only to Joshua and then to them both when Andrew followed him one late fall afternoon. Joshua was angry at being followed and found out but then he gave in and led Andrew to a little space inside a dense thicket of rhododendron where they sat and talked about nothing in particular, which Andrew didn't mind, glad just to be there with his brother.

And then there were the evenings when Joshua was late for supper, taking his time coming home from practice or playing with friends, and Andrew and his parents would be sitting at the kitchen table, food steaming on their plates, and when his mother or his father asked him where his brother was, Andrew would shake his head even if he knew.

He could be anywhere, he thought. He's only missing to those who cannot find him.

He held the letter to his nose and smelled the faint scent of the Lucky Strike Joshua was probably smoking when he wrote it, musty sweet. He imagined the cigarette in the fingers of one hand while he balanced a pad of paper on his knee and wrote with the other, dog tags at the end of a chain around his neck, gently swaying over the words. Andrew closed his eyes and tried to picture his brother's face, but then there was the sound of someone taking the stairs two at a time, whooping as he went, then Steve bursting through the door and letting it slam open against the wall as he crossed the room in a few long strides and leaned down to look into Andrew's face.

"Assignments are up," he said, smiling and wiggling his eyebrows. "I got Intelligence."

"Far out," said Andrew, his voice flat.

"Far fucking out no shit," said Steve, kissing the palm of his hand with a loud smack and leaning forward to slap it on the poster of Ann-Margret above his desk. "And you, poor bastard, you also got your wish. Ground kissing, treefuckinghugging infantry." He walked across the room and laid his books on his desk. "While I'm down in Saigon grilling gooks and sleeping in a real bed, you'll be humping 60 pounds of shit through the highlands, not to mention getting shot at by every pissed off gook in Southeast Asia."

Andrew folded the letter and slid it into the pocket of his shirt.

"Just remember," said Steve, tapping his finger against his temple, "when you're out there pinned down by a zillion gooks, it'll be me who warned your CO not to go out there. You'll wish he'd listened to me." He made a quick fake smile, his teeth white and clenched. "We got drill tomorrow?"

"Every Wednesday."

Steve looked at him. "What's the matter?"

Andrew said nothing for a moment, silenced by the heaviness in his chest.

"They can't find my brother."

A low whistle from Steve, "Oh, Jeez, no. Where?"

"Khesahn."

Steve shook his head. "They're in a load of shit up there."

"I know."

"When'd you find out?"

"Just now. My mom called."

They were silent, the space between them feeling large and empty.

"Sorry to have to tell you now," said Steve, "but the Colonel wants to see you."

"What about?"

"I don't know. He just said he wants to see you."

Andrew rolled out of bed.

"I'm really sorry, Drew."

"Me, too," said Andrew, putting on his coat and noticing his uniform in the shadows of the closet, the light reflecting off the three silver diamonds on the epaulets, the insignia of the Cadet Colonel, the highest ranking student in the corps. And next to the uniform, his varsity jacket and the hand-me-down flannel shirt that his mother had pulled from his father's closet in a fit of spring cleaning—*he doesn't wear it anymore, he'll never miss it*—and that Andrew liked especially for how soft and broken in it felt against his skin when he first put it on, like slipping into some tender essence of his father that he otherwise hardly knew. Staring into the closet, it came to him again, a feeling he'd had before, that he was somehow the sum of such things that attached him to teams and schools and his country and its history, to his mother and his father and his brother, and that this is all he was or needed to be, someone with a place in the scheme of things, a place bounded by rules and obligations and understandings of what was what and what mattered and what did not, in return for which he got to know who he was and where he did belong.

He walked across the green, remembering the day he told his mother he had joined the Army, just a month after his brother had joined the Marines. It was after dinner and he leapt to his feet to clear the table.

"Thank you," she said, and he looked over his shoulder as a tremor went across his face, which he hoped would appear as a smile. He stood for a moment before the sink, looking out the window at the trees and the lawn and the setting sun, and when he turned around, his father had left the room and it was just the two of them.

That was when he told her.

At first she said nothing, staring at him until he looked away.

"Why won't you look at me?"

He looked at her, then away again with a shrug.

"Help me understand," she said. "Is it because of Josh? Are you doing this because your brother did it?"

"No."

"You think it's just coincidence that you signed up a few weeks after him?"

"It was my last chance. You can't get in once you're a junior."

"Your brother did."

"He enlisted. He's not an officer."

"So? You *want* to be an Army officer? That's your goal?"

"No."

"Then why?"

"Because I would've been drafted when I graduated," he said, grabbing at the words and pushing them into the air between them, like frantically stuffing rags into a hole in a sinking boat. "I'm not going to med school or law school and there's no reason they wouldn't take me." He looked at her, waiting for her to say something, but when she did not, he began to feel more sure of himself. "So, if I have to go, I might as well go as an officer."

"Assuming you didn't refuse the draft," she said.

He blinked, startled.

"I'd go to jail for that."

"Or Canada."

He looked down at the floor.

"I can't do that," he said, not looking up.

"And why not?"

"Because."

"Because what? You have a duty?"

He nodded.

"To what?"

Looking at her, surprised that she would ask, he could only mutter, "You know."

"No," she said, "I don't. You'll have to tell me."

"The country—"

"But what *is* it?"

"What do you mean, Mom?" he said.

"I mean what exactly is it that you owe?"

Andrew stood there for a moment, unable at first to form the thought and then to find the words.

"You can't just take," he said. "You have to give something back."

"Well, Andrew," she said, nodding, "that is undeniably a good and noble thing. But is there a reason why you need to do it in just this way? You could join the Peace Corps, you—"

"What's wrong with the Army?"

"What's wrong?" she said. "What's wrong with going halfway around the world to risk your life? Have you thought about the fact that you might be killed? Do you know how many bodies they're shipping home every day?"

"Sure I have," he said, his mind struggling to keep up with the words coming out of his mouth, "I am . . . and . . . I won't get killed."

"You won't get killed," she said, "no," her voice softer now, "you probably won't. You'll come home. Just like your father. And I will never see you again."

There was a long silence.

"I think you don't know why you're doing this," she said. "And that's not good enough."

He leaned against the sink, hands in his pockets, his face growing hot, nothing coming to his mind except wanting to be anywhere other than here.

Then she turned and looked at him, her face softening with understanding.

"This is because of Joshua—"

"No, Mom, it's not—"

"You'd be ashamed not to go."

He shook his head but she looked at him, her gaze unwavering until his head became still.

"You're caught," she said, almost in a whisper as she looked out the window. "We both are."

She closed her eyes.

"All you brave young men," she said with a sigh. "Going off to war because you're afraid not to."

And then, without a word, she pushed off from the counter and went down the hall and out the door.

Andrew stepped into the ROTC building and wiped the moisture from his eyes, thinking it was from the cold, then stamped the snow from his boots with such ferocity that the sound echoed through the halls. Since leaving the dorm, fear and worry had hardened into anger that now softened and disassembled, leaving only fear.

"How are your exams going?" said the Colonel as he took Andrew's elbow in one hand and shook his hand with the other.

"Fine, sir. I'm all done."

"Good. Good. Sit down. Tell me, how's your brother?"

He paused for a moment, unsure of what to say.

"Fine, sir."

"Good. Good," said the Colonel as he went behind his desk and sat down in the chair. "Well then," he said looking up at Andrew and licking his lips. "All ready for the winter term?"

"Yes, sir."

"Good. Good."

The Colonel leaned forward.

"Look," he said. "The reason I asked you to come is this. I won't beat around the bush. There's something I want you to do. Of course you're free to say no, but I hope you'll see the merit of it and agree."

Andrew nodded.

"There's a new history course—Topics in Southeast Asian History it's called. That's your major isn't it? History?"

"Yes, sir."

"Are you familiar with the course?"

"I've heard of it."

"Are you enrolled?"

"No, sir."

"Uh-huh. Well, it's supposedly on Southeast Asian History, but I have reason to think otherwise. It's being taught by a Professor Petersen. Do you know him?"

"No, sir. He's new."

"Yes, I should think so. At any rate," the Colonel said, clasping and unclasping his hands, "I believe what he's really up to is a bit of indoctrination."

"Really, sir."

"Yes. Really. Anti-war. Pro-VC. The classroom is no place for that sort of thing. Ideology and propaganda don't belong in school. This isn't Russia."

Andrew nodded and shifted in his chair.

"You're wondering what all this has to do with you."

"Yes, sir."

"Well, then, I'll tell you. I need someone to observe the class and let me know what's going on. I'd do it myself but I'd stick out, you see. You're a history major and it's a big class, so no one would take any particular notice of you." The Colonel cleared his throat. "There is no one I would trust more for this assignment. You're the best Cadet Colonel we've ever had."

"You want me to spy for you."

"Well," he said, sitting back in the chair, "that's putting it a bit strongly, I think. No, I'd say I'm asking you to be my eyes and ears. Call it a recon mission."

Andrew licked the sweat from his lip.

"You want me to tell you what he's teaching."

"Exactly. That's all. You don't even have to register or go to every class. Just sit in back and get a sense of things. And write down what you can."

The Colonel stood and walked to the window overlooking the green, his hands clasped behind his back.

"Every day," he said, "young men like you put their lives on the line to defend the freedom of the Vietnamese people. Do you have any idea what it's like for troops in the field to hear about protests and subversion back home?"

The Colonel turned to face him, hands still behind his back.

"How do you imagine your brother feels when he reads about people marching in the streets, encouraging the enemy, waving Vietcong flags, vilifying our Commander in Chief, making the communists out to be some kind of heroes. Not to mention using colleges as platforms for indoctrinating young people and turning them against their own country. Just how do you think he feels?"

Andrew tried to swallow, but his throat was so dry the motion caught half-way down and there was a moment of panic when it seemed he might choke on it and so he tried to focus his mind on the effort by staring out the window at the snow covered ground.

And then it came over him that all he wanted to do was lie down somewhere by the river and listen to the water and look up into the sky, but he knew the Colonel was waiting for him and he knew what he was expected to say, and somewhere inside himself it seemed so obvious and so natural, like the impulse to raise your hand to a place over your heart when someone begins to recite the Pledge of Allegiance or to stand at the opening notes of "The Star Spangled Banner." He knew just what to say, what shits they are, these bastards who turn on their own country, the kind of thing he might nod at when it came from Joe or Steve, but never actually say himself, which he realized now for the first time, how much these were other people's words and not his own. He could feel the anger behind them, but lacking depth and staying power, and so in its place there invariably entered something softer and closer to doubt.

"I don't know, sir."

"You don't know?"

Andrew's mind was a blank, casting about for words as he shifted in the chair, the air in the room suddenly thick and close.

"Well," said the Colonel, his voice beginning to rise, "I'd say stabbed in the back, for one. Young men like your brother. What did you say his name was?"

Andrew had to push the words into the air in front of his face, tears crowding around his eyes, "Josh, sir," blinking them away.

"Yes," said the Colonel, "brave young men like Josh."

In the silence Andrew could feel the Colonel looking at him and he tried to raise his eyes but could only manage a glance at the Colonel squaring his jaw around the words, "So, how about it? What do you say?"

Andrew paused, feeling himself suspended between the old familiar comfort of being taken into the confidence of adults, made one of them, it seemed, by the simple act of being chosen, elevated above the rest, the coach taking him aside—*because only you will understand*—whispering the game-winning play, the nod between them—*yes, I can do this*—the hand on the shoulder—*I know*—suspended between that and some vague foreboding sense of betrayal, of things not spoken, secrets still held close, of letting go at one end before something solid takes hold at the other, things not being what they seem. He looked at the Colonel and for an instant saw his father's face, the light reflecting from his glasses, obscuring his eyes, and unable to see any other way to escape this room, this conversation, this moment caught in a gaping void between worlds, Andrew nodded and mouthed the words, "Okay, sir," and the Colonel made a sound which Andrew knew meant he hadn't heard, and so he said the words again, louder, filling the room.

Andrew hurried down the stairs and out into the sunlit air that smelled of old snow, fear wrapping itself around a growing awareness that he had crossed a line he could not see, and so had no clear idea of where he was or who or what he'd left behind on the other side.

Andrew squared his hat in the mirror and pulled the bill down over his eyes so he could barely see without having to lift his head. It gave him, he thought, a mysterious and intimidating edge, but now he stared into the mirror and felt slightly foolish, too small for the uniform, a boy trying on something belonging to his father.

In his mind he heard his mother's voice, *you don't know why you're doing this*, and then there was the sight of her going down the hall and out the back door, and then the panic rising up inside of him as he ran through the living room and out the front door, circling around behind the dorm where he saw her walking fast down the moonlit cinder path toward the chapel. A vee of Canada geese passed overhead, silhouetted against the sky, honking encouragement to the lone goose out in front. She stopped and looked up and he thought she said something before walking on but he couldn't make out the words. She passed a boy on his way to the library but didn't slow her pace, and the boy turned as she passed and watched her for a moment as if surprised to see the history teacher's wife in such a state.

Andrew ran down the grassy slope and across the lawn as his mother disappeared into the chapel. He entered by a side door and went up to the balcony, standing in the doorway and looking down on the great room empty save for her and the stillness lit by lamps along the wall and what remained of dusk beyond the windows. She was sitting near the front, her head slightly bowed. In the silence he became aware of the organ breathing into the air above the pews, a low murmur, like a slow elongated pulse, coalescing into a stillness that emerged like a boat drifting out of fog.

She rested her hands on the back of the pew in front and laid her head down and began to cry. His eyes filled at the sound of a bawl escaping into the air amidst sobs pouring out of her with the unguarded freedom of what he imagined could only be a broken heart.

And then she was quiet and he saw her take a tissue from her pocket and wipe her nose and lean down and wipe a spot on the floor beneath her. When she stood, he stepped back from the doorway and behind the wall, leaning against it as he closed his eyes, his heart beating hard.

Standing in his room, staring into the mirror, he tried to think of the reason he was doing this, the good-enough reason, but all that came was the look on his brother's face the last time he saw him, the soft, cocky smile as he grabbed Andrew behind the neck and pulled him in for a hug, patting him on the back and whispering, "See ya," before gently pushing him away.

It seemed so simple for his brother, as simple as the look on his father's face when asking about Andrew's Army training or hearing the news that he'd been named Cadet Colonel. He tried to see the expression in the air in front of him now, the clarity in his father's eyes, the banishment of doubt, the simplicity of knowing what is true.

And yet, he thought, Joshua's letter had none of that, unable to sleep or stop shaking, just like their father, dragged from his bed by nightmares night after night. What sort of truth is that?

Everyone said Andrew looked just like his father—the blue eyes and square jaw, the straight, elegant nose, all drawn together around a sense of economy and proportion. A handsome face, but with something more, the sense one got from a well-designed tool or instrument that felt just right in the hand, a balanced blend of form and function, even beautiful in a way.

A sharp rap sounded on the door. "You coming?" said Joe, his voice edged with care and softness since he heard the news.

On the way out they picked up Steve who was standing on the front steps having a smoke and trying to master the fine art of lighting a Zippo by snapping his fingers against the wheel, turning to join them as they went by. They walked to the field house where drill was held in winter, and as they rounded the corner at the far edge of the parking lot Steve made a low whistle, "Holy shit," pointing to a crowd of demonstrators gathered outside the main doors, and then he turned to look up toward an open window in a dorm across the street where someone had just cranked up the volume on their stereo playing "Eve of Destruction."

"Welcome back and fuck you very much," he said.

"If they so much as touch me," said Joe, balling his fists. "Doesn't it piss you off?"

"Oh, hell," said Steve, "they're just a bunch of pissant commie scum."

"Let's just go inside," said Andrew, the words barely out of his mouth when he saw her, Ruth Koszinski, standing out in front, holding high above her head a sign in large red letters, BRING THE WAR HOME, pumping it up and down as she chanted with the crowd, "Hell no, don't go! Hell no, don't go!"

Andrew looked at her and stood very still as if she might not notice that he was there if he did not move, and then there was his brother's voice in his mind *not for you* and then someone taking his arm, a voice nearby, the sound of his name and Joe saying something about going around to the other side, and Andrew suddenly aware as if startled awake. He made a sheepish little smile and shrugged and off they went past the corner of the field house and then across the street to the side doors, only to find them locked. Andrew stood, hands in his pockets, looking up the sidewalk toward the parking lot.

"Fuck it," said Joe. "Let's just do it. Mount up. Lock'n load."

Andrew shook his head and fell in behind the other two, the rhythmic chant swelling as they drew near. He lowered his head and leaned into it, focusing on the polished black toes of his shoes and the crisp sound of leather soles against the pavement, melding into a single cadence as the three men fell into step with one another. He was comforted by the sound, the unity and power of it, but then suddenly they were wading into the crowd that grudgingly gave way to let them pass, the chant rising to envelop them as they made their way toward the doors. And then someone leaned in close to Andrew's downturned face and spoke in a normal voice that seemed, in the midst of such a din, almost intimate, so startling he couldn't help but lift his head, and when he did he was looking into her eyes, only inches away, earnest and blue, staring into his.

"Don't go," she said. "Just . . . don't . . . go." And he straightened up and looked at her, unable to move.

"What?" he said, even though he had heard every word, now drifting off to a distant corner of his mind.

"Don't go," she said, leaning in closer still.

He was frozen to the spot, his knees suddenly weak beneath him, and yet wanting to scream into her face, *you have no idea, you don't understand, you don't know what you're saying, you have no right*, and then suddenly, without warning, wanting to cry just as he felt Joe take him by the arm and pull him toward the door. But Andrew shook him off, turning and stepping toward her, "I have to," through gritted teeth, "I *have* to go."

But, "No," she said, so simply, so matter of fact, "you do not."

And then Joe took his arm again, but this time with both hands and no intention of letting go, "Come on Andy, we're late. Time to bug out. Let's go."

And he turned and followed him inside.

4

For weeks, whenever Andrew looked at Petersen he thought of Leon Trotsky, the Russian revolutionary who believed in action over theory and fled Stalin's reign of terror only to be murdered by an assassin who tracked him down in Mexico and drove an ice pick into his brain. It was the wire-rim glasses that made Andrew think of him, an image from a movie or book he'd long since forgotten, of communists sitting at small tables in smoke filled rooms, soft caps on their heads, conspiring as they drank hot tea from glass mugs. That image along with Petersen's thin, angular body suggested the spare existence of one who made revolution and was therefore always on the run even when seemingly at rest. And the shock of hair over his forehead, which he didn't bother with, as if he had more pressing things to do.

From his perch in the last row where he could lean his head against the wall and look down over the heads of other students, Andrew saw in Petersen a figure of both menace and fascination. For the first few days he barely heard the lectures, so fixed was he on the face turned downward to the notes spread out on the lectern, pausing to rearrange them as though he'd lost his way among pages he'd neglected to number. His voice was soft and yet every word was edged with the earnest intent of someone who did not foresee a second chance to get it right.

Andrew kept trying to see in the face before him some hint of the evil that he was coming to believe had seized his brother and carried him away, what the Colonel was intent on finding here, but every time he thought he had a fix on it, something intervened, a thoughtful expression or the gentle way Petersen fielded a difficult question.

Andrew's notes were sparse because he heard nothing he thought would be of use, little mention of Vietnam, and even then nothing more recent than the first coming of Europeans hundreds of years ago. And so he doodled, often sketching Petersen behind the lectern. Once he found himself adding a pair of short horns to the head and a tail meandering out behind with a little fork at the end, and when he looked up to see the student next to him staring at the sketch, he hurriedly covered it with his hand.

Ruth Koszinski sat in the far back corner a few rows down from the last, and Andrew made a point of arriving late and leaving just as students closed their notebooks and stirred into motion. Once, she came in late and just as she was sitting down she glanced at him, her eyes fixed on his face just long enough for him to see she knew who he was.

He started marking his calendar to keep track of how long his brother had been missing, leafing through the months ahead to figure how long was long enough for him to reappear. What was at first measured in days became weeks gradually slipping into a vaguely unbounded unit of time he could not bring himself to try to name.

Toward the end of February he asked the Colonel to relieve him of the assignment, but the Colonel urged him on, which he still could not resist, something in the tone of voice, a dead certainty that Andrew could not match. Besides, spying on Petersen gave him something to do, a point of focus, a way to attend to his lost brother without actually having to think about him and where he was and the time that was running out, one step removed in his mind, obscured and cushioned by a thick veil of history. And there was also the recurring sight of Ruth Koszinski, her head bent over her notes or looking up at Petersen. He wondered if she found the man attractive, his intellect filling the room. She must, he thought, for that was what he saw in her, that same intensity radiating outward all around and yet also turned inward on itself.

It was the sound of a single word that reached into the deep pool of Andrew's drifting mind and pulled him toward the light just above the surface, something about the Portuguese and pepper and spices, *colonialism*, and then the Dutch, English, and Spanish, with the French arriving last, worried they were too late to get a large enough piece of the action to turn themselves into a global power.

"They are, of course, entirely up to it," said Petersen. "They are driven by adventurism and greed and a missionary zeal to spread their culture to people they regard as backward, which," he said with a little smile, "if you've ever been to Paris, you know includes most people in the world." He paused for the soft wave of laughter to ripple across the room.

Andrew picked up his pen and began to write.

"So, how do the French do colonialism? They begin by installing missionaries and commercial enterprises and then use any excuse to resort to force. They make impossible demands, and when the mandarins object, the French bring their warships close to shore and shell the towns and cities and then demand still more concessions as the price of peace."

Andrew looked at Ruth, her head bent low as she wrote, her free hand at the back of her neck, fingers combing through her hair.

"When the Emperor Tu Duc finally surrenders to the French in 1861, he sends a plea for help to Abraham Lincoln, but the President does not reply, having problems of his own. By 1883, Vietnam no longer exists as a country by that name. Rice becomes a crop for export, driving peasants from the land to work as cheap labor in factories and mines."

Andrew laid the pen on the desk and shook his fingers to relieve the ache, looking about the room and picking up a shift in mood, students leaning in as if Petersen had lowered his voice and made it harder for them to hear. But, if anything, he had grown louder, each sentence more crisp and distinct than the one before.

And then came the name Andrew had been waiting for.

"Ho Chi Minh signed on as a merchant seaman in 1913 and sailed around the world. Ho visited San Francisco and lived in Brooklyn for a year and then worked in London as a pastry chef in a five-star hotel."

Andrew looked at Petersen saying the name with lips softly rounded to form the word, noting the easy familiarity of Petersen not bothering to speak the full name, as if nothing else was necessary to identify the man, which, of course, was true, *Ho* the architect of war, of history itself it seemed, visionary *Ho*, inscrutable *Ho*, implacable *Ho*, who loomed Fu-Manchu-like in Andrew's mind, the quintessence of evil and yet, like evil, also fascinating, holding out the promise of a secret that Andrew felt compelled to know.

Petersen looked at his watch and shuffled his papers. "That's it for today," he said. "You'll notice we're taking a bit of detour that's not on the syllabus."

A voice from the crowd asked about additional things to read and Petersen smiled at the murmurs of approval as he shook his head. "I'm not being nice," he said. "I just don't know what you could read in a few weeks without having to live in the library. You'll have to settle for me. I'll hand out a bibliography next time for the more motivated among you."

Andrew, pen in his teeth, was the first one out the door and was across the slush covered street before he'd even put on his coat. He hurried across the green with no idea of where he was going until he was mounting the stairs to the second floor of the ROTC building and suddenly he thought of Ruth Koszinski combing her fingers through the fine hair at the back of her neck. He remembered his anger at the field house, but also how when he looked at her or heard the sound of her voice, something crowded the anger out, the way she leaned over that afternoon, her face so close to his in the crowd, and spoke to him with the intimate tone of someone who knew things, mysterious and secret, unmistakably implying that some of what she knew was about him. He slowed several stairs from the top and stood, one foot up and one foot down, his breath hollow in his ears as if he were under water. Above him, a conversation drifted from the Colonel's office where Major Kilgore sat just inside the open door, his leg slung over the arm of the chair, pant leg hiked up over a line of pale skin above the black sock. Andrew leaned against the wall as he heard the Major laugh at something the

Colonel said and bark a reply. But Andrew couldn't make out the words, turning away down the stairs, feeling suddenly out of place, afraid of being discovered, as if he would be called to account for something he as yet did not know he had done, hurrying down the stairs and out the door into the cold.

He stood in the middle of the green, breathing hard as he tried to focus his mind on what had just happened, what it was about the name of Ho Chi Minh that had such power to turn him around in his mind, produce so much confusion, and send him off in a direction that took him to a place that, when he got there, made no sense at all. He felt the fear coming back into his body as he stood at the top of the stairs, hearing the Major's voice and not wanting him to know. But what was there to know? What had he done? What had he heard?

Students passing by made him suddenly conscious of standing in the middle of the green and he turned to join the flow across the street to the student center where he checked his mail and went to the snack bar for a cup of coffee. He settled into a chair by a large window on the south wall and looked out at the water dripping off icicles hanging from the roof, glistening in the sun against a deep blue sky.

"Where's your costume?"

He turned, startled by the voice, his mouth falling open as he looked up into the face of Ruth Koszinski who stood just a few feet away, a book bag slung over her shoulder, her cheeks red from the cold.

"What?"

"Where's the uniform?"

He felt the color rising in his face, embarrassed at his seeming inability to comprehend the question, going back and forth between its obvious meaning, which made no sense for her to ask, and something else he could not see, finally giving in with a shrug, muttering, "My closet," and then she said, not missing a beat, "Oh, and you?"

He made an awkward little smile, unused to feeling so inept, bordering on stupid. "What do you mean?"

"Never mind," she said, not taking her eyes from his face as he looked away, fingering the handle on the cup.

"You liking the class?" she said.

He hesitated, managing a little nod.

"I was surprised to see you there."

"It's my major."

"Still," she said, "I'm surprised."

"Oh."

"You must be boning up."

"For what?"

"Vietnam. You're all set to go, aren't you?"

He just looked at her.

"So, now you'll know what you're getting into. Be prepared," she said, making a soft little punch with her fist in the air. "I'll bet you were a Boy Scout."

He said nothing, feeling his mind catching up to the conversation, ready now to match her word for word.

"I thought as much," she said. "Eagle Scout, I'll bet."

Andrew didn't move.

"Am I wrong?" she said.

"About what?"

"Ah," she said, nodding "that's good. Very good," a faint edge coming into her voice as she turned away, "See ya."

He was glad to see her leave and yet wanted her to stay even though he had no idea what to do with her if she did. Her eyes seemed a deeper blue than he remembered, especially the left one that was like an open window he could fall into if he wasn't careful. And the corners of her eyes had drawn up in a knowing little smile as she turned, which he wondered about as he watched her thread her way among the tables and disappear through the door.

At the next class, Petersen gave out a bibliography and Andrew spent the entire afternoon in the library reading about the French.

Toward evening he was back in the dorm, lying on his bed and looking up into the fading light. From the floor above, The Doors sang "Light My Fire" and loud talk and laughter rose and fell, a window flung open, someone shouting to someone in the street, and then Andrew was wondering at the fact that everything could be so bad over there where his brother was or had last been seen, and yet so normal here, when Steve walked in, a pile of books in one hand and his coat dangling on the floor from the other.

"So," he said, "how's the master spy?"

Andrew looked at him.

"Yes?" said Steve, drawing out the word.

Andrew shook his head and looked away.

"What?" said Steve.

Silence, and then, "Did you know," said Andrew, "about the French?"

"Which French?"

"The ones in Vietnam."

"I don't know. I suppose. What about them?"

"Nothing."

"Right," said Steve, his books landing on the desk with a thump. "I thought this was Asian History."

"It is," said Andrew. "The French were in Vietnam." He propped himself up on an elbow. "Are you listening?"

"Yeah, yeah," said Steve, waving his hand, "so what about it?"

"Nothing."

"Come on, tell me—"

"Never mind."

"Tell Stevie what the big bad Frenchie did to the poor little Vietnamese."

"I said never mind."

"No *Liberté, Egalité, Fraternité?*"

Andrew looked at him, his face implacable, staring him down.

Steve shrugged and slung the coat over his shoulder. "Okay. Whatever. You eat yet?"

Andrew shook his head.

"What's the matter with you, anyway?" said Steve. And then a softening came over his face. "Oh, shit," he said, "I forgot, your brother. I'm sorry."

"It's all right."

There was a silence and then Steve took a deep breath and let it out on a sigh. "Well," he said, "I get that you're upset, but Christ, Drew, who cares what the French did a hundred years ago?"

"Not that long ago."

"Is that guy Petersen getting to you?"

Andrew shook his head.

"Well," said Steve. "I say fuck it and let 'em eat cake and I'm for dinner. A man's gotta eat. You coming?"

Andrew shook his head. Steve nodded and turned and was out the door, breaking into an off-key rendition of the Rolling Stones getting no satisfaction, his voice fading down the stairs.

Andrew put his hands behind his head to resume staring at the ceiling.

So, he thought, the French are the bad guys, which means the good guys are . . . what . . . the VC . . . no, hardly . . . then the U.S., but then why do we come to help the French . . . so, then, there *are* no good guys, and that makes no sense at all.

He sat up, swinging his legs over the edge of the bed.

Comment allez vous? Bien, merci, et vous? Voulez vous coucher avec moi? He did a rough count of how many years of French he'd taken, dividing it into the number of things he was still able to say and then factoring in their probable significance in his life, and he knew without actually doing the math that the result would be a very, very small number. Better that than German, he thought, remembering the look of carefully contained disgust that came over his father's face whenever he heard the sound of it, which was pretty often, considering that Mr. Grundig, who taught German, was housemaster in the other half of the dorm and the walls were thin enough to hear him if he was feeling bombastic which was fairly often.

But there has to be a good guy, he thought, just like you have to have an up if you're going to have a down. And then Petersen's face came into his mind, his intense, penetrating gaze looking out over the class, and Andrew knew in that moment that Petersen was going to find a way to connect the French beast to the United States and use that to drag America down into the mud by making it seem that this country, a beacon of freedom and hope to the world, *land of the free and home of the brave*, words that Andrew took to mean something real and always had from even before he knew what they meant, singing the song in school, mouthing the words, trying to keep up with the melody. He could see it coming now. Petersen was going to make the French evil into something American and then smear it over everyone, including Joshua. That's what he'll try to get us to think, he thought, and to hate our country the way he probably does. Except, why would an American want to do that?

Snow swirled in the air outside the window. The lecture hall smelled of damp wool and the radiator softly clanged along the wall as Petersen spoke.

"When the Japanese invade in 1940, they leave the French in charge to run the country for them. When the war ends, Roosevelt is against letting the French back in unless they agree to eventual independence."

Andrew scribbled in the margin, *U.S. against French.*

"But then Roosevelt dies and with the French hinting they might go communist if they don't get their way, the U.S. changes its mind."

Andrew put down the pen.

"Ho writes eight letters to President Truman, reminding him of U.S. policy against colonialism. Truman does not reply."

Andrew picked up the pen and forged ahead, *Vietminh Congress proclaims independence; warns UN to live up to anti-colonial principles (UN & Atlantic Charters). Ho's 4th of July speech—*

Petersen stepped to the side as he leaned an elbow on the lectern.

"Listen to the words he uses here—

'*We hold the truth that all men are created equal, that they are endowed by their Creator with certain inalienable rights, among them life, liberty, and the pursuit of happiness.*'

"Sound familiar?" said Petersen, stepping behind the lectern and raising his fist to his lips as he cleared his throat.

"That same year, the last Emperor of Vietnam, Bao Di, who has no real power, sends a message to Charles de Gaulle, President of France.

'*You would understand better if you could see what is happening here, if you could feel this desire for independence which is in everyone's heart and which no human force can any longer restrain. Even if you come to re-establish a French administration here, it will no longer be obeyed: each village will be a nest of resistance, each former collaborator an enemy, and your officials and colonists will themselves ask to leave this atmosphere which they will be unable to breathe.*'

"So," said Petersen, looking up from his notes. "What do you suppose happens now?"

The students watched him, waiting for an answer until they realized it was he who was waiting for them. Finally, a young man raised his hand.

"They leave?" laughter rippling across the room, the student making a little smile, a shrug.

"Well," said Petersen, "actually that's not such a silly idea. Here you have the Atlantic and UN Charters against colonialism, not to mention our own Declaration of Independence." He leaned forward, curling his fingers over the front edge of the lectern. "Surely it makes sense that the French would get the hint, not to mention the U.S., that's just had its own sacred text read back to it from halfway around the world."

He stopped and in the deepening silence Andrew rocked slowly forward and back in the chair, knowing what was coming now.

"But no," said Petersen, "the French return in force. And who provides the ships and planes to transport the French divisions?" He paused, looking from one side of the room to the other. "The United States of America."

A soft rustling among the students slowly grew into a chorus of creaking chairs and clearing throats.

ask him why

A hand going up, "What about the communists?"

yes

"What about them?"

ask the question

"Isn't that why the U.S. supported the French? To stop the communists from taking over?"

yes

"Good question," said Petersen. "Communism certainly plays a key roll in this. As does capitalism, of course." He stepped away from the lectern and sat on a chair near the edge of the platform, leaning forward, forearms resting on his knees as he looked out over the room.

"Let's consider Ho's point of view. The French come back and rule just like they did before, with a modern military backed by billions of U.S. dollars. Suppose you're Ho Chi Minh. What do you do? Where do you go for help? The U.N.? But Vietnam isn't a member of the U.N., it's part of France. It'd be like Vermont going to the U.N."

Andrew felt his mind begin to disconnect from the train of Petersen's thought, still following the argument, but observing it from a height, like a hawk circling a field in search of a mouse, looking for a sign, some flaw that would make it all come unraveled, all of it untrue, sudden and full of relief, like the sun breaking through the clouds, some magical sleight of intellect, a mind trick so graceful and seamless that it would all be over, transformed into something else, *and Joshua*

Petersen sat back in the chair and folded his arms across his chest.

Joshua's face, his eyes, oh Joshua

"So. What can he do? Maybe he should negotiate, except the French insist the Vietnamese first give up any claim to independence, so that doesn't get very far. What else, then?"

come home

"Running out of options here, aren't we. Maybe they could try Gandhi's tactics, civil disobedience, passive resistance, that sort of thing."

leave him alone

"Except the Vietnamese are a warrior people who've always hated foreign interference and domination."

let him go

"Not unlike the U.S., actually. 'Don't tread on me.' Not much room for Gandhi there—"

please

It took awhile for Andrew to become aware of the silence in the room and, then, looking up from his desk, to notice the faces turned in his direction. And then it dawned on him that the words that he thought were only in his mind had somehow found a way out into the air, and he quickly began to gather up his things.

"Excuse me," said Petersen.

Andrew stood up to leave.

"Young man," came Petersen's voice. Andrew tried to move against the sheer weight of attention and the certain knowledge that Petersen was talking to him and no one else, only to him.

"You said something," said Petersen.

Andrew shrugged.

"What was it?"

"Nothing."

"I'd like to know."

Andrew tried to think of the word, but there were so many of them and he could not be sure just which had managed to escape.

"He said 'please'," came the voice of the student beside him and a faint ripple of laughter went through the room, but Andrew could not help but notice Petersen not joining in.

"Is there something you want to say?" said Petersen.

"No," said Andrew, still standing in front of his chair, books in his hands.

"Are you sure? I'd like to hear it."

Andrew stood there in front of everyone for what seemed a very long time, longer than he thought he could bear, except that after awhile it seemed less difficult than before, time slowing almost to a stop, and there was something in the way Petersen looked at him, all the time in the world, patiently waiting him out, and then it occurred to him that maybe Petersen really did want to know, but exactly what it was, Andrew could not see, shaking his head, "I don't know."

"Give it a try."

Andrew stood awhile longer before clearing his lungs with a sigh. "It just seems to me," he said, looking down, "that anyone would be better than the communists. Even the French."

"Well," said Petersen, "that may be. And maybe not." He paused, his eyes fixed on Andrew's downturned face as he spoke in soft, measured tones, as if his words might tip over something fragile if he weren't careful. "Either way, though, in the end you go with whoever's got what you need to survive. And the Chinese are just across the border with all the equipment it takes to make an army that could match the French. Perhaps even the Americans."

Andrew felt a greater sadness than he'd ever known bearing down on him with such a weight that he could barely move. And then he was aware that Petersen had stopped talking and was looking up at him. "I'd be interested to know what you're thinking," he said.

For a moment Andrew's mind was blank, but then the words just started coming out of him, "It just seems you're making it out like the U.S. is one of the bad guys. But we're not. And they're not the good guys. They're just a bunch of killers," the last coming out so softly that only the student next to him could make it out, looking away in silence.

"Well," said Petersen, "maybe there aren't any good guys, except in the movies. Now there's a thought."

He stepped toward the edge of the platform.

"I'm just trying to point out that to explain something as complex as Vietnam, it takes more than calling it communist aggression. Or good versus evil. Or killing, although there's plenty of that on both sides. But you have to realize they're human beings who believe they're up against something that threatens what really matters to them."

Andrew, feeling suddenly exposed standing in front of his chair, sat down.

Petersen's voice dropped to a soft and measured tone, almost intimate, speaking to the whole class now. "In a way, Ho Chi Minh is no more extreme in what he's prepared to do to unify his country than was . . . say . . . Abraham Lincoln. Lincoln did, after all, state that he would do whatever it took to keep the Union together. Even if it meant a bloody civil war. Or keeping blacks in slavery."

He looked around the room.

"Didn't know that, did you? They didn't teach you that in high school. The Great Emancipator. Well, it's right there. 'If I could save the Union without freeing *any* slave, I would do it.' He wrote that in 1862 in a letter to the *New York Herald Tribune*. You can look it up.

"Ho Chi Minh is certainly a communist," said Petersen, "and you don't have to like that. But, I think we do have to acknowledge that a communist isn't all that he is. He's also a patriot who loves his country, just like Lincoln, and he turned to communism because the capitalists all sided with the French. It all came back to where was the man supposed to go? And when he turned to China and Russia for help, the U.S. sat back and said, 'Aha, see, we always knew he was just a communist.' Damned if he did and damned if he didn't."

Andrew leaned back in the chair and pressed his fingertips into his eyes, feeling suddenly tired and wanting only to be away from this place, from everywhere.

Petersen looked up for a moment and then shrugged and turned away.

Andrew inhabited the library, missing classes and coming back late to the dorm, sometimes after the others had gone to sleep. Outside the library, in classrooms or the dining hall or his room, he felt vulnerable and exposed, as if everyone were looking at him because he'd forgotten to get dressed before leaving his room or was talking to someone who wasn't there. But in the library, sitting on the floor in the dimly lit stacks or barricaded by books piled high on a study table in a far corner of the reserve room, he felt safe, enveloped in a stillness that calmed his mind, if only for awhile. He often thought of his brother, but in a quieter and less agitated way than on the outside, for now he was on a mission to bring his brother home, because he had come to believe, although he would have been hard pressed to find the words, that if he could catch up to the history that had reached out and grabbed hold of his brother, and somehow show that Petersen was wrong, then Joshua would be found, no longer missing, no longer lost.

Day by day he concentrated on building a case and getting ahead of the class so that he could anticipate Petersen's next move. Then he waited for the flaw, the moment when the lecture departed from the text to reveal the lie. Any lie would do, even a mere distortion of fact, the kind of thing most students would never even notice, a slender thread he could pull until it all came undone.

But week after week the moment did not arrive. The readings were diverse, published in France or Britain or Canada, some in the U.S., and extending back more than a hundred years. And yet there was a consistency among them that he found disturbing, and, even more, the realization that Petersen had read them all, probably more than once, and could tell by Andrew's pointed questions that he was reading them as well, like a dog sniffing at his heels and occasionally loping a slow circle around him just to show that he could.

He had to leave the library to go to class and to sleep and eat and shower and change his clothes. And there was also the matter of his growing interest in Ruth Koszinski, which drew him to the snack bar almost every day at the same time as before, where he bought coffee and a donut and sat at the same table by the window and waited for upwards of an hour before going back to work.

He was watching a nuthatch flit across the snow when he looked up to see her standing beside him, her smile taking him by surprise. "Mind if I sit?"

He shook his head.

"I'm Ruth," she said. "Ruth Koszinski."

"I know," he said, then spoke his name.

"I knew the Carson part," she said, "but not the Andrew."

He looked at her, puzzled. She tapped the right side of her chest, just above her breast, which he couldn't help but notice.

"Your name tag. On your uniform."

"Oh."

"You're the man in charge, right?"

"What do you mean?"

"The Army. ROTC. All the brass on your shoulders."

"Oh, that."

"Yeah, that. So tell me, how did it happen?"

"How did what happen?"

"How you got to be the big cheese," she said. "Are you the best shot? The most gung-ho? First one over the wall?"

"Why do you want to know?" he said. "Am I some kind of project?"

"Maybe. Let's just say I'm fascinated when an intelligent man winds up leading the charge. I love a good contradiction. So, how'd you wind up being the . . . " she looked at him.

"Cadet Colonel," he said.

"Whatever."

"How'd you wind up carrying signs and harassing people?"

"I asked you first," she said.

Andrew looked out the window and saw a faint reflection of her in the glass, her eyes fixed on him as she waited for an answer, and he felt himself suspended between the urge to tell her to go fuck herself and the desire to tell her everything she wanted to know.

"Okay," she said, "I'll go first if that's what it takes. I grew up in New York and everyone in my family—well, not everyone, but my father certainly and my mother—are the sort of people who get pissed off about things. Not just anything, but bad things, like violence and cruelty and stealing people's land and exploiting their labor and sucking the life out of them. And of course nationalism—"

"What's wrong with that?"

"Oh," she said, "don't get me started. Sometime when I know you better. A lot better." She reached for his coffee. "Mind if I have a sip?"

"No," he said, sitting back in the chair, "go ahead."

She took a sip of coffee, then wrinkled her lips and shook her head. "Too much sugar."

"Sorry."

"That's all right. Anyway . . . where was I . . . "

"Growing up in New York."

"Oh, right. Anyway, growing up with them made it easy to see the war for what it is." She fixed her eyes on his face and smiled. "So," she said, "that's me. What's your excuse?"

"Why should I tell you?"

"Well, you've got me there," she said and then her eyes widened, leading the rest of her face into a look that was both guileless and disarming.

Andrew couldn't help but smile as he sat forward, elbows on the table. "Well," he said, his voice so quiet she had to lean in to hear, "okay, but it's not what you think."

"You're not the best shot?"

"No."

"Or first one over the wall?"

He shook his head.

"How disappointing," she said.

"At the end of basic training we had this graduation parade and they needed someone to be brigade commander."

"Which is—"

"The guy who stands in front of all the troops and tells them what to do."

"And?"

"I tried out."

"You auditioned."

"You could say that."

"And you did this . . . why?"

"Because . . . I don't know. Free pizza. A night off. Who knows. Anyway, we stood out there with a sergeant a hundred yards off and yelled commands at him. I guess I yelled the best, because they chose me."

"That's it? You had the biggest mouth?"

He smiled. "I guess. So they made me sergeant major my junior year and colonel the next."

"Jesus. No wonder everything's all screwed up."

"What's your major?" said Andrew.

"No major. I'm a grad student."

"What department?"

"English."

"Really. Huh. So, what'll you do with that? Teach?"

"Oh, God, no. I'm gonna write."

"Really. Write what?"

"Books. Novels."

"So what're you doing in Southeast Asian History? Not to mention U.S. History."

She lifted her eyebrows and tilted back her head, taking the measure of him.

"You noticed."

"Sort of."

"Sort of, my foot. I take the class because I want to know what's going on. A better question is what you're doing there."

"I told you before. It's my major."

"Right," she said. "And?"

He looked at her for a moment. "You're awfully sure of yourself."

She looked out the window, then back at him. "I guess I am. Aren't you?"

He tried to meet the steady gaze coming from her eyes, but after a moment he turned his head and looked out the window. The nuthatch was gone.

She leaned on the table and gently wagged a finger in the air as she spoke. "You've got about as much business going to Vietnam as my Aunt Fanny."

"Really," he said. "How's she like it over there?"

"Not much. She's dead. Got hit by a cab on Second Avenue."

He looked at her—nodding her head slowly up and down, not taking her eyes from his face—and could think of nothing to say.

He stopped taking notes because he forgot about the Colonel and thought he knew what Petersen was going to say before he said it. Instead, he looked at him the whole time, not a stare or simply paying attention like an audience at a play. It was rather a look that felt to Petersen, who couldn't help but notice, as if the young man in the back row were looking right through him at something just behind his head. It was unnerving to be watched in this way and he occasionally lost his place and had to look down at his notes to rediscover the thread.

If Andrew were taking notes, he would have written something like

Vietnamese defeat French at Dienbienphu; French want to negotiate but U.S. opposed (why?)

1954 Geneva Accord declares cease fire and then temporarily divides Vietnam into north and south (<u>not</u> two countries)

> *Provides for elections (1956) and eventual unification*
> *U.S. & Vietnamese don't sign Accord. U.S. says it won't interfere—no use of force*
> *U.S. calls north/south line an international boundary even though Eisenhower agrees it's not*
>> *Calls presence of north troops in south 'external aggression'*
>> *North insists Vietnam is one country*
> *U.S. secretly sends arms & combat teams in violation of Geneva Accords. Blocks elections (why?)*
> *U.S. backs Diem—catholic, nationalist(ha!), lived in U.S.*
>> *Tries to crush Vietminh—repression also in north*
> *Kennedy (1962) asked if U.S. troops engaged in fighting*
>> *Answer—"No"*
> *Diem represses Buddhists, closes nightclubs, etc. Street protests, Buddhists set themselves on fire. U.S. backs a coup, Diem & brother murdered (1963), no investigation*
>> *Kennedy assassinated (November)*

At the end of class Petersen gathered his notes and slid them into his briefcase before looking up, but Andrew was already gone.

Andrew lay awake in the middle of the night, staring up at the ceiling, the room unlit even by the moon, cradling his head in his hands, the last letter from his brother lying open on his chest.

He remembered a spring afternoon, when they were boys, and they went down to the pond in the bird sanctuary and Joshua invented a game that came to him when he stepped out on the ice and heard it crack beneath his feet. He was close enough to shore that the only danger was getting wet, but he was startled by the sound and as he moved away from it he discovered that the right amount of forward motion could keep him from letting down his full weight upon the ice. And so it became a game between them, to see how far they could outrun the failing ice.

Andrew read the letter again and thought of the smile on his brother's face, which had appeared in his mind just a few hours ago when his weariness took on a weight that he could no longer sustain with the forward motion of his desperate attempt to keep his brother alive and bring him home. It came to him at the least expected moment, in the men's room of the library after Petersen's class, standing over the urinal, watching the flow around the porcelain, the soft gurgle down the drain, and suddenly the progression of days and weeks that seemed without end came to a halt with nothing to follow except the thought that now sought entrance to his mind. He closed his eyes to fight against its incursion through his weariness, incredulous at being taken so completely by surprise, and then a moment of panic as he tried to keep it at bay *no . . . no* to find a way to make it impossible, and yet, inexorably, slowly filling with the dread certainty that Joshua was dead.

He lay in bed, his mind in an uproar. It was too late to catch up with history, for whatever it was, it had swallowed up his brother and would never give him back.

He got out of bed and dressed in the dark, careful not to wake Steve and Joe, then went out across the green and into the woods. He tried to calm his mind but it did no good, and by the time he got back to his room, he was in a rage, slamming the door and standing with his back against it, allowing the tears to flow.

They asked him what was the matter, their voices sounding young in the dark, but he could only shake his head until they turned on the light and finally understood and climbed out of bed and went to him and sat him in a chair and stayed up with him into the night, trying to calm him down. When they all finally went back to bed, Andrew was still wide awake, his mind racing from one thought to another, and so he got up again and began to drink, going through the half-empty bottles in the little bar Joe made in the wood shop junior year.

But no matter how drunk he got, Andrew couldn't keep an image from coming into his mind, a picture itself so dark he could barely make it out. And yet he sensed its every detail—the jungle canopy dense and high above the ground, the body stretched out in the shadows, face down, crumpled, the joints suddenly come undone, bones dissolving and muscle melting into air. And the silence, except for the droning of the flies.

Someone shook him by the shoulder, removed and from a distance, as if his arm were asleep, leaving behind no more than the idea of being touched and moved

come on get up it's late

floating somewhere between the voice and the bed, eyelids thick and heavy, tongue large in his mouth, a dull pain wrapped around the back of his neck

"come on"

a sudden jerk of his arm as he shook away the hand

"you're gonna miss your first class"

"leave me the fuck alone"

muffled voices

"pissed"

"let him be"

the door closing, Andrew sinking down into something like sleep

walking across a field of hay, his brother looming above him even though he's only two years older, the sun high and hot on their faces, blades of grass dangling from their mouths and the feeling that life is easy, walking beside his brother, their voices low and familiar "Race you to the trees," his brother's little smile cast over his shoulder before setting off at a dead run, Andrew running after in slow motion, the distance lengthening with every stride Josh! Wait up! the clouds growing dark and the wind turning cold as he runs, pumping his legs through the hay until he trips and falls, scrambling to his feet, looking out over the field, the hay turning grey beneath the changing sky, running to the edge of the woods and looking in, no sign of where his brother has gone, calling out his name and beginning to cry, a boy alone with darkness coming on and the wind moving through the trees

Andrew woke in a cold sweat and sat on the edge of the bed, his head in his hands, rubbing his temples, trying to clear his mind and make the pain go away.

Petersen had already begun when Andrew arrived and stood in the doorway at the back of the room, leaning against the jamb for support. His hair was uncombed and flecked with snow and a light stubble of beard covered the smooth skin of his face. His head hurt and he felt queasy from lack of food and the drinking that ended only a few hours before. His mind moved slowly, swimming in mud, and yet there was something almost graceful in the unimpeded flow and clarity of his thoughts.

He stared down the aisle at Petersen who looked up from his notes to where Andrew stood in the doorway. Petersen went on with what he was saying, then looked up again.

"Why don't you join us?" he said, gesturing with his hand.

When Andrew noticed the light reflecting back from Petersen's glasses, a wave of fear passed through him and it was all he could do to keep from throwing up. Everyone turned to look at him standing there breathing through his mouth, wanting to turn and run away but unable to move from the spot where he had placed himself, his mind struggling to catch up as Petersen looked at him, "Is there a problem?"

Andrew's mind overflowed with words and yet he could think of nothing to say, tears gathering along the rims of his eyes, panic tightening his chest as he watched the arrival of what seemed from the distant perspective of his floundering mind a moment of truth that might linger for no more than an instant before moving on and leaving him behind. Panic at the impending loss and panic that it might not be lost soon enough to save him from having to step into the room and find the words to speak to this man who looked up at him, patiently waiting him out like his father at the other end of a chess board, already knowing his next move and the next one after that, right down to the end.

"Hello?" came the voice from down below, then a titter of laughter from the crowd, a pause, "Will you join us?" and something in the tone, some lack of guile, pulling Andrew into the room, and when he spoke, the words came out too loud, as if he were trying to rise above a great commotion in his mind.

"Why don't you?"

A silence, Petersen turning his head as if to catch the words, a small uncertain smile, "Why don't I what?"

Andrew watched himself passing by the point of no return to encounter the strangely calming certainty of no going back, of nothing left to protect, everything already lost, hearing the words come out of him, "Take our side for once," his voice breaking, "you always take their side."

Petersen looked at him, the light reflecting from his glasses as he moved his head.

"Whose side?"

"You know what I mean."

The room was quiet, the students all turned in their seats, and Andrew had to make an effort to keep from looking to where he knew he would see Ruth Koszinski regarding him with an expression he didn't even want to think about. His tongue felt large and dead in the sour dryness of his mouth and a dull pain crawled up the back of his head. The room was hot and stuffy, his skin clammy as sweat rolled down the furrow of his spine.

"Well," said Petersen, looking down, fingers stroking his forehead.

"Don't you know who they are?" Andrew called out from the doorway, "Who they're killing over there? Don't you care?"

He pushed off from the jamb, his legs trembling beneath him, "How can you take their side?"

"I do care. And it's not that simple—"

"Yes, it is that simple," said Andrew, tears welling in his eyes and before they could escape he turned and walked away, not looking back to see Petersen gazing up the aisle, lips parted, poised over something to say, but now with no one to say it to. Nor did he see Ruth Koszinski gather up her things and follow him out the door.

He was halfway across the green when she fell in beside him, matching him step for step.

"So," she said, "where're you off to?"

He looked at her, then away.

"Nowhere."

"You can say that again."

"Just leave me alone."

"I don't think I can do that."

He stopped and turned.

"Why the hell not?"

"Because I think you're making a mistake."

"Well," he said, walking away, "that's my business."

"Not really," she said, catching up again.

"Whose, then. Yours?"

"Actually—"

"I'm not your fucking project—"

"—mine and everyone else's," she said. "You think this war is just about you?"

He stopped and stepped back from her, palms in front of him to keep a distance.

"Look," he said, teeth clenched, "just . . . " and then he sighed and looked at the ground, "just . . . don't."

She wrinkled her face and gave her head a little shake. "Not good enough, Andrew."

He looked at her, his eyes hard.

"I don't even know you," he said.

"Maybe you should."

"Right. That's what I need. I need to know some . . . what . . . New York . . . peacenik," he said, waving an arm in the air as if trying to find the words in the snow drifting down.

"That's right," she said. "That's just what I am. And what does that make you? A warnik? Is that what you are? Is that your thing?

Is that what God put you here for? Go halfway around the world and kick the living shit out of some little country that can barely feed itself?"

"It's not about that."

"Oh," she said, "and how would you know what it's about? Do you know *anything* about Vietnam? Can you find it on a fucking map?"

"Fuck you."

"You wish," she said, looking right at him, her eyes deep and wide as they followed his every move, like an angler with a fish on the end of a line.

He shook his head and walked away, but she was close behind, the silence punctuated by the sharp crunch of their footsteps on the packed snow. And then he heard her voice, breathless, earnest, and low from just over his shoulder.

"You cannot kill people . . . or offer yourself to be killed . . . without knowing why."

He walked on, eyes wild, looking straight ahead.

"Petersen knows things you don't," she said. "Ask him. Fight with him. But don't run away."

"I'm not."

"You could've fooled me."

"Probably not hard to do."

"Oh, come on, you can do better than that."

"Maybe not," he said. "You don't know me."

"No. I don't."

"Then why bother?"

She came to a stop, calling after him, "I don't know."

She watched the distance increase for a moment, then shook her head and took off after him again, passing him by and turning to walk backwards in front of him.

"Maybe I bother because you're not like the others."

"You think so."

"They're all half dead, Andrew. They just do what they're told."

"I do what I'm told."

"Yes, you do. But you're also stirred up about it."

"And you think that matters."

"It does about this."

He tried to pass her but she matched him step for step until he stopped, hands on his hips, looking down at the ground.

"I think the truth matters to you," she said. "I saw it in your face that day."

She took a step toward him, mindful of the held rage in front of her.

"And I think it matters enough to turn yourself inside out if that's what it takes. Which is what I think you're doing. Which is why I bother."

"You do," he said, still looking at the ground.

"Yes."

"Well," he said, "good for you," walking past her and away. He did not look back, nor did she turn to watch him go.

The college was nestled in the hills of northern New Hampshire along the eastern shore of the Connecticut River, which was where Andrew took himself now, to the boathouse where the crew kept its shell and the outing club stored kayaks and canoes. Joe drove by and rolled down the window and offered him a ride but Andrew waved him on. At the bridge at the bottom of the hill he turned down the dirt road leading to the boathouse and the dock. When he saw the parking lot empty he felt relieved to be alone.

He stopped at the edge of the lot to throw up in a ditch.

He wiped his face with snow and went to the boathouse where he took a chair from the porch down to the dock and sat looking out over the ice.

He tried to get his mind to reassemble the fragments of memory beginning with the moment he realized he was talking from the back of the room, the words, the nausea, the sensation of sinking into dread.

He looked down at the ice. In a few months it would warm and shift and crack and students would make bets, guessing the first day that a stone, rolled from the end of the dock, would find too little ice to hold it up and sink down and out of sight. He closed his eyes and listened to the tap of snow landing on his parka and thought of his brother and wished he were found and home, that they were all found and home. And then it began, softly at first, somewhere in his throat, a murmur deepening to a moan and then rising on a wail that radiated outward until his entire body bent to the effort of the scream, a long, devouring scream that rolled across the ice and reverberated off the hills along the far shore.

On Saturday nights, there being little to do in the hills of New Hampshire, Andrew's roommates often went drinking in the bars of nearby towns. Their favorite was across the river in Vermont, a place called Harlan's Taproom which was owned and run not by anyone of that name, but by a round and cheerful woman named Dorothy who insisted on being called Dot and always seemed glad to see them even if she couldn't recall their names. Andrew never went because he didn't like the way it made him feel, getting drunk, especially the day after. And so he always waved them off when Steve jingled car keys in the air and wiggled his eyebrows as he motioned with his hand to suggest tipping back a bottle before his puckered lips.

But this Saturday, to their surprise, Andrew pulled on his coat and followed them out the door, Joe making whooping noises to celebrate winning him over. They piled into Steve's rusted green Ford and drove down the hill and over the bridge into Vermont. Talk in the car was loud and boisterous, but although Andrew smiled from time to time, he remained held somewhere inside himself where they could not reach.

Dot pronounced him cute and asked where they'd been keeping him all this time. Joe and Steve ordered boilermakers and Andrew, after watching her pour the beer and whiskey, signaled with a downturned finger that he would have the same. They oohed and aahed as he lifted the tiny glass of whiskey to his lips and tipped it all the way back, stifling the urge to cough as the fumes clutched at his throat. They drank and shot pool and played shuffleboard and drank some more. The bar filled with the local trade who looked at them askance but left them to themselves, glancing over when the volume of their commentary on the drinks or a hanging disk or a scratched cue ball was too much to ignore. Andrew lost track of time and the flow of money from his pocket, and as the evening wore on he felt something let go inside, laughing and moving in ways that were large and rough. He sat on the edge of a chair and it tipped forward, spilling him onto the floor, the pool cue leaving his hand and clattering on the tile. He lay on his back and looked up at the ceiling, enjoying how the room seemed to spin and the floating, timeless feeling on the edge of numb oblivion.

The bar closed at 2:00a.m. and they staggered across the gravel lot to the car, hooting and shouting at patrons as they drove away.

"Where to next?" said Andrew.

Steve shook his head. "No place."

"Whatd'ya mean?"

"Everything's closed."

"Not possible."

"Nothin'," said Steve.

"Squat," said Joe.

"Diddly," said Steve. "In case you haven't noticed, my friend, this here is the boonies, where we're at. As drunk as you are is as drunk as you get."

"Shit," said Andrew, "I'm not drunk. You call this drunk? This isn't drunk."

Joe snorted. "Get in the car, asshole. You're out of your mind."

"You're the asshole."

"No, you're the asshole."

"You're both assholes," said Steve. "Get in the fucking car."

"*You're* the asshole," they said, pushing him up against the car.

"All right. All right," said Steve. "We're all assholes!"

"That's better!" said Joe.

"Right!" said Andrew. "Assholes stick together! *Semper fi!*"

"*Semper fi?*" said Joe. "What the fuck are you? Some kind of fucking Marine?"

"Right," said Andrew, wedging himself into the back seat. "Fucking Marine," his voice sliding off into a quiet, private place, "right on . . . fucking . . . fucking Marine."

"Jesus, it's dark," said Steve, turning the car onto the road.

"Turn on the fucking headlights," said Joe.

"Oh shit."

"Fucking Marine," from the back seat.

"What?" said Joe.

"Fucking Marine."

Joe shook his head and looked out at the road.

Still west of the river, they slowed at a stop sign and Andrew, leaning his head back against the seat, turned to look out the rear window as the car moved past the sign.

"Whoa," he said, "stop the car."

"What?" said Steve, the car jerking to a stop.

Andrew was looking out the window at the sign on its post illuminated in the red glow of the tail lights. He pounded the back of the seat until Joe pulled forward so that Andrew could open the door and step out into the cold. He walked back to the sign and stood in front of it, looking up. Then he reached out and took the post in his hands and began to rock it in the frozen ground.

They looked at him, then at each other.

"Fucking wild man," said Joe.

They got out of the car and walked toward the sound of Andrew grunting as he tried to pull the signpost from the ground.

"Drewski," said Joe, "you wild man. What the fuck you doing?"

But Andrew heard only the sound coming from within himself, the low primal groan that stood guard above the rage he funneled through his arms and legs, a rage that would have this sign, post and all, torn up from the ground, or have nothing at all. Sweat poured down his face, even in the cold. He backed up and then threw his body against the post. Pain shot through his shoulder but he didn't care, wrapping his arms around the post and trying to lift it out. But it would not come. He stepped back and kicked at it, little cries escaping his throat. And then he screamed and hurled himself against it one last time and something deep in the frozen ground cracked and gave way and he lifted the sign into the air and stood panting beside it.

Joe and Steve stood in silence, their mouths open.

"Open the trunk," said Andrew.

"What?" said Steve.

"Open the fucking trunk!"

"It won't fit. It's too big."

Andrew stood still for a moment, his breath fogging in front of his face. "Through the window, then."

"You gotta be kidding."

"Open the fucking door."

"Take it easy," said Joe, putting a hand on his shoulder.

"You take it easy!" Andrew yelled, shrugging him off. "*You* take it goddamn fucking easy!" And then he was flailing his arms in the air, punching and swinging in every direction as they fell on him and wrestled him down to the cold pavement and tried to hold him there, panting fog into the air. And then, slowly, his arms went limp and fell, his legs stopped kicking, and the tears came, driven by great choking sobs that seemed to empty him out onto the road until he gasped and heaved another breath inside to begin all over again. They waited with him, motionless where they fell the three of them together, until slowly, beneath a canopy of stars, he surrendered to the arms that held and then softened around him, and sank down as the earth opened to receive him, and someone began to rock him gently back and forth.

5

Andrew stood outside Petersen's office and through the frosted glass watched the figure inside the room move against the light. Twice he raised his hand to the door and twice he dropped it to his side. He was turning to walk away when the door opened.

"Are you looking for me?"

"No."

Petersen smiled. "Just passing by?"

Andrew looked down at the floor.

"Why don't you come in and we can talk."

The office was small with two wooden desks joined in an L in a far corner. Shelves overflowed with books piled at all angles and in such a way as to make the walls seem to lean inward. The room was lit by a single lamp on the desk and there was a faint smell of tobacco in the air.

"Have a seat."

"That's okay."

"Really," said Petersen, looking at him with steady eyes. "Sit down. Please."

Andrew sat.

"I don't think I know your name."

Andrew said his name.

"So, Andrew, what brings you here?"

"You don't know?"

"I can guess, but I'd rather hear it from you."

Andrew shifted in the chair. "I came to apologize."

"For what?"

"The way I was in class."

"You mean getting angry?"

Andrew nodded.

"Well," said Petersen, "the fact is I didn't mind that. It was kind of interesting, actually. What bothered me was the hit-and-run thing. I would've admired you more if you'd stuck around to finish what you started."

Andrew felt his face grow hot.

"Why are you taking my course?"

"It's my major," said Andrew, looking at him and then away.

"But why *this* course."

A shrug. "It looked interesting."

"Uh-huh," said Petersen, bringing himself forward in the chair. "So, what got you so upset?"

Andrew stared at the man's hands, the fingers short and ringless.

Petersen looked at him, studying his face. "You said I always take their side."

Andrew made a little nod without looking up.

"Is there something you want to ask?"

Andrew looked at him.

"Are you saying we're wrong? We're on the wrong side?"

Petersen was quiet for a moment.

"It doesn't really matter what I think. I'm not the one living your life. What matters is what you think."

"But I don't know."

"Well, that's a start."

"Not much of one."

"Oh, no," said Petersen, "not knowing is a hell of a good start."

"I don't see how."

"It's an opening to what you don't know. Somewhere in there is the truth, or at least what's true for you."

"What don't you know?"

Petersen smiled. "For one thing, whether my work makes any difference."

"Then why do it?"

"Another thing I don't know. Except that it feels like what I'm here to do."

Andrew looked at Petersen staring at a pencil in his hand that he played with, pressing one end and the other against the desk until he laid it down, the corners of his mouth drawing back in a pensive little smile as he looked up at Andrew.

"What are you thinking?" said Peterson, his voice gentle and close.

"I was wondering why you call it civil war when one country invades another."

"I don't think I do."

"Then why—"

"You're assuming North and South Vietnam are separate countries."

"You mean the Geneva Convention."

"Right."

"Then why does everyone talk about the North making war on the South?"

"Not everyone does," said Petersen, "especially outside the U.S. And no country goes to war without claiming it's in the right."

"And you think that's what we're doing?"

Petersen looked at him, but said nothing.

"So it's just a civil war?"

"You tell me," said Petersen. "What would you call it when two halves of the same country fight over whether to be united or apart and on what terms? What would you call Lincoln's war to force the South to stay in a Union they didn't want? Aggression? Should freedom-loving nations have intervened on the South's behalf? Sent half a million troops to help them out?"

Andrew shook his head.

"And yet," said Petersen, "people living in places like Georgia and Mississippi certainly *felt* invaded when they saw the Yankees coming. So, it's not a simple thing."

"Then what are we doing over there?"

Andrew waited for the answer, but Petersen just looked at him, then tilted his head and rested it on his hand.

"I'm wondering," said Petersen, "if your question is political or historical, or maybe something personal."

Andrew became aware of his hand deep in the pocket of his coat, wrapped around the letter from his brother. He felt the edge of the paper press against his skin and rubbed his finger back and forth, distracting himself from the tears coming into his eyes. He got to his feet, looking down at the floor.

"I have to go," he said, his voice low. "I'm sorry about the other day."

Petersen said something that Andrew did not hear in his hurry to get out the door.

Andrew sealed the note in an envelope and took it to the address he found in the student directory, an apartment on the edge of campus, down Main Street just past the Gulf station. As he neared the house he looked from one window to another and imagined her standing behind a curtain watching him approach, rehearsing what she'd say, selecting the words to tell him off. He stood on the porch and rang the bell beneath her name and waited, looking through the lace curtain across the glass, braced for the sight of her coming down the stairs.

When no one came he looked at the envelope and felt suddenly foolish and pathetic, that she must think so little of him that even a moment to put him in his place was more than she had to spare. He went down the steps and walked away. But just past the Gulf station he stopped and looked up at the sky and then turned and walked back to the house and up the stairs and slipped the envelope through the mail slot in the door.

Late in the afternoon she saw it on the floor when she swung open the door. She took it upstairs where she uncapped a bottle of beer and propped her feet on the kitchen table as she opened the letter.

Dear Ruth,
  I'm sorry for what I said. Andrew

She smiled and folded the page, drawing her thumbnail across the crease to make it sharp. She lifted the bottle by the neck and took a sip, then lowered it down, letting it swing between two fingers as she looked out at the darkness coming on and the lights of the town.

Peterson leaned back in the chair and knit his fingers behind his head.

"It's not easy to think your country might be doing something wrong," he said. "It's mine, too, you know."

"But you think it's wrong to fight the communists."

"I think," said Peterson, dropping his hands into his lap, "that it's wrong for a superpower to destroy a third world country in the name of saving it from its own people. And I think it's wrong to prop up one corrupt, repressive regime after another and pretend we're defending freedom and democracy. The U.S. government refuses to see that this is a holy war for the Vietminh, not because they're communists, but Vietnamese."

"Are you?"

"What."

"A communist."

"Ha!" said Peterson, tilting back his head, "I was wondering when you'd get around to that."

Andrew made a nervous little smile as Petersen sat back in the chair.

"Let me tell you something. It's possible to criticize the 'good guys,'" making little quotes with his fingers, "and not be one of the 'bad guys.'" He shook his head. "No," he said, "I wouldn't call myself a communist. I have a lot of respect for Marx—I'm a Marxist at heart—but I'm not a communist in the modern sense of the word. And I'm not trying to make one out of you. I just think before you go off and risk your life making war against people, you might want to know why."

"That's what my brother said."

He looked at Petersen, then away, suddenly remembering the sound of Ruth Koszinski's voice, so close to his ear she might as well have been inside his head.

"And where is he?"

"Over there."

"And you'll be going soon."

Andrew nodded.

"And you don't know what you're getting into."

Andrew didn't move.

"Which is why you're here," said Petersen, almost to himself. "And how *would* you know? What does your brother say?"

"Nothing good."

"And your father?

"My father . . . what about him?"

"How does he feel about all of this?"

"He thinks we should go."

"Did he?"

Andrew nodded.

"He saw combat?"

He nodded again.

"And has he told you what it was like?"

Andrew looked surprised. "No. He doesn't talk about it."

"Really. Never?"

"No."

"Unh huh," said Petersen, his eyes narrowing. Andrew looked down and in the silence felt himself go heavy and numb, his lungs emptying and blood slowing in his veins.

"Andrew."

"He's missing," Andrew said, his lips barely moving.

"Your father?"

He shook his head.

Petersen sat up, his eyes going soft as he removed his glasses and rubbed the bridge of his nose.

"Your brother."

"Yes."

"I am so sorry."

He'll be all right, Andrew thought to say, *he's a Marine*, but all that he could do was look down into his lap, knowing it wasn't true, not anymore, if it ever was. Which he realized only now it could not have been, that it was never true, that from the day his brother joined the Marines he was not and could not be all right ever again, from that day, if not long before.

"I'm sorry," he said, glancing at the sadness in Petersen's face as he took his coat and made his way out the door.

Andrew could see the note on his door as he mounted the last stair, and thought it was another message from his mother.

Dear Andrew,
I wasn't home when you came by. But I'm here now and don't plan on going anywhere.

R

When Ruth swung open the door she looked at him and saw not the Colonel of the Corps but a young man diminished and hunched over, shivering on the stoop, eyes puffy and red.

"Come in," she said, watching him walk past without looking at her.

"I'm this way," she said, motioning toward the stairs, but he got it wrong and started down the hall and she reached out and took his hand which was cold and she had to pull open the fingers to get a hold on it, the muscles in his hand tense against her before giving in.

"Come on," she said, "it's just a little ways."

The room was warm and small, an old couch along a wall, a chair and table, a long bookcase. Through a doorway he could see the corner of a bed and through another a kitchen with a table and chairs. She sat him on the couch.

"You want your coat off?" she said, her voice tender and soft.

He shook his head.

"You want a beer? Some coffee?"

He nodded.

She tilted her head to the side as if adjusting the angle and then made a pained little smile. "Which one?" she said. "The beer, I'll bet."

He nodded without lifting his head and she looked at him for a moment before walking away into the kitchen. He heard the refrigerator door open and close, the sound of a drawer sliding out, the soft click of the opener working against the cap. He wondered why he came, looking around the room, the walls bare except for an unframed Matisse print and a poster that read, "War is Good for Business. Invest Your Son."

She stood in the doorway, a bottle in each hand, and looked at him seeming to make himself as small and dense as possible, shoulders sunk down, legs and feet pressed together. He didn't see her because his eyes were fixed on the poster.

She handed him a beer.

"Thanks," he said, resting it on his thigh.

She took off her shoes and climbed onto the far end of the couch, pulling her legs up in front of her. She sipped the beer.

"How are you doing?" she said.

"Okay."

"You're really in it, aren't you."

He nodded, suddenly feeling tired.

"You were looking at my poster."

He nodded again.

"What do you think of it?"

"I don't know."

She sipped the beer.

"You want to talk about what's going on?"

He shook his head and looked down at the bottle.

They sat in silence for awhile and then she leaned over and took a book from the little table in front of the couch and opened it on her legs and began to read, her manner taking on the unselfconscious ease of someone passing the time while waiting for a bus.

He leaned back and his cheeks puffed out with a sigh. He looked at the bottle, then lifted it to his lips and took a drink, tilting it high in the air. He brought the bottle down and rested it on his thigh, working a thumbnail under the edge of the label.

"What did you mean?" he said.

"When?"

"At the field house."

She thought for a moment. "I meant I don't want you to go. Any of you."

"And you think I don't have to."

"You always have a choice."

"But I made a commitment. I signed up."

"That just makes it harder."

"What do you mean?"

"I mean it's not the only thing. Sometimes you change your mind. You need the courage of your doubts."

"You mean convictions."

"No," she said, "doubts. Convictions are easy. Everyone's got them. But not everyone dares to doubt."

"Sometimes you have to do things you don't want to do."

"Sure," she said, "but not if it's wrong. You think it's some kind of virtue to honor a commitment that's wrong?"

"You don't understand," he said. "People are counting on me—"

"They always—"

"—and it won't make a difference anyway because they'll just draft me."

"If they can find you."

"You mean run away."

"That," she said, "or refuse to go."

"Except to jail."

"Probably." She took a sip.

In the silence she looked at him with her head resting on the heel of her hand. He glanced at her and thought how much he liked the way she looked and imagined laying his head down in her lap.

"There's this story about Henry David Thoreau," she said, "and his buddy Ralph Waldo Emerson. Thoreau was in jail for civil disobedience. He refused to pay poll taxes because they were used to support slavery and the war against Mexico, which he considered unjust. Which, of course, it was. Anyway, Emerson visits him and takes one look at his old friend says, 'What are you doing in here?' And so Thoreau fixes him a look and says, 'What are you doing out there?'"

"My dad wouldn't understand."

"Why not?"

He stared down at the bottle for a long time.

"Well," he said, not looking up, "let me put it this way. My dad is varsity lacrosse coach at the school I went to, and I played defense my senior year. The last game was against our big rival, and they had this guy we couldn't stop. He kept getting by us and it was like no matter where he threw the ball it always wound up in the goal. My dad got more and more pissed. I could tell by the way he walked up and down in front of the bench, and every once in awhile he'd stop and fold his arms across his chest and stand there staring at me over on the far side of the field. And then this guy starts bringing the ball down again and my dad just yells, "Hit him!" and I could tell he was talking to me. He was always trying to get me to hit guys, but I'd rather go for the ball. Anyway he keeps yelling for me to hit him. I'd never heard him so worked up. Everyone was staring at him, players on the bench, guys on the field. His face was all red. I could see the muscles in his neck. So . . . I started to run. I guess the guy didn't see me coming. He probably didn't hear my dad. I was running as fast I could, leaning down just before I got to him so I could hit him low, and there was this big crunch and he stopped like he'd hit a wall. Except he didn't just stop, because I was going pretty fast and he came right up off the ground and went backwards through the air. I remember looking up and seeing him. His arms went out to the side and his gloves came off and when he hit the ground his helmet rolled away like a hubcap coming off a car. I was down on one knee and I remember being scared that maybe I'd really hurt him. The ref blew the whistle and I got up and went over and leaned down and asked him if he was okay. His eyes were open but he didn't say anything for a long time. And then he got his breath back and he said, 'Was that you?' And I said yeah and he just nodded and said, 'Well fuck you then,' and I said okay and walked back down the field. Our goalie stood there shaking his head like he couldn't believe it. And then I looked over at the bench and my dad was standing there, but not looking at me at all, like I'd just done something I should have done all along."

She closed the book and set the bottle on the table, then watched him as he stared at the poster on the wall.

"Did you win?"

"Yeah," he said, his voice just above a whisper. "We won."

She took a sip of beer.

"Were you crying before?"

He paused and then nodded.

"How come?"

"I don't know," he said, drawing a finger around the opening of the bottle as if wiping something away. "I was over talking with Petersen."

"About what?"

"The war. And to apologize. He asked me about my brother." He looked at her. "I have a brother." His eyes narrowed. "He's missing."

"In Vietnam?"

He nodded.

"How long?"

"I don't know. A long time, I guess. I lose track."

"That explains a lot."

"Does it?" He shook his head. "Everything moves so fast. I can't keep up. I read everything on Petersen's list and the more I read the less I feel like I know anything. Nothing's what I thought. But it can't be right. How can it be?"

"What's his name? Your brother."

"Joshua."

"The angel who made the walls come tumbling down."

Andrew nods.

"And you love your brother."

"He's lost," he said. "I don't know what to do."

"You think you're going to find him in all those books?"

He looked out the window.

"Maybe," he said, looking at her and then quickly away. "No," shaking his head, "not anymore," glancing at his watch, "I should go."

"You don't have to."

He looked at the poster that kept drawing his attention as if it were staring at him and not the other way around. He wiped his eyes with the back of his hand.

"I don't want him to be dead," he said, the words thick in his throat. He laid his face against his sleeve, then stood and looked down to zip up his coat.

"If you go," she said, "go because you want to."

He paused, the zipper halfway up, and looked at her.

"Do you want to?" she said.

"You don't mind if I stay awhile?"

She made a little smile and shook her head.

"You know," she said, holding her third bottle of beer up to the light to see how much was left, "what I can't figure out is why with such big brains and all those libraries full of books, we fuck up so much." She got up from the couch and went over to the record player.

"You'd think the more we knew the smarter we'd be," flicking the switch on the phonograph, "but we're not," a pause and then the Beatles singing "Sgt. Pepper's Lonely Hearts Club Band."

"You don't think what we have now is any better than . . . say . . . feudalism?"

"Not really." She drained the bottle and a soft burp escaped her lips.

"Well," he said, waving her off, "that's . . . just . . . dumb."

"Really?" she said. "Okay, so tell me—what's better?"

"Everything. Indoor plumbing, cars, phones—"

"Oh, sure," she said, "stuff and more stuff, and while you're at it, don't forget machine guns and hydrogen bombs, and tell me, what good is a standard of living if you kill everyone and blow it all up?"

He looked at her. "They did not have democracy in the Middle Ages—"

"But for whom?"

"Or the Bill of Rights—"

"You think blacks have democracy—"

"Or freedom of the press—"

"Working people? Poor people? Vietnamese?"

He couldn't take his eyes off her, the way she leaned in, fingers waving beneath her face, the air electric with her voice. She sat back and looked down into her lap.

"I get carried away," she said, surprising him with this sudden appearance of something like humility.

"No," he said, "that's all right. But you are definitely wrong."

"I am not."

"No, I mean you're right, but . . . "

She looked at him and began to smile, "but . . . "

"But . . . "

"But but . . . " making fun of him now.

"Because some things really are better."

"Yes," she said, "and not."

"All right. I get that."

"Which was my point."

They sat quietly for a moment, listening to the Beatles getting by with a little help from their friends.

"I do get this bug up my ass sometimes," she said. "I can't seem to help it." She looked at him. "Then again, it's the way I am and, fact is, I kind of like it."

He smiled. "I can tell."

"But sometimes," she said, pointing a finger in the air, "the bug needs a little something to calm it down."

She got up and went into the kitchen. A drawer opened and closed and then she returned and plopped down on the table a small plastic bag and a package of cigarette papers.

"Is that what I think it is?"

"I certainly hope so," she said with a toss of her head.

"That's illegal."

"Certainly is. So's the war."

He watched the calm authority with which she assembled it, the paper in her fingers, the line of marijuana sprinkled along its length, and then folding and rolling and finally bending down her head and passing the tip of her tongue from one end to the other to moisten and seal it shut. He followed the motion of her tongue in particular, then looked at the window.

"Shouldn't we close the shades or something?"

"If you want," she said. "Go ahead."

He stood at the window and held his face close to the glass. He could feel the cold outside. The air was streaked with rain, the road slick and black beneath the streetlight.

He pulled down the shade and walked back to the couch and put his hands in his pockets as he watched her hold a match to the end of the joint and take a few shallow puffs to get it going. Then she drew in a lungful of smoke and held out the joint to him. He took it, unsure how to hold it, trying to remember what it looked like in her hand, not like a cigarette, which he'd held before, but something else.

124

"You look awfully serious for a guy about to get high."

"I'm breaking a rule. A really big one."

"Well," she said, "I'm guessing you've done pretty much everything you were supposed to do up to now. Just like your brother. Maybe it's time to break some rules."

He watched her lift her hand to demonstrate, the tips of her thumb and forefinger pinched together, and raise her eyebrows as he moved the joint in his fingers and brought it to his lips. It wasn't like a cigarette, the smoke more pungent, almost sweet. He pulled it deep into his lungs and held it there, stifling the urge to cough, determined not to let it go. He waited for some alteration of reality to sweep over him, but he felt the same as before. He handed it back to her and sat down where she patted the cushion beside her. She took another drag and handed it to him and he made a little shrug and filled his lungs again. And then he felt it, a lightness in his mind, a letting go, a slowing down, something coming softly undone.

When he moved
the music of The Doors drifting in the air
something about the end
the motion
   so slow

          and

      smooth
      it seemed all in his mind
without the encumbrance of a body
        and its puzzling relation to gravity

"How you doing?" she said.

He turned his head and looked at her and smiled without moving his lips. He thought of words to say but was content just to look. There was something profoundly calming about the silence inside himself, the ease of his inertia whether staying at rest or following a motion once begun, of his head or his hand or even just his eyes.

"What were you staring at?" she said.

He thought for a moment and then slowly moved his lips around the word, "doorknob," conscious of the time it took to form the word and push it like a heavy bubble into the air.

She looked at the door and smiled.

"It's very . . . " he said, his voice slow and making a little sigh, "doorish . . . and . . . knobby."

He looked at the shiny brass against the white of the door, wondering how something so small and insignificant could draw his attention to every contour, the way the light played on the scratches and dents, imagining the inner workings of the lock, at peace, like himself, to be at rest or in motion, fulfilling its purpose, borne along by something it neither comprehended nor needed to

gravity suddenly releasing its hold to let him rise from the couch like a balloon with nothing to hold him down, gripping the arm, but it making no difference as he rose up and up and yet everything else seeming just the same, the cushions still beneath him, and then everything in reverse, sinking down to become the pure essence of weight itself, passing through the floor to the apartment below and then the concrete of the basement floor and into the earth

laughter doubling on itself cascading into tears running down his face and somewhere the sound of her laughter and his own blending to a single sound and her hand briefly lighting on his knee and something stirring inside him and a strange mental apparition of happiness and his brother found and the war gone away

quiet, slouched down, staring at the poster on the wall, waiting for her to say something, but her just looking at him, her eyes reminding him of the light playing off the brass and how it filled his mind

"I'm hungry."

A smile, "the munchies," she said, pointing toward the kitchen as she rose from the couch, "oh I do love the munchies."

He stood behind her at the counter and noticed the smell of her hair and the slope of her shoulder and the shadowy hollow where her skin disappeared beneath the collar of her shirt. She reached up and tucked a lock of hair behind her ear and he wondered if he was the only one ever to notice that singular little movement.

They sat in the living room and ate most of a banana cream pie and a bag of chocolate kisses. She rolled another joint and put on a Janis Joplin record and they lay back on the couch, feet propped on the little table, listening to the music as they smoked.

"She's the best," she said.

"You think?"

"You don't?"

He shrugged. "I don't know," he said, "she's a little . . . " he looked at her.

"Raaaw," she said.

He nodded.

"Ohh," she said, "That's what I like her for. Raw is good. Raw is real."

He looked at her mouth moving around the words as she sang along, her throat long and open, and wanted to kiss her but he couldn't seem to move.

Andrew woke without the memory of falling asleep on the couch or how he came to have a pillow beneath his head or a blanket down the length of him. He opened his eyes and saw the poster on the wall, the words dark in the shadow of early morning light, but not so dark that he couldn't make them out. He listened for sounds of her, but heard only the radiator creak as it expanded to receive the heat.

He was relieved to find himself fully clothed except for his shoes which he didn't remember taking off. He did remember the joints and the food and laughter and talk and the sight of her head laid back as she sang along with Janis Joplin. And the rawness of the music and the bite of the smoke in his throat and the sense of wanting and yet being unable to move and then stumbling upon a still and silent place inside the wanting that grew with every pulsebeat of desire until it was large enough to hold it all.

He sat up and looked out the window. The sun was just clearing the tops of the trees across the street, turning the grey bark a dull golden yellow. Through the open bedroom door he heard her move beneath the covers. He threw back the blanket and put on his shoes and got up and took his coat from the back of a chair and didn't wait to put it on before turning the brass knob and stepping out into the hall and closing the door behind as softly as he could.

She lay in bed and listened to the footsteps quickly padding down the stairs, the pause at the front door as he put on his coat, the door opening, and then the little slam as he pulled it shut, pulling too hard because it stuck, the glass rattling in the frame. She went to the window and held back the curtain as she watched him walk up the street, head down, hands in his pockets, not looking back.

6

As weeks dragged into months, the hope Anne clung to so tenaciously, defiantly, sank into a slow and desiccating grief. She and William moved together and yet apart, each off somewhere in the company of a version of Joshua known only to themselves. They did not make love, rarely even touched, except in passing or sometimes in the dark, on the edge of sleep, a hand laid gently on the other's back, tentative, pausing for a moment before pulling back, like someone opening the wrong door.

William dreamed the dream, sometimes more than once a night. But now he woke standing alone in the kitchen or the hall, forehead pressed against the wall, bathed in sweat, with only the silence and the memory of rounding the corner and waking before he got to the other side.

Sometimes he showered and climbed into bed and looked at the shape of her outlined against the light coming through the window, his hand spread on the cool expanse between them. Or he dressed and went outside where he smoked on the terrace and thought about what was happening. More and more, night blended into day, blurring the line between reality and dream, the crisp, clear demarcations of his mind giving way to something more shadowy, fluid, and dark.

Most disturbing was the day in class when the subject was the battle of Fredericksburg and he was diagraming the opposing lines at Marye's Heights where the attack by fourteen Union brigades was funneled across a half mile of open fields, their destination a low stone wall concealing ranks of confederates standing in a sunken road from which they poured down a steady hail of fire upon them.

He spoke as he drew little arrows for each brigade following on the one before.

"A disaster all around," he said. "General Longstreet predicted from his vantage point behind the wall that a chicken could not live on that field when they opened up on it, and later, his commander, General Lee, watching the slaughter unfold, turned to his General and said that it was well that war was so terrible so they would not grow too fond of it."

Then the chalk tripped on a little rise in the surface of the board, an imperfection in the slate, and broke in half, leaving the stub extending just beyond his fingers and resting against the spot where it stumbled and fell. He stared at the spot, and as the clock ticked on the wall above him, the spot became a blue cap on top of a man's head. Slowly he began to circle it with the chalk as if to slow the man's advance or surround him with something like a wall, circling round and round, bearing down so that small pieces of the chalk crumbled away.

And then he stopped and spoke, his voice softly confiding to the slab of stone hanging on the wall.

"Like snow," he said, "like snow falling on warm ground."

The room was quiet and still. He touched his forehead to the cool stone and smelled the chalk. A chair creaked and he snapped his head, like waking from nodding off, then blinked and turned to look at them, wondering what they'd heard and seen.

"Of course," he said, quickly taking a breath, "Lincoln was appalled. 'If there is a worse place than Hell,' he was heard to say, 'I am in it.'"

Still, he could feel their eyes upon him as he leafed through his notes, unable to remember what came next. Finally he looked up and said, "That's enough for today," and gathered his things and walked from the room as if that was his plan all along.

He had tried to write it down, like she asked. But it seemed inconceivable to put it on a page where it would exist outside himself, constant and real. And so it either came out seeming trivial and pathetic—the awful food, the lack of sleep and sex, the stench, the never being clean or dry—or it didn't come at all, too enormous for words on a scrap of paper.

For weeks after that awful night, he could feel her waiting, believing she'd found a way in, the air so thickened by her hope and anticipation that he dreaded going home. But there was nowhere else to go.

And then, late one Sunday afternoon as they sat reading in the living room, she sighed and closed the book in her lap and stared down at the cover until he felt a shift in her attention. He did not look up from the sentence he had read over and over again.

"I can't wait any more," she said.

He stared hard at the page.

She cleared her throat.

"What did you say?" he said.

She wondered if this was how people go insane, hanging off the edge of something that isn't there until they open their eyes and see their fingers grasping nothing but the air, then fall and keep on falling. She thought of Lyndon Johnson on television the other night, announcing he wouldn't run for President again, and suddenly she saw a man trying to save himself and wished that she too could just resign or decline to run again.

I will not be your mother anymore. I will not be your wife.

"Don't do this," she said, closing her eyes.

He was quiet for a moment, closing the book, marking the place with his finger, then pulling the finger out.

"I tried," he said.

She looked at him.

"I threw them away."

"Why?"

"It was no good," he said, and then a silence. "Besides, I can't see the point."

"I need to know."

"But I don't," he said. "And I'm not willing to dredge up something that happened more than twenty years ago just to satisfy some . . . morbid curiosity."

Suddenly she was on her feet, the book falling to the floor.

"Morbid curiosity?" she said, her voice rising. "You think that's what it is?"

"I just don't see why we have to dwell on it."

"*You* don't see," she said. "You think *I'm* the one who dwells on this?"

"Look," he said, his voice rising to match hers, "the war affected me like it did everyone else. But I've had to get on with my life."

"And you think you have?"

He looked at her.

"Every man has his own way of dealing with this," he said, "and you have to let me have mine."

"Except that whatever that is," she said, "it clearly doesn't work."

"It does for me."

"You can't be serious."

He went to the sink and poured a glass of water.

"You think this works for you," she said. "What exactly is it that works? I'd really like to know."

She walked to where he leaned against the sink and stared out the window.

"Silence?" she said. "You think that works? Except for twenty years of walking around the house, crying in your sleep. Is that what you call 'dealing with it'?"

She leaned forward to see his face in the dim light through the window.

"And you never draw anymore. Except for little diagrams of battlefields. Don't you wonder about that, what became of you?"

He didn't move, his eyes fixed straight ahead.

"And what about us?" she said. "Does that work for you, too? Going around like ghosts so you don't have to face whatever it was that happened to you. Is that how it's supposed to be for the rest of our lives?"

His eyes went dead in his face, the color draining away, and as she saw it happen her voice took on a hard and throaty edge.

"And our boys," she said, "marching in their father's footsteps, and one already missing. Josh is probably out looking for you. And now it's Andrew's 'turn' as you call it."

The words caught in her throat and she pushed away from the counter.

"Goddamn it," she said, "I am not going to cry."

And then she was back again, looking into his face, her voice rising.

"What the hell are you waiting for? What does it take? Do you wait until there's nothing left to lose? The boys gone? And me? Is that it?"

She looked at him, her eyes searching his face, then turned to look out the window.

"Well," she said, stepping back from the sink, "you'll have to count me out. I can't live the rest of my life this way."

His stomach suddenly went light with fear.

"What am I supposed to say?"

She stood in the middle of the room, resting a hand on the back of a chair, a sudden weariness coming over her.

"Nothing," she said. "Nothing at all."

"Don't you understand," he said. "I don't know how to do this."

She whirled around behind him.

"Look at me," she said, her voice flat and hard.

Slowly, he faced her, leaning back against the sink. Her eyes were dark and without a grain of sympathy.

"I don't care," she said, the words coming even and slow. "I don't care if you don't know how." She took a step toward him. "You just start," she said. "The way you do anything."

"But where—?"

"Anywhere!"

In the silence she could see a faint tremble in the muscles of his face, a darting movement of his eyes, and for a moment she felt herself soften at the sight of him, so newly vulnerable. But then she balled her fists, fingernails digging into her palms to steel herself against it.

He looked at her and all he could think was that she might leave him if he failed to do what she wanted, this thing that felt impossible. His breath was shallow and the blood pulsed in his ears.

"You wouldn't leave," he said.

She shook her head. "I cannot do this anymore. I won't."

He settled the corners of his mouth.

"Okay," he said, and thought a softness came into her eyes.

She went to the couch, sitting at one end, curling her legs in front of her. He followed and sat at the other end, feet on the floor, looking straight ahead, holding his hands in his lap to keep them still.

He was quiet for what seemed a long time to them both, staring at the wall, his fingers softly working one another in his lap.

"What?" she said.

"I was thinking," he said, "about the men I knew." He paused and looked at her, then away, shaking his head. "There was one named Ray . . . or Roy. I don't remember. It doesn't matter. None of them made it. They were all killed. North Africa. Italy. I stopped making friends. It was easier that way."

He looked at her. "What do you want to know?"

"Everything."

He looked back at the wall and was quiet for so long that she became aware of the ticking of the clock on the mantle. Then he began to speak, his voice flat and soft.

"You're dirty all the time. Same clothes for weeks. You're either boiling hot or freezing cold. Depends on the time of day and where you are. But you're never just okay. You hurt from the weight you have to carry. You sleep on the ground. You wake up not knowing where you are. The food's terrible. And usually cold. When you're on the move, you shit and piss wherever you can and try not to step in the next guy's." He looked at her. "You have no idea how much shit comes out of an army."

He looked away and sighed.

"And of course all you think about is home, and staying alive because that's the only way you'll get there."

He looked at her, fixing his gaze on her eyes.

"I thought about you. All the time. Sometimes, I closed my eyes and tried to see you. Smell you. Hear your voice. Sometimes I didn't know if you were real or something I'd made up."

She noticed his hands, the fingers of one gently exploring the other like a blind person becoming acquainted with someone's face.

"What was the fighting like?" she said.

He was still for a moment.

"A lot of waiting, actually," he said. "Waiting for someone to tell you where to go. Which gives you time to worry about what'll happen when you get there. And then . . . chaos. Just chaos." He shook his head. "You find out in the first five seconds that for all that training, all ten weeks of it, you don't know a thing, because nothing ever turns out like the drills and maneuvers. The generals have their maps and plans and strategies, but they're miles away and once they throw you into it, all you've got is instinct and luck and one another. Everything else comes the hard way. If you live that long."

"And the dream," she said.

He sighed and looked away.

"I don't remember."

"Tell me anyway," she said. "Imagine it's your last chance."

In the silence she watched his mind working behind his eyes, his face smooth and almost soft in the half light.

"There's just bits and pieces."

"I don't care."

He paused.

"Okay. I'm running. In a street. Someone is shooting at me."

"Then what?"

"I don't know. There's a basement of some kind and stairs and a hallway. I'm running down a hall."

"And . . ."

"And then I wake up."

She leaned forward. "What's at the end of the hall?"

His face was still for a moment.

"I don't know."

"It just stops? No doors? No windows? Nobody?"

"I guess," he said, then, "No," shaking his head, "there's a corner."

"And around the corner?"

"I don't know." He looked at her. "I really don't. That's where it always ends. I wake up."

Her gaze dropped to where his hands gripped each other in his lap, the knuckles turning white.

"Can we stop now?" he said.

She hesitated, then nodded.

"Please don't go," he said.

The silence grew around them, their eyes fixed on each other.

"This is just the beginning," she said.

"I know."

Late in the night William stood outside and looked across the lawn and remembered the softness in her voice and the shadowy light from the window slanting across her face. And then, coming into his mind like something strange and unexpected, he recalled how beautiful Anne looked and how beautiful she had always been. He closed his eyes and saw her standing in front of him in his father's garage, smiling as she rubbed a thumb across his cheek, leaning forward, eyes half-closed, kissing him. There was the smell of her and the palpable sense of wanting that flowed through her hand laid against his hip so lightly he barely knew it was there. He remembered how he missed her, longed for her, when he was away, clung to the idea of her as if it might be enough to get him home.

He opened his eyes and suddenly a great loneliness came over him, being far away and missing her for as far back as he could remember, missing her even though from where he stood, he could see the window beyond which she slept even now. He flicked the cigarette out across the lawn, the arc ending in a thin line of dirty snow.

William always found comfort in faculty meetings and the company of men who'd been in one war or another, except for a few who were unfit or the wrong age. For all they had in common, though, they never spoke of it, the silent bass note in the harmony of their ease with one another.

To the uninformed observer, their jackets and bow ties and learned demeanor might suggest a life of the mind, but these were also highly physical men who had discovered their bodies not through the demands of athletics, but through the nearness of death. It was the imminent destruction of the body that made them feel alive with an intensity they had not known before. But when they survived and came home, they inhabited a strange and middle region, neither dead nor fully alive, but intensely physical nonetheless. It could be seen in how they carried themselves with a sense of purpose and self-conscious muscularity found even in their laughter, a percussive clapping of the air, the danger they endured having magnified everything into something larger than life and yet, at the same time, smaller and more brittle.

As he climbed the broad marble steps to the third floor of Adams Hall, William felt himself walking with slow and careful movements as if noting how each muscle worked with all the others. At the top of the stairs he went through the double oak doors into the faculty room, the paneled walls lined on three sides with high windows looking out onto the campus. The men stood in little knots of laughter and animated talk. He took a place next to Cliff Eagleton, an instructor in history who had served in his regiment. William put his hands in his pockets and listened to the talk as one might sit beside a stream to hear the water flowing by.

"No," said Cliff, "by far the best was the car in the library. Nothing else comes close."

A young teacher stood on the far side of the group, a puzzled look on his face.

"You weren't here then," said Cliff. "It was just after we built the new addition with the plate glass windows—'63, I think it was. Anyway, the seniors—or so we assume—got hold of Jim Perlmutter's red mustang convertible and rolled the damn thing down through the double doors into the new wing. It looked like a goddamn showroom. Funniest thing you ever saw."

"Unless you were Jim," said another and the men all laughed. William looked down at his shoes.

"How'd you get it out of there?"

"I can't remember," said Cliff. "You remember, Bill?"

For a moment they looked at him.

"Bill?"

He lifted his head, startled. "What?"

"The car. Do you know how we got it out?"

"No," he said, and then Jack entered the room and the little knots of men slowly came unraveled as they chose their seats. Cliff sat down next to William.

"You all right?"

William nodded.

"No news, I suppose."

"No."

"It's a rotten business, having to wait."

William said nothing, staring toward the front of the room where Jack sorted through some papers on the desk.

"How's Anne holding up?"

"Okay."

Cliff nodded, looking away and then back. "Say," he said, "why don't you come with me this year. It might do you good."

"Come where?"

"The reunion."

"What reunion?"

Cliff rolled his eyes. "The same one I've been trying to get you to for how many years?"

"Oh," said William, shaking his head. "No. I don't think so."

"It's in Boston. You don't have to get on a plane or even a train. So there's no excuse."

"That's not the reason."

"I know that. I'm just trying to wear you down."

William looked around the room and it occurred to him this was as close to an Army reunion as he intended to get.

"Don't you ever wonder what happened to guys you knew?" said Cliff. "How they're doing?"

William looked at him.

"No," he said, "I don't."

Anne and William embarked on a running conversation through which he introduced her, bit by bit, to the particulars of war. But as she listened, in the kitchen or the living room or the shadows over their bed or walking through the bird sanctuary, she felt an old familiar distance reassert itself in the recounting of a story strangely not his own, once removed in the way historians are, reflected in the measured tone of his voice, not cold, but merely factual. And slowly it dawned on her that he had retreated still further in the face of her advance and was now lodged safely in a castle keep built just inside the ruined walls she had so laboriously torn down.

But still she pressed on, wanting to know every detail, the taste of food, the names of things, the proper procedure for clearing a jammed rifle in the heat of battle. Anything to keep him talking while she worked the nailfile in the mortar, loosening the stones one by one.

They crossed North Africa and then landed in Sicily and worked their way up the Italian peninsula. They rested in England before wading ashore on the Normandy beaches, where almost everything, it seemed, went wrong, and then went on through the French hedgerows where everything that didn't go wrong on the beaches lay waiting for them. He seemed almost relieved to be telling it, coming to her to fill in some bit left out in the previous account. Even the nightmares stopped. But she was uneasy with the stories in the telling of which he was often both animated and yet strangely unmoved and unaffected, no fear or horror, none of the anguish that had drawn her from her bed night after night to go find him in the darkened hallway.

"You must have been afraid all the time," she said.

"Something like that."

It was early April, during spring break, and they were walking down the gravel road through the sanctuary.

"Tell me," she said.

He was quiet as he walked, hands in his pockets, looking down at the ground, turning to her to make a smile.

"There's so much to choose from," he said, then walked a few more steps before he stopped.

"I remember we were going through this town," he said, walking on. "We were a long way in from the beach. I think it was mid-July . . . a sunny afternoon. We were just going along when all of a sudden we were in someone's back yard, and I saw a flower garden along a stone wall. It was beautiful, in full bloom, and I stopped and I was looking at it when I started wondering how to paint it." He looked at her. "It surprised me, you know, because I wasn't a painter and I didn't think that way. But there I was, standing there looking at this garden." He walked on for awhile in silence, looking down at the road, and then he stopped and looked up at the sky. "And then all hell broke loose. There were automatic weapons going off all over the place. Machine gun rounds ticked little chips of stone off the wall"—he bobbed his finger through the air to mimic their advance—"like they're marching right down to me."

"What did you do?"

"I jumped over the wall."

He stopped and looked down at the road.

"Anyway," he said, looking up, "I'm on my back and listening to the roar of all this going on and squeezing my eyes shut to keep out the bits of stone falling on my face. And then I notice something else, soft, like goose down, and I open my eyes and the air is full of flowers, all these colors drifting down out of the blue."

He shook his head and started to walk again. "It was the guns. Tearing up the beds and kicking bits of flowers into the air. Only I didn't realize it at first. It was like I was turned upside down and the garden was up in the sky or something."

She waited for him to circle round and come back to the fear, but he was quiet now, walking down the road, hands in his pockets, a bemused little smile on his lips as he replayed in his mind the tail end of the story.

She took the file from the crack where she'd been digging and laid her ear against the stone, but there was only the pulsing of her own blood.

At first, Anne didn't notice it, set down on the floor, too big to fit in the narrow box. She was focused on the letters in her hand, as she always was, rifling through them, trying to look unconcerned, but never fooling those who knew what she was looking for, the pale yellow envelope from Western Union. There was a phone bill and a letter from her mother, and various things addressed to William, but she didn't look at those, so intent was she on that particular shade that reminded her of daffodils just past their prime.

She let go the shallow breath she'd been holding and was just about to turn and leave when her eye was drawn to the handwriting on the package on the floor, just as a familiar voice might reach out from a crowd and turn her head in its direction.

She knew what it was.

There was a ringing in her ears, her mind going numb as she steadied herself against the wall, her mouth open to the quick breaths going in and out, a voice behind her, soft and seeming far away, but not hearing as she bent down and watched her fingers slip beneath the twine just above where Joshua's name was written in her own distinctive hand.

As if alone in a narrow tunnel that echoed and magnified every sound, she moved down the hall, the letters in one hand and the package dangling from the other. Faces smiled at her and she heard her name but only nodded and kept on going, the package swinging with her step and tapping against her thigh. And then she was out the door and swimming against a tide of boys streaming inside in search of mail from home or girlfriends. Her eyes were wide and stung and blurred around the edges as she forged ahead, bumping into boys who muttered apologies she didn't hear.

She stood inside the door, leaning back against it until she heard the click of the latch, the letters dropping to the floor leaving only the package in her hands. The brown paper was soiled and the corners bruised. There was her own name and address in the upper left corner and then his just as she wrote it that cold and snowy afternoon.

And there was the stamp in large red letters, that wasn't there when she sent it off —

UNDELIVERABLE RETURN TO SENDER

She felt the meager weight of it, the cookies dry and hard by now, this small parcel of her love returning now to her hands, undeliverable.

When William came through the door that evening, he called her name as he took off his coat, but the only sound was the television turned up louder than usual and water running in the kitchen. He turned down the volume on the television before stepping into the kitchen where he found her standing at the sink, hands resting on the edge, steam rising in front of her face as she stared out the window. He leaned against the jamb and could tell from the stillness of her body that she was looking far beyond the horizon, her gaze following the curvature of the earth to the place where she imagined her boy was waiting to come home. Next to her, on the counter, was a small package wrapped in brown paper and twine.

He said her name again but she didn't move and so he walked across the kitchen and leaned down to look up into her face, her eyes dark and full.

"What is it?"

She stared out the window.

"Anne," his voice soft.

"They sent it back," she said, the words catching in her throat.

"Sent what back?"

And then the tears rolled down her face as she reached to the counter and took the package in both hands and turned and held it out to him, her face twisted in pain, collapsing in on itself. He looked at her, then down, his face uncomprehending, and then his cheeks and mouth sank down as he looked up at her.

"Oh, God."

"They sent it back."

"They should never have done that."

"They sent it back."

"Someone made a mistake. Oh, Annie."

And he took her in his arms and held her while she cried, her heart seeming to break against him. And when she drew back and saw the tears on his face and realized they were not her own, she grabbed hold of him with a ferocity that pulled a moan from somewhere deep inside him, and she held on tight, feeling them both adrift in a little boat in the midst of a sea gone mad, tossing and pitching, taking on water, in imminent danger of foundering.

7

Andrew skulked from place to place with the furtive self-consciousness of a fugitive. Walking across campus and hearing a woman's voice call out, he would snap his head toward the sound, then, realizing it wasn't her, lower his shoulders and hurry on. He stayed away from Petersen's class and didn't check his mail or take coffee in the snack bar.

And then he was summoned by the Colonel.

"I'm eager to hear what you've found," he said, leaning back in his chair.

Andrew stood in the doorway.

"Come in. Sit down."

"That's okay."

The Colonel held his hand out over the desk, beckoning with an open palm.

"No," he said, his voice flat and even, "I'd like you come in and sit down."

Andrew sat in a chair by the door.

"So, tell me."

Andrew licked his lips. "There isn't much to tell."

"Really. What does that mean, exactly?"

Andrew shifted in the chair. "It's just a history class."

The Colonel leaned forward. "I knew that. But what sort of history?"

"Just . . . you know . . . history."

The Colonel looked at Andrew for a moment, eyes narrowed, assessing the situation. "Including Vietnam."

"Yes, sir."

"And?"

Andrew looked at him, then away and back again.

"I'm not sure what you mean."

He watched the Colonel work the muscles in his jaw.

"Andrew, tell me. Were you clear about what I asked you to do?"

"I think so, sir."

"Then why all the beating around the bush?"

Andrew cleared his throat, willing himself to look into the Colonel's face. "I didn't think I was."

"Just a history course."

"Yes, sir."

"Not anti-war, not pro-VC."

Andrew shook his head.

"You mean to tell me he takes no position?"

"No, sir. He does."

"Then he's against the war."

"Yes, sir."

"And so it's hardly just a history course."

"But he doesn't make a point of it. Not really."

"What the hell is that supposed to mean?"

Andrew pressed himself into the chair. "He wants us to make up our own minds."

The Colonel leaned back and folded his arms across his chest as he fixed his gaze on Andrew's face and held it there in the silence.

"And have you made up your mind?"

Andrew tried to swallow, but his mouth had gone dry. "It's complicated," he said, the words coming out in the midst of clearing his throat.

"What did you say?"

"It's complicated."

He waited for the Colonel to say something, but there was only silence.

"The war," said Andrew. "The history. It's complicated."

"Complicated," said the Colonel, nodding, "I'm sure it is. And how is that?"

Andrew had been here so many times before, the interrogation, the pursuit, the closing off of avenues of escape one by one, homing in on the singular destination already selected by the interrogator, all the rest detail. But now something strange and new was entering in, some doubt about the outcome that before was always known. Something in the Colonel's face, the grim finality of the nod like a fisherman resigned at last to the baitless hook, the broken line, and it occurred to Andrew that in this moment he knew more about the history of Vietnam than the older man sitting across the room from him might ever know, a fact the Colonel was trying to conceal with his air of confidence, leaning back in the chair, his gaze fixed on Andrew's face, the nod, as if everything were under control.

"The French," said Andrew, his voice dropping as if there was nothing more that needed to be said.

The Colonel sighed, rocking forward in the chair, already impatient to play it out and have it done. "And what about them?"

Andrew looked at this watch. "I have a class, sir."

"And I asked you a question," said the Colonel, looking up from the desk.

Andrew looked at the Colonel and felt both afraid and unafraid at the same time, as if one half of him was braced for the punishment he was sure would follow, knowing you do not cross a man like the Colonel, who is used to having his way, has built a life around commanding obedience and respect, always on the right side of an argument even when he was not, while the other half was carried along by a sense of letting go that he had never felt before, his heart expanding into the knowledge that there was more in the world than what the Colonel might think of him or do, and when at last Andrew spoke, the words came out with a pure simplicity that startled them both.

"I know."

The Colonel blinked. "And I suppose you think the communists are better than the French," he said, his voice picking up the pace as if to recover some lost momentum, but the look in his eyes giving away that whatever he was trying to gain was already lost.

"It is their country," Andrew heard himself say in a voice so soft and measured he barely recognized himself.

"You think so," said the Colonel, staring hard at him, waiting for a reply, but Andrew just looked at him, then watched the Colonel's head dip forward in the faint gesture of a nod, "and the United States," said the Colonel, the nod growing more pronounced, "just how does your country figure in this complicated little history of yours."

Andrew recognized this moment, the unveiling of contempt and then the trump card, love of country, tossed casually on the table, the anticipation of shame crawling hot up the back of his neck followed by the urge to cry, the longing to be forgiven and brought back into what he himself had already thrown away. He recognized the moment, saw it coming, and then, inexplicably, watched it pass him by.

In the long silence the radiator creaked against the wall.

"I see," said the Colonel, abruptly sitting forward, the chair banging as it came down. "I think we're done," he said. "Thank you for coming in. You can stop going to Petersen's class."

Andrew nodded, rising from the chair and turning toward the door.

"Carson," said the Colonel. "You do understand the nature of a contract, do you not? Such as the one you made with the United States Army?"

Andrew looked at him. "Yes."

"Good," said the Colonel looking down at the papers on his desk and lifting a pen in his hand.

It was snowing when Andrew stepped outside and he was halfway across the green when he saw her coming. He walked toward her with the slow, steady pace of a man accepting his fate.

"I'm sorry," he said, holding up his hands.

"You should be. What's the matter with you?"

"I don't know."

"You just up and disappear? You don't even leave a note?"

He shook his head.

"I'd like to know why you left," she said.

He looked at the dirty snow on the ground, then up into her face. "It was . . . awkward."

"Awkward how?"

"I didn't know what to say."

"I was asleep."

"I mean when you woke up."

"How about, Good morning, Ruth, thanks for the good time last night and by the way aren't you're looking especially fine."

He looked into her eyes and thought to say she was, but did not. "Haven't you ever woken up feeling strange?"

Rolling her eyes, "Have I."

"And you left a note?"

"Hell, I made coffee," she said. "Breakfast, even. You do know how to make coffee."

"Of course."

She took a deep breath.

"Look," she said, "if we're going to know each other, and it seems we are, then you gotta be straight with me. No slinking off at dawn. You feel funny and you gotta go, that's okay. But you leave a note that says you're feeling funny and you gotta go. You know what I'm saying?"

"You are, you know," he said.

"Are what?"

"Especially fine."

"And you are so especially full of shit, you know that?"

"Yes," he said, his face serious, "I think I do. Sometimes."

"Good," she said, "so long as we're clear."

"Right."

They looked at each other through the snow falling in the small space between them, the flakes large and wet as they landed with a soft tap on her shoulder and clung to the length of hair that fell down over her forehead. He was watching his foot make a little arc in the snow when she leaned forward and took the collar of his coat and pulled him gently down and kissed him on the mouth.

"I gotta go," she said, her lips still close to his. "I'm home after 6:00."

She turned and he watched her walk away across the green, remembering the kiss, so sudden and full of intent and yet so yielding and soft. He touched his lips and followed her progress across the street and then around the corner and she was gone.

For the better part of an hour Andrew wandered the aisles of the A&P in search of something they might make into supper. He'd never shopped before, except for canned goods and beer and snacks, and he realized he had little idea of where a meal actually came from. He finally took a box of spaghetti and a jar of sauce and a little jar of grated cheese and was approaching the cashier when he thought of something more and went back to the produce section for iceberg lettuce and a tomato. He thought to buy a bottle of wine but remembered her fondness for beer and felt unsure, standing on the corner outside the A&P, the bag of groceries on his arm.

When she opened the door she noticed the bag with the bottle of wine showing out the top and the six-pack of beer in his hand.

"A man bearing food," she said, smiling.

She led the way upstairs and went to the kitchen and lit the stove beneath a large cast iron skillet. He stood in the doorway and wondered why she didn't kiss him when he arrived. He set the bag on the counter and watched her chop onion and green pepper and garlic and throw them into the pan.

"The sauce needs a little help," she said. "It always does. There's just so much you can put in a jar."

She looked at him standing back from her, hands in his pockets, on his face a little frown.

"Oh, shit," she said, "I hurt your feelings," a sigh, "I'm sorry. I'm such an idiot sometimes." She took a step toward him. "It was sweet of you to buy groceries. Really. You just need practice is all. How about you make the salad," and then she kissed him and he smiled.

"There's some stuff in the fridge if you want to jazz it up a little."

He rooted until he found a drawer full of greens—scallions, peppers, mushrooms, and different kinds of lettuce, none of them iceberg—far more than he'd ever seen in a salad before. He tore the lettuce into a bowl, the smell of olive oil and garlic drifting over from where she stood in front of the stove. When he turned his head to pick up a pepper he looked at her eyes intent on the end of the wooden spoon in her hand, a lock of hair dangling down in front of her face, the long line of her nose, and he felt himself suddenly wanting to cry with no idea of why, but he shook it off and set himself to coring and slicing the pepper.

She told him about what he missed in Petersen's class, but he'd read so far ahead that he recognized most of it.

"Do you think Petersen was ever in the service?" he said.

"The military? I doubt it."

"Do you have brothers in?"

"I don't have any brothers."

"Was your father?"

"Oh, God, no," she said. "He was a CO."

"Really?"

"The only thing he served in was prison, until they let him out so he could clean hospital bedpans."

"Why was he a CO?"

"The usual reason, killing is wrong and war never solves anything."

"Sometimes it does."

"No," she said, opening the jar of sauce and pouring it into the pan, "it's always a bad idea. Gandhi was right. Violence doesn't work."

"Not even World War Two?"

"God, no. It was one of the worst."

"You don't think we had to stop Hitler."

"Sure we did."

"So—"

"But war is the worst way to do it. Look at it. Billions of dollars and most of Europe in rubble and how many people dead just to stop Hitler and Tojo?"

She tapped the spoon against the edge of the pan and looked at him. "Fifty-five *million*," she said, "and mostly civilians. And for what? To make the world safe? So we could have Korea and Vietnam and the Cold War and the bomb hanging over our heads? Fifty-five million people had to die to get to that?"

He said, almost without thinking, "But how would you stop Hitler?" but in his mind he was asking himself what would be worth the loss of his brother's life, what cause would make it acceptable, and how would he find his brother in numbers so large they left no trace of who he was, the things he'd done and said and thought and felt and what it meant that he had been alive.

"I don't know," she said. "We're supposed to be so smart, I'm sure we'd come up with a better way if we really wanted to. There are all kinds of ways to beat a tyrant. Gandhi got rid of the British without firing a shot." She looked at him and shrugged. "War is dumb. It always fails, even when you win, and even then the real winners are the fat cats who sell the guns."

He looked down and picked at the lettuce. She drained the pasta through a cloud of steam over the sink. He took the salad to the table by the window.

"There's something I didn't tell you," he said. "About Petersen's class. Why I'm there."

She leaned back against the stove, looking at him.

"The Colonel asked me to."

"Really," she said. "Why?"

"To see if Petersen is anti-war."

"A spy," she said, lifting her eyebrows.

He looked at her, then away with a nod.

"He called me in today."

"Petersen."

"No, the Colonel."

"And?"

"I told him it was just a history course."

"You lied," she said, making a little smile. "Some spy you turned out to be."

"I had to tell him something."

"Did he buy it?"

Andrew shook his head.

"Was he mad?"

"You could say that."

"Well," she said, "good for you."

"I guess."

"Are you worried about what he'll do?"

"I don't know. There isn't much. It's not like I broke a rule or anything."

"The hell it isn't."

He looked at her. "Right."

"That's a good one," she said, grinning, "just a history course."

"Whatever that is."

They stood in silence for a moment, staring at each other across the room.

"My father teaches history," he said.

The snow came down hard, the flakes big and wet, the kind of late winter snow that can lay several inches on the ground in a matter of hours and then melt away the next day. They finished eating and she stood in the doorway watching him wash the dishes.

"This I know how to do," he said, looking out the window over the sink. "It's really coming down."

"You should stay over," she said.

"I don't know," he said, drying his hands on a towel. "The couch is kind of lumpy."

"That's not what I had in mind."

He looked at her.

"Your face is turning red," she said.

"No it's not."

She smiled. "Yes," she said. "Really. It is."

"You're worried," she said, sitting beside him on the couch, passing him the joint after giving him a kiss that was so long and so sweet that she could tell it all but stopped his mind.

He looked down at the joint in his fingers. "Well," he said, "I'm not exactly . . . what you'd call . . . prepared."

"You mean no toothbrush and clean underwear."

"Well, that, too . . . "

"Ah," she said, "no rubbers. No problem. I'm on the pill."

He looked at her.

"You have that worried look again," she said. "You think that makes me bad?"

"No."

"I think maybe you do. But you're wrong. I just don't want to worry about whether a man can spare a few minutes to think more about me than he does about himself."

"I did," he said.

"Did what?"

"Thought about you."

She smiled. "So you did."

He took a shower and stepped into the hall, a towel around his waist, and she passed by, dressed in a white terry cloth robe, leaning in to kiss him, her fingers lightly resting on his belly, and he felt himself harden beneath the towel and wondered if she could tell.

Her room was furnished with a double bed, a small wooden chair tucked in a corner, a bookshelf rising nearly to the ceiling. The head of the bed was beneath a window that looked out onto a side yard. The closet door was ajar and a sweatshirt hung from the knob.

He draped the towel over the chair and stood for a moment in the dark room lit only by the streetlamp across the way, his mind filling with the memory of her fingers on his skin, the sound of running water coming from the other side of the wall, closing his eyes to imagine it flowing over her body. And then the sound of the water turning off and the shower curtain pulled back and suddenly he felt exposed, leaning down to pick up his underwear from where he dropped it on the floor, then thinking no, not after a shower, and slipping into his jeans and shirt and sitting down on the bed to wait in the stillness.

She stepped into the room and sat beside him. From the living room came the sound of Judy Collins singing "Mr. Tambourine Man."

"You've never done this before, have you."

He paused and then shook his head.

"That's okay, I have."

He swallowed.

"But not a lot if you're worried about that."

"I'm not."

"Good," she said, "because that's who I am. Ruth Koszinski who's done it before but not a lot."

She leaned forward and kissed him and her robe, tied loosely around her, fell open just enough to reveal the smooth upper slope of her breasts and he put his arms around her and kissed her and then she smiled and he made a little gasp too soft for her to hear as she stood and let the robe drop from her shoulders and smiled to see his eyes pass slowly over her body illumined in the dim light of the streetlamp coming through the air outside the window, thick with snow.

Standing by the bookcase, she struck a match and lit a pair of candles.

"Come on," she said, helping him unbutton his shirt. He slid out of his pants and crawled beneath the covers.

"The first thing," she said, "is that when you go slow, you don't miss so much." She turned and lay on her back. "So, take the tour," she said, smiling at the ceiling, "and feel free to ask questions."

"Take the tour—"

She began to laugh.

"Well, let's see," he said, hiking himself up on his elbows.

Her laughter quieted to a smile and she closed her eyes.

He traced around her ear, gently tugging the lobe before dropping down the line of her jaw and then up and over her nose and down again and across her lips and drawing from her a little murmur as she rubbed them with her finger.

"Tickles," she said. "Do you know lips have more nerve endings per square inch than almost any part of your body?"

"No," he said, tracing the hollow at the base of her throat, "I didn't know that."

"Well they do."

"Amazing," he said, drawing the covers down around her waist, drawing from her a soft little gasp as he circled down and around first one breast and then the other, spiraling up until he lightly came to rest on a nipple, hard beneath his finger.

"Are they always like this?"

"No," she said, the word seeming to come a beat or two behind the thought. "That's nice. The circling part."

His finger circumnavigated the nipple and with a murmur she raised her arms over her head and laid her knuckles against the windowpane, her breasts lifting with the motion.

"What's this?" he said, touching a small mark below her left breast.

"A birthmark. Looks a little like Italy, don't you think?"

He cocked his head to one side as if to correct the view. "I guess so," he said, trying to remember the shape of Italy. "How cool."

"I'm gonna live there someday," she said, "and write all morning and drink coffee in little cafes all afternoon."

"Like Hemingway."

"No," she said, "that was Spain, I think. Besides, he didn't like women much."

He slid his fingers down between her breasts to the soft rise of her belly and her hand lit on his shoulder as her other arm rose from the bed, the hand waving gently back and forth above her hip, dreamy in the air, as if following a piece of music.

He leaned down and smelled her skin, the scent faintly nutty, and felt her fingers in his hair, her hand coming to rest on his head as he drew his cheek across her belly, sinking down into the softness.

"That's nice," she said. "You could do that again," and he did before pushing the covers halfway down her thighs.

"Atta boy," she said with a little bark of a laugh. And then she kicked away the covers and drew her knees up off the bed and let them fall outward to the side, opening herself to him.

He was stunned by the sight of her. He'd seen pictures of this in magazines boys would smuggle into the dorms. And there was the time he stumbled in upon his mother in the bathroom after she'd taken a shower, leaning down to dry her foot resting on the toilet seat, her breast pressing against her thigh as she looked up and said, "Eeek! A man!" in mock distress and waved him back through the doorway and into the hall. So he had some idea of the inside of a woman's thigh and the little mound of hair above and what lay beneath, but none of that seemed to matter now. This was entirely new. He stopped breathing in the stillness that slowly settled over the room. She played her fingers through the hair over the tender spot at the nape of his neck and he felt his cock go soft. He filled his lungs with air as he began to wander across the smooth expanse of her, pausing to run a fingertip around her navel, drawing from her another little laugh, but softer and more girlish than before, now dipping down to the little hollow where her pelvis met her thighs, his fingers spread to take the measure of her hip, his thumb passing down the low ridge of bone. He was surprised by the softness of the skin inside her thighs, softer, he thought than anything he'd ever felt before. As he pulled himself toward the foot of the bed, he looked down toward a faint sweet smell and was for a moment suspended over the dark mound of hair and the darker lips below standing out from her like wrinkled petals on some exotic flower. Reaching down, he drew a finger lightly along the outer edge, just enough to make it move in the dim light, drawing a little moan from her as she raised her hips to meet his hand and he felt himself grow hard against the sheet.

"That's really nice," she said, her voice drifting away.

Drawn to the pace and rhythm of her movement beneath his hand as they mirrored each other, following and being followed at the same time, he looked up across her belly and breasts to her face slightly raised, lips parted as she breathed through her teeth, licking her lips, "Make me wet," and for a moment him not knowing what to do until she drew her fingers across her tongue and floated them down to the little space between them.

"Nothing like spit," she said with a little smile, and so he wet his finger and touched her, now warm and slippery until suddenly her hand appeared again, taking his finger and bringing the tip to rest on a button of flesh where the lips came together to form a little hood.

"Go easy," she said. "A little goes a long way."

He touched the tip of her and felt her pelvis rotate downward with the arching of her back, marveling that something so small, so illusive beneath his finger could cause such pleasure, watching her giving in, the rise and fall of her belly below her hands laid gently on her breasts, then reaching down to seek him out, her fingers circling around him, soft but sure in their intent as he made a little gasp and then forgot what he was doing.

"Don't stop," she said.

He put his finger back in motion and closed his eyes to focus on the sweetness of her touch blending seamlessly with his own, flowing through her and back to him again.

"I think it's time," she said, her voice breathy and low.

He hesitated, unsure of what she meant, then rose to his knees, his mind filling with images of lying between her legs, hips pumping in the air, until suddenly she was up and rolling toward him, hands on his shoulders pushing him onto his back until she was above him, straddling his hips, up on her knees as she reached down and found him and with a single motion slid him deep inside a sweetness beyond anything he'd ever thought to know, not only the sensation, but the idea of being inside, taken in and held by this woman who looked down at him with such tenderness, smiling at the look on his face that seemed puzzled and ecstatic at the same time.

She moved against him, rocking her pelvis forward and back, eyes closed.

He felt it coming just before it arrived and his heart sank, thinking he should have lasted longer but having no idea of how, unable to hold it back, nor wanting to. He pushed upward with his pelvis, wanting to thrust inside her, but he was pinned beneath the weight of her and gave himself over to the rhythm of her movement back and forth as the sweet release spread from the middle of his body down to his toes at one end and his lips at the other. On she went, seeming oblivious to him now, quickening her pace as he looked up at her, leaning back with her hands on his knees as she arched away from him, her face toward the ceiling, mouth open as she breathed fast and deep, and then crying out, high in her throat at first and then dropping to a deeper place, leaving him amazed and transfixed by the sound and sight of her.

She took a deep breath and let it out on a sigh, then looked down at him as he felt himself go soft inside her.

"You okay?"

He nodded.

"Not what you expected."

He looked away, then back at her. "Well," he said, "as you said," a little shrug, "never done it before."

"Can't say that again. You, my friend, just got properly laid."

She leaned down against his chest, then lifted her head and kissed him, long and slow, her tongue exploring his mouth.

"I like the way you touched me," she said. "Nice and slow."

"I think you're beautiful."

"You don't have to say that."

"But you are."

"Yeah, yeah," she said, looking away with a faint smile on her face.

He could feel his slow, shrinking withdrawal from her until he was no longer inside. She looked at him with a little pout. "What goes up must come down," she said, then rolled away and lay on her back beside him. A few minutes went by and then she turned to him. "So," she said, "tell me the story of your life."

He made a little laugh. "You're kidding."

"Not at all. Where were you born?"

"A dinky little town near Boston."

"And your favorite thing to do when you were a kid?"

He was quiet for awhile, staring up at a small brown spot on the ceiling where water had seeped through a long time ago.

"Other than beating off," she said, watching the smile break over his face and then just as quickly fade.

"These are not hard questions," she said. "Unless you had a rotten childhood."

"No. It was fine."

"And . . . ?"

He shrugged. "I was thinking about my brother."

He looked away out the window at the snow.

"Mostly I try not to," he said, "and when I do, I try to imagine him doing something, hiding out somewhere," and then his voice dropping almost to a whisper, "but I think he's really dead."

"No—"

"Yes. I do."

"But you don't know that."

In the dim light she made out a thin wet line running down from the corner of his eye. He said nothing. A car went by, tires muffled by the snow, headlights playing across the wall and ceiling and then leaving them in the light of the candles and the streetlamp across the way.

"Maybe it'd help if you had s'more," she said.

He looked at her. "I'm not hungry."

She looked away, her face puzzled, then softening into a tender smile. "I wasn't talking marshmallows," she said, her hand sliding down beneath the covers. She played her fingers through the fine hair and then began gently stroking him, watching his eyes close and his chest rise as he filled himself with air.

"Oh, my," she said, her voice soft and close to his ear, "it's a miracle." And then she gently took him by the shoulder and pulled him toward her, laying back and spreading her legs out wide.

"Take your time," she said. "This one's all for you." He held himself above her as she guided him inside and he felt something in the region of his heart begin to come undone as she took him by the hips and pulled him deep, and then he lost himself in the motion of them together, like waves across a beach, flowing in and pulling back until he opened like a flower inside her, the coming sweet and warm, the murmur of her assent as he slowed and began to cry, the tears falling on her breast, her fingers gentle in his hair. He laid himself down on top of her and she wrapped her arms around him, turning her head to look out the window at the air thick with snow.

Andrew woke in the middle of the night and lay in the dark, looking at her sleeping beside him and wondering if it was love, this tender wanting, this affinity of one body for another. The house creaked and he thought of his father's nocturnal wanderings, getting up to see what was the matter only to be shushed by his mother and sent back to bed. He stared out at the snow coming down so hard he couldn't make out the house across the way, and he imagined his father sleeping in that house, holding close the secret he had harbored as long as Andrew could remember. And then he felt himself wanting to know, not as he had before, driven only by a boy's curiosity about his father, but springing from the nascent belief that somewhere within that secret he might find not only his father, but his brother and himself.

He looked down at her hand lying palm upward against the sheet, fingers curled, long and slender in the air. He imagined them passing lightly across her tongue before dropping down to turn a page or waving in the air to emphasize a point. In the dim light, the outer joints made little jerking motions that made him wonder at the content of her dreams. And then suddenly she turned and rolled away and he felt a lonely emptiness in the pit of his stomach. He watched her sleep, then slid over, coming near and spooning in behind, his arm around her, hand across her belly, his face in close to her hair.

All night long the moist air swirled up from the south to meet the cold front sweeping down from the north and what began as an early spring curiosity turned into a full-fledged blizzard. When Andrew woke, Ruth was standing at the window looking out. A snowplow labored past and as she turned her head to follow its progress he looked at her face outlined against a white sky and remembered the little murmur as he came inside her, her hands on his hips, the intention of a smile on her face.

She looked at him. "It's a friggin' blizzard," she said. "I can hardly see the fence." Then she smiled. "Let's be snowed in. All day. Let's just eat and sleep and read and who knows what else."

"So," he said, passing a forkful of scrambled egg into his mouth, "what you're saying is there's a conspiracy to wage an illegal war and lie to the American people."

"Absolutely," she said, folding her leg beneath her on the kitchen chair.

He shook his head.

"What?" she said.

"Conspiracy?"

"Yes."

"All those guys? McNamara? Johnson? Humphrey? Rusk? The FBI? The Supreme Court? The CIA? The Joint Chiefs—"

"The Department of Agriculture."

He smiled, "Come on."

"Come on where?"

"Reality. It isn't possible."

"The hell it's not. Look," she said, "the one thing you can count on is that governments lie. Especially when they're out of their minds, which is most of the time, and this one for sure. But, they can't let anyone know, so they blunder and flounder and bluff it out and lie to cover their ass, which is, of course, the first rule. Never admit you're wrong and always cover your ass."

"I think that's two rules," he said, wagging his fork in the air.

"Whatever. Either way, the arrogant little shits act as though not being caught in a lie is the same as telling the truth."

He nodded with a slow shake of his head from side to side. "Okay," he said, "but lies don't mean conspiracy."

"It does when it's one long lie from the beginning. We lied when we signed the Atlantic Charter against colonialism. We lied when we said they could hold elections and when we promised not to interfere." She slid her leg from beneath her and planted her foot on the floor. "And we've been lying ever since, all this bullshit about defending democracy and saving the Vietnamese. We could care less. We have no idea who they are and no interest in finding out. We just assume they want what we want and think like we do and if they don't, well, fuck 'em. The only thing we care about is being right and thinking we're number one and making sure capitalism goddamn well rules the world."

He looked at her eyes, wide open and blazing with light.

"I know, I know," she said, looking away. "I can't help it. This is important."

"I know that."

"Well, you should. They eat up guys like you for snacks."

He watched his fork poke through the bits of egg on his plate and in his mind saw his brother's face the morning after he announced he'd joined the Marines, closing the suitcase and looking up at Andrew lying on the top bunk, the sadness on Joshua's face barely visible in the pre-dawn light, the sound of rain putting a chill in the air.

"Andrew," she said, her voice earnest and low, "this thing they're running is a death machine, pure and simple. They suit you up in nice little uniforms and tell you how special you are and how it's your duty and your big chance to let everyone see what brave and patriotic men you are. And off you go. But once they've got you, they turn away and you don't exist anymore. You're just a thing to them, part of the mass, a grain of wheat thrown into the mill with all the rest. And when they've ground you up, they pause to say what a shame, such a noble sacrifice, all the while they're reaching in the sack for more."

From outside the window there was the sound of a snowplow lumbering by as he looked down and slowly moved his fork back and forth, mashing the egg against the plate.

Two days later Ruth threw open the door and came into the apartment with a whoop.

"What's got you lit up?" he said.

She stopped in the middle of the room.

"Bobby Kennedy's running for president," she said, trying to catch her breath. "It's so great I can hardly stand it."

"Why?"

"Why's he running?"

"Why can't you stand it?"

"Because it means we've got a chance to elect a president who's against the fucking war. McCarthy's good, but McCarthy and Kennedy are *really* good. They don't like each other, but between them we just might stop Lyndon's boy from getting the nomination."

She started to do a little dance, her hands raised loosely in the air as she chanted, "Dump the hump. Dump the hump." She stopped before the puzzled look on his face. "The hump?" she said, "Hubert H. Humphrey? Vice President of the United States?"

"Oh."

"You never heard 'dump the hump' before?" she said, bugging out her eyes. "Where've you been?"

"You know where I've been."

"Oh," she said, nodding, "right."

8

Anne longed for the sweet mundane, for her ordinary life to reassert itself and crowd out thoughts of her boys and the inescapable marking in her mind every time she encountered a calendar, of how long it had been since someone, somewhere knew where Joshua was. She would try to make up her mind that he was dead, but then she couldn't bring herself to grieve what she couldn't see or touch. And then she'd have a burst of energy, full of hope and the conviction that it was inconceivable that she would never see him again, riding it like a wave until she happened to turn on the news or pass by a newspaper left open on a table, standing there, suspended between worlds as if trying to remember a dream, her eyes filling with tears.

One day in the middle of April she went to the bird sanctuary and sat by the pond to watch cedar waxwings dip low over the water and a great blue heron stand motionless on one leg among the grasses along the far shore. She took herself there after a cold morning rain and sat on the swimming dock pulled out on the beach where boys would come to swim when the weather turned warm, to pass the time between final exams and graduation. She stared into the fog softening the woods and in the stillness a limb let go from the upper reaches of a tree on the far side of the pond and she tracked its descent marked by the bending of lesser branches giving way below. Slowly the fog yielded to sun and she watched a sliver of light make its way to the base of the tree, threading among the other trees like water, she imagined, seeking out some patch of ground, returning to a place it had been before, a place where it belonged.

As May approached she washed windows, cleaned the apartment, and tended the small flower garden along the backside of the dorm. She cleared out winter debris, noting damage and what needed replacing. Her favorite part was loosening the soil, down on her knees, the sound of the trowel digging under, encountering a stone, the loamy scent rising into the air around her face. She sat back on her heels and wondered what she was doing, digging in a garden while her boy was lost somewhere off in hell, and then it came to her that she was merely occupying herself as a mother must at such a time, unable to take on the mantle of Demeter and go after him herself. And then her mind began to play with the word, *occupy*, images of armies moving in the night, taking over houses, eating up food, raping mothers and daughters, shooting everyone, imposing curfews. That's what I am, she thought—occupied, taken over, confined to a few small rooms and the windows looking out, afraid each moment of what might happen next, dreaming of waking in the morning to the silence of absence and the fullness of the world restored to what it was.

She stood at the kitchen sink, looking out, a glass of water in her hand. The sky was grey and low. A breeze blew across the great lawn, billowing curtains into the room. And then it began to rain, tentative at first, as if scattered by hand, then driving down, spotting the slate walkways and sending boys scurrying for cover.

She went into the living room and sat down at the piano, closing her eyes as she rested her fingers on the keys, the ivory cool against her skin. She was still for a moment, and then it began with the index finger of her left hand and the thumb followed by the thumb and fingers of the right as each applied its ascending weight, pressing down to move the hammers to sound the strings and make the tone that filled the room. The feel of it always pulled her in, the sure connection between muscle and sound, one motion transformed into another.

It was a Bach prelude she had learned as a child, a simple piece to play but like so much that seemed beautiful to her, simple only on the surface. It unfolded as a seamless web of arpeggios, each proceeding upward, reaching in its own small way for something higher while the pattern of the whole sank gently down. She played hoping for an accident, an unforseen moment when the music would take her someplace and she would stumble into it and suddenly know exactly who she was. It might happen when her fingers sounded out a certain cadence of chords or inserted a passing tone, reaching, straining for the next to span a great divide, aching to connect, to dance in the air and then come together, spiraling down to wrap around something deep and elemental.

Such moments had been ever more rare since the boys were born, and when they did occur, often passed unnoticed. Most of the time she felt like a ship plowing through a wide and boundless sea, the wake that marked her passing soon commingling with the rest, leaving the impression she had never passed that way at all.

She finished the Bach and began a Mozart Sonata—which her teacher in high school, a French woman who went by the name of Madam Schultzy and wore jeans and tied bright scarves around her head and gave lessons from her home—called the "Sonata Facile."

"Meaning what? Easy?"

"No," said Madam, shaking her head. "Smooth. Flowing. As *if* it were easy, but not really, you know?"

"You mean without effort."

And then Madam smiled and nodded and said nothing more.

Anne played, eyes closed, head back, music filling the room, and was halfway through when suddenly she stopped, unable to remember what came next. She stared at the keyboard, her mind a blank, shaking her head, beginning again, a phrase or two before the gap, playing up to it only to stop, go back, begin and still not get past the hole in her memory. With a sigh she slumped her wrists against the keyboard and felt herself full of holes and loss, no longer a suitable container for music or anything else that seemed to matter. She lowered the cover over the keyboard and stared at the scratches and nicks in the ebony finish.

The back door opened and several sets of feet scraped against the mat and she wondered who William had brought home for lunch. She listened for Jack's voice or Cliff or one of the others, but there was only William saying, "If you'd wait here, for just a moment," and then his footsteps down the hall and the sight of him she would never forget, arms hanging at his sides, standing in the doorway, not leaning against the jamb with hands in his pockets as he usually did.

He cleared his throat.

"There are some officers here to see us."

She made a quick little smile of disbelief.

"The police?" she said and only then noticed the paleness in his face.

"No," he said. "They're Marines."

She imagined it was invisible to everyone around her, the feeling as she watched them enter the room, a captain and a lieutenant, dress blue uniforms immaculate, hats in their hands, hair short against their heads. For so long she had lived so close to the impending reality of Joshua's death that she thought the arrival of the news would be a small distance to cross, but now she knew she was wrong as everything inside her slowly turned to dust and drifted away on a dry hot wind, leaving her emptied out, arid and hollow, a husk on legs. She could tell their discomfort from how stiffly they stood, waiting to be invited to sit. But she didn't care. She looked at William, his hand gesturing them toward the couch, face ashen and full of pain, but she didn't care about that either. They could set her house on fire. They could cut her open, put out her eyes, beat her to death, and she could feel no part of her that would care.

The officers sat, one next to the other, a matched set, she thought as she wondered why they bothered sending two. She listened to the talk, mostly directed at William, their sensing something in her that steered them toward the man. She noted it was the captain who did the talking, the lieutenant quiet beside him, perhaps observing and learning how.

"As you know, your son has been missing for some time. We're very sorry to have to bring you the news that he's been found and did not survive his wounds."

Suddenly alert, "You mean he was alive when you found him?"

"No, ma'am. I'm sorry if I gave that impression. I meant to say that he was wounded some time ago and was dead at the time he was found."

A little nod as she looked away.

"On behalf of the Marine Corps," he said, "we want to offer our sincere condolences. Your son died in the service of his country—"

"How?"

The captain looked at the lieutenant, then at William and back at her.

"I'm not sure what you mean, ma'am."

"How did he die?"

"He was shot, ma'am."

"Where?"

"We believe it was about 30 miles south of Khesanh."

"No," she said, shaking her head. "I mean where was he shot."

He looked at her, his face uncomprehending, then lifted his chin with an abrupt little nod.

"I'm afraid we don't have that information, ma'am."

Before he could finish the sentence she had already retreated to a place inside herself, solitary and quiet except for the wind moaning through the emptiness. Then William was touching her arm and there was his voice sounding faint and far away.

"What," she said.

"The captain says he can be buried at Arlington if we want."

"Or here, ma'am," the captain hurried to say. "It's entirely up to you."

"Here," she said.

"And, of course," said the captain, "he'll be buried with military honors," but she wasn't listening now and as that became apparent, the officers pursed their lips and put their hands on their knees to push themselves to their feet. They shook William's hand and nodded at her sitting in the chair and then made their way down the hall, the voices low. The door opened and closed and in the stillness that settled over her, she heard the breath moving in and out of the hollow shell she had become. And then William was next to her, a hand on her shoulder, but she shrugged him off as she stood and walked into the kitchen, her breath coming faster now with something hard and dark coalescing beneath it as she stood at the sink and stared out the window, aware of him standing just behind her, looking over her shoulder.

"I hate you," she said, her voice barely above a whisper, him leaning in close, thinking he hadn't heard.

"What?"

"I hate you," she said, motionless and still as the words floated past her lips, "I hate you all. All you men and your precious manhood, your fraternity of death. Most of all I hate the silence. When you could've done something to stop it."

Her eyes stinging for want of tears, she stared unblinking out the window as he turned and walked down the hall to his little room, shutting the door softly behind.

William sat at the desk, his face cradled in his hands, and allowed the tears to come, but without making a sound that might be heard beyond the room, sinking down into the enormity of his loss, not only of his son, but what he imagined to be everything else as well.

Andrew returned his father's call, sitting on the floor of the phone booth, knees drawn up to his face as he listened to the familiar voice, the carefully measured evenness of tone. Andrew did not move and when he spoke it was only to say yes or no and even then he had to clear his throat to make way for the sound. He turned his head and closed his eyes as if against a bright sun.

"I don't know," he said, shaking his head and then a muffled goodbye and the phone sliding down from his ear to rest on his shoulder as he stared up at the graffiti scratched in the wall of the booth. And then he was on his feet, struggling with the door, pulling it back with a clatter and across the hall in a few steps and out the door.

He ran across campus and down Main Street past the Gulf station. He took the porch steps two at a time and rang the bell, leaning his head against the glass while he waited, rang again and looked through the window, shading his eyes with his hand, but no one came.

He sat down on the porch, his back against the wall, his breath coming shallow and slow, his insides frozen and numb. He couldn't think of him, for every time he tried to form an image or a memory or the cold fact that his brother was truly dead, his body found, identified beyond a doubt, it slowly came apart like a fine smoke and was gone.

He watched the sun drop beneath a line of trees along the ridge of a distant hill, and then he saw her coming down the street and the quickening of her step when she caught sight of him on the porch, a frown appearing on her face, her eyes fixed on him until she stood beside him, looking down.

"They found him," he said, and without a word she reached down and took his hand.

"Come on."

For a moment he couldn't move, so weary and heavy with wanting only to lie down right where he was and rid himself of consciousness, something deeper than sleep, but gently she pulled him to his feet and kept hold of his hand as she fumbled with the keys and unlocked the door and led him inside and up the stairs. She took off his coat and sat him on the couch and stood over him, laying her hand on his head, and there was something about the tenderness that loosened the strings binding his grief, the tears pouring out of him and then the deep rending sobs of one whose heart is cracking open and spilling out into the room. She sat beside him and wrapped her arms around his shoulders, his tears wetting her face as she rocked him back and forth, little murmurs coming from deep in her throat as he cried and cried, stopping for awhile to catch his breath and stare at the poster on the wall before starting in again, rocking back and forth, until finally she laid him down beneath a blanket and he fell asleep while she was in the kitchen making tea.

"When is he coming home?" said Anne.

"He doesn't know."

"But he is coming."

"Of course. It'll be at least a week before we can hold the funeral. There's plenty of time."

Anne no longer watched the evening news. She sat on the steps overlooking the great lawn and stared at the sun as it lowered in the sky above the trees. And as she sat and stared, her chin resting on the heel of her hand, boys passing by on the way to the library, she replayed in her mind each conversation, searching for the moment, the opening she failed to step through, the one thing she might have said to keep her boy from going away and what she still might say to save the one he left behind.

She drifted in the yawning gulf between a mother's impulse to save her children and the fact of having already given them up. At first it was a blank and empty space, like her mind when she realized while driving along in the car that she couldn't remember the last stretch of road. And then, slowly, it filled with the special sort of guilt and shame reserved for elders who betray the young, engulfing her in a terrible sense of loneliness and loss.

She saved her crying for when William was out of the house, feeling her grief separate and distinct from his own and not wanting to soften her anger against him, which she knew she might do the moment he tried to comfort her.

Sometimes she curled up in bed to cry, gazing out the window at the sky. Or she drew a bath and sat in the water, steam rising into the air as the tears poured out of her. Most of the time, however, the grief wove itself into the ordinary moments of her life. Suddenly her eyes would fill in the middle of doing the dishes or brushing her hair or picking a box of cereal off the shelf at the market or making the bed or lifting a bit of food toward her mouth. And then she'd stop and let it come or, depending on where she was, stuff it back inside and continue on.

She could not escape William's desire to talk her out of hating him, the way he hovered nearby, glancing at her, words crowding in behind his lips, but saying nothing, knowing that to speak openly of any emotion might unleash a depth of feeling he'd be unable to contain. And so he regarded the hatred she felt for him now as one more thing to endure, one more memory to steel himself against, one more act of violence added to all the rest.

Andrew made the rounds of his professors, who told him to go home and not worry about final exams. He couldn't bring himself to tell Petersen and so Ruth went instead. Petersen wrote to tell him how sorry he was, hoping that, *in all of this you will find what is true for you.* Andrew read the letter and slid it into the notebook where he kept the last one from his brother.

The Colonel nodded gravely when he heard the news and looked out the window for a moment, rubbing his chin as Andrew stood in the middle of the room.

"So now it's up to you," said the Colonel, turning from the window. "The torch is passed. And you'll soon have your chance to honor your brother's memory and make him proud."

Andrew could think of nothing to say. He stared into the Colonel's eyes until the man looked away, unnerved, clearing his throat, trying to recover, "and when is the funeral?"

"Next week. They have to bring him home," repeating the word in his mind, *him,* so full of life, and just who or what is left to come home?

"Yes, of course," said the Colonel. "And then you'll be back for graduation and your commission," laying a hand on Andrew's shoulder as he steered him gently toward the door. "Sometimes," he said, "it takes a jolt like this to bring us to our senses, to make us see what's really important."

Andrew looked down at the hand the Colonel held out to him, the West Point ring on the finger, the age spots on the back of the hand, and for a moment he thought of Mr. Hruska, who taught math down the hall from where his father taught history, who coached the varsity wrestling team and liked to play what he thought of as a little game, enticing boys into shaking hands and then not letting go and slowly increasing the pressure until the pain brought the boy to his knees, the wonder of it being the way the boys kept coming back, as if they might discover the secret of escaping the grip. They never did.

Andrew said nothing, or even looked into the man's face to see just who it was before he took the hand held out to him and then let it go and walked away.

When the body arrived on a train from Boston, the campus was in the full bloom of spring. For days Anne imagined him on his way, the body in a zippered bag, the skin lifeless against the black plastic, and somewhere, just over his heart, perhaps, a sad little wound, the one that brought him down and drained out the life that was his. And she imagined him surrounded by the remains of other mothers' sons, the nameless unlucky ones she always imagined would die instead of her own. But now she saw them all together in the same dark tunnel lumbering through the night, engines straining against the load, bearing them home.

She went to the closet in William's study where Joshua left his things when he went away, her knees weak beneath her as she stood before the open door and took in the scent of him drifting from the shadows. She reached in and took the navy blue suit they bought together at Simpson's downtown, and went to the bedroom and laid it out on the bed. She stared down at it, remembering that afternoon, her sitting in the chair by the wall, waiting for him to emerge from the dressing room and then seeing him so straight and tall, eyebrows lifted in search of her opinion, and how he allowed himself a smile when he saw the look on her face as she thought how handsome, how much like his father, a look that could only come from the first woman ever to love him.

She asked William to take the suit to the funeral home and he agreed, but as he was about to leave she changed her mind and without explanation followed him to the car. He sat for a moment behind the wheel, looking out over the hood as he tried to identify the content of her silence, and then, without a word, turned the key in the ignition and drove downtown.

He handed the suit to the undertaker who stood in silence for a moment as he looked from their faces to the suit held awkwardly in his hands.

"May I suggest a closed casket might be best," he said.

There was a pause and then Anne drew a sharp breath in through her nose.

"Where is he?"

The man looked at William and then at Anne, his face perplexed as if he'd been asked to tell her something she already knew, and so wondered if she was asking something else. He motioned with his head in the direction of the door behind him. "Here," he said, with a little shrug, "in back."

"I want to see him."

And then William understood the strange and heavy silence in the car. He said nothing, looking at her and then at the man whose eyes darted between them.

"Oh," said the undertaker, clearing his throat. "I don't know if that would be a good idea."

"I want to see my son."

He looked at William, then nodded and turned and motioned them through the door. They passed down a corridor into a large room at the end. In the middle was a row of tables, each bearing a casket. As she looked at the dark boxes it came to her suddenly that one of them was the one in which Joshua lay at this very moment as she stood looking at it. Her breath quickened and rose up high in her chest. The man stood by one of the caskets and when he raised his hand to scratch his nose she could see it tremble. William was between them, looking back at her, his face dark with sadness and anger. She laid her hand on her stomach and closed her eyes and tried to draw the air deep inside her as she stepped toward the box.

"Mrs. Carson, I really don't think—"

"Open it. Please."

"But," and then he paused, looking at William and then back at her, "Mrs. Carson. Please."

"My God, Anne," said William. "It's just his remains. There's nothing to see."

"No," said the undertaker, wringing his hands. "Actually, he died only recently. But still, Mrs. Carson—"

She looked at him, her eyes so wide and hard that it made him blink and step back as she spoke, her voice low and even, the words coming slowly through her teeth.

"When it's your son inside the box, you can decide. But not when it's mine."

"Anne," said William, but she could tell what he was about to say from the level, bloodless tone, and she lifted her hand to silence him.

"Or you," she said. "If you don't want to see then don't look." She turned to him. "Or go." And then she watched him turn, shaking his head, and walk away through the door.

The undertaker's face was pinched and the lips pressed into a thin line as he stepped in front of the table and turned to the casket, pausing before inserting his fingers beneath the lid and raising it into the air, stepping back and standing aside, eyes cast down.

"I'll be with him now," she said.

"As you wish," he said, not looking at her as he walked crisply from the room and closed the door.

And then, in the silence the two men left behind, she felt herself sinking toward the floor, although strangely to her, she was standing still, and then realized it was her heart sinking down, tired of beating, of holding its place amongst everything else, wanting only to stop, to stop everything, to be cradled by the earth all around. She saw sunlight coming through a window into air so still it seemed it might shatter if she moved against it. Then she stepped forward, looking from one end to the other to see how he lay in the box beneath the sheet. She looked at the rumpled form and knew in her mind that in this moment she could turn away, that if her hand reached in and pulled back the sheet, it would be her will and nothing else that made it so.

Without a sound she reached in and drew it slowly away, startled by the realness of the familiar sandy hair and the sudden memory of watching him sleep when he was a boy, the shape of his lips, wanting to reach down and brush back the hair that had fallen across his forehead, but without inserting herself into his dreams.

And then she stepped back in horror, her hand rising to her mouth when she saw what was left of his face.

The left side was almost completely gone, the jaw and most of the cheek below the eye shot away, leaving behind a ragged, gaping hole of dark tissue and remnants of teeth and bone. She couldn't take her eyes from the sight of him, unable to let go, as if holding a live wire. She began to tremble, her eyes wide and bright with tears, but she refused to make a sound, determined to stand her ground and feel the brunt of the betrayal that had brought him here and to bear the weight of her own complicity. Tears rolled down her cheeks, breaths coming gusty and hard through the fingers laid across her mouth and nose, and when she could hold it in no longer and a sob broke out from her, she turned toward the door, but her legs would not carry her away and she could only turn back again.

She half expected to find him suddenly gone, hoping what she saw was merely a figment of her fear, but when she looked down into the box he was still there, the remains of his face unmistakable. She touched his cheek, quickly pulling back from the cool, waxy skin. She thought to speak to him, of love and sorrow and regret, but no words would come for there was no one here to say them to. She was staring at an emptied out container, a shell abandoned on a beach.

She looked up and about the room, at the sun coming through the window, casting a long panel of angled light across the floor, and felt the utter irretrievable loss of her boy.

She closed her eyes and shook her head as she wiped her hand across her nose, then reached up and pulled the lid down, pausing for a moment to feel the wood beneath her fingers before she turned and walked away, her footsteps the only sound.

"Where the hell you been?" said Steve as Andrew walked into the room, stopping just inside the door, his hand still on the knob.

"I've been staying with someone."

A smile crept over Steve's face. "And who might she be?"

Andrew shook his head as he stepped into the room and closed the door.

Steve made a little whoop and clapped his hands, "Laid at last!"

Andrew opened the closet and pulled his suitcase from the shelf.

"What's the matter?"

He set the suitcase on the bed.

"They found my brother."

"He's okay—"

"No."

"He isn't dead."

Andrew looked at him. "I've gotta go home."

Steve was still for a moment, his hands suspended in the air by his waist, and then he startled them both by stepping forward and taking Andrew in his arms.

"God, Drew," he said, stepping back, "I'm really sorry. Is there anything I can do?"

Andrew shook his head.

Ruth drove him to the bus station in her car, an old powder blue VW covered with anti-war stickers.

"Will you be all right?" she said.

He stared out the window at a group of boys making their boisterous way home from school, and thought of the poster in Ruth's apartment.

"Probably not," he said, looking at her. "The thing is, I don't know what'll be worse, the funeral or seeing my dad."

"How come?"

"I've changed," he said, "and he'll know." He snapped his fingers. "Just like that, he'll sniff it out."

"You don't know what this will do to him," she said. "It may change him, too."

"Not my dad. He's a rock."

"Maybe so," she said, "but even rocks can break."

"Not this one."

He kissed her goodbye and as the bus pulled away and he looked back and saw her disappear behind the corner, he felt suddenly alone and afraid as he never had before, some fabric that had held him all his life now unraveling all around him, loosening its hold on his heart. He sat staring out the window, his bag beside him to discourage anyone from sitting there. He laid a hand on his belly to calm himself. He wished for sleep or something to occupy his mind but there was only the sight of low grey clouds scudding across the sky and the road stretching south where he did not want to go.

Andrew saw his parents standing beside each other and yet apart, not touching, his father's hands in his pockets, his mother's arms across her chest, her face looking open and raw as if her skin might suddenly produce tears. His stomach went light as he made a little smile and raised his hand to wave, but they made no sign of seeing him through the tinted glass.

His mother's eyes were wet when she stepped forward and took him in her arms while his father stood beside them, his hand on Andrew's shoulder. She held him for a long time before stepping back to look into his face. "Okay, then. Let's go home."

He sat in the back seat. His mother turned and looked at him. "How are you doing?"

"Okay," he said. "It's just hard to believe."

"I know."

He really is gone, he thought to say, but did not, watching her nod and glance over at his father staring through the windshield.

They climbed the hill toward the school and passed a playing field where the lacrosse team was practicing.

"How's the team this year?"

"Pretty good."

He waited for his father to say more but there was only the sound of the car straining up the hill and his mother giving him a weak little smile before turning her head away.

Andrew put his suitcase in his old room. He stared down at the lower bunk where Joshua had slept, by right of seniority, being the older, and remembered the late nights, leaning over the edge to peer down at his brother lying on his back, hands folded behind his head, his voice drifting up through the dark, the muffled laughter at something funny, the silence as they listened for footsteps down the hall.

In the living room William put on his jacket.

"I have a class. You okay?"

"No."

Late in the afternoon Andrew went to the bird sanctuary and walked down the road, noticing the smells, the sound of birds calling out, his shoes against the gravel. And then he rounded a familiar corner bordered by a dense thicket of rhododendron. He stood in front of it, his eyes fixed on the memory of the darkened center where the light could barely reach. Then he looked up and down the road and, seeing no one, stepped inside, dropping to his hands and knees as he crawled toward a small hollow space just big enough for two if they pulled their knees up to their chests. And then he sat and lowered his head and began to cry.

In the evening Andrew and his mother watched television while William graded papers in his study. She stood to leave when *Gunsmoke* came on.

"That's okay," he said, "we don't have to watch it—"

"No, you go ahead," but he was already stepping over to turn it off.

She sat on the couch, picking up a book from the table.

"The quiet is nice," she said.

A door opened down the hall and his father walked into the kitchen and rummaged through a drawer.

"Mind if I join you?" said Andrew.

William looked up from the pack of cigarettes in his hand.

"You smoking now?"

"No. I just feel like having one."

"All right."

They sat on the steps overlooking the lawn and boys going in and out of the library across the way.

"Not much has changed," said Andrew.

His father blew a plume of smoke into the air.

"Not much."

There was a long silence.

"Dad."

"What?"

"How come you never talk about the war?"

He felt his father shift, as if rearranging himself in his clothes.

"Which one?" the edge in his father's voice making Andrew's mouth go dry.

"Yours."

"You've been talking to your mother."

"No. Not about this."

His father sighed. "I don't talk about it because I don't see the point."

"But would you mind?"

"Now?"

"Yes."

"No. I mean yes. I would mind. It's not the time for it."

They sat in silence, Andrew's stomach quick with fear as he struggled to form the next sentence in his mind. His father seemed enormous sitting beside him, his muscles tight and coiled like an animal preparing to strike.

"Maybe it is," said Andrew. "For me, anyway."

His father stood and flicked the glowing cigarette out over the lawn.

"Not for me."

Andrew looked up at his father standing over him.

"If now isn't okay, then maybe some other time. I could come down before graduation."

"It's not a good idea."

"Why not?"

"Because there's nothing I can say to prepare you. It's something you have to find out for yourself."

Andrew drew on the cigarette, then flicked it into the dark. "You mean like Josh," he said, bracing himself.

Two boys emerged from the dorm with voices loud and full of laughter as they made their way to the library. Andrew's father stood still in the darkness, watching them, then turned and went inside.

Andrew took the lower bunk and was dropping off to sleep when the door opened and he saw his mother step in and close it behind her. She walked softly across the room and stood by the bed, looking up into the top bunk, then down to where he lay.

"Are you awake?" she whispered.

"Unh-huh."

"You're sleeping down there."

"I thought I would," he said, his voice small in the dark. "Is that okay?"

"Of course," she said, sitting down. He tried to make out from the dim outline of her face if she was crying, but he couldn't tell for sure. "I thought maybe you'd want to talk about tomorrow," she said.

"I'm all right."

"I know."

He felt her hand cool against his forehead, her fingers combing back the hair.

"Are you and Dad okay?"

She withdrew her hand and laid it in her lap.

"Not really," she said. "But don't worry about that. You've got more important things to think about." She paused, leaning down close to his face, "Andrew, I have to say this—"

"Mom—"

"No, Andrew," straightening herself as he sat up in the bed, "I've lost your brother and I'm not going to lose you, too."

"I know, Mom, but—"

"No, honey, you don't. You can't. Not this. Not until you've had children of your own, and even then you won't be their mother," her voice dropping to a whisper and the words coming faster than before. "You won't know what it's like to raise a child and then give him up to this. I should have stopped him, but I didn't think I had the right and I didn't know how, and now I don't know how to stop you—"

"It's okay, Mom—"

"No," she said, "it's not. Don't you see. It never will be okay," wiping the back of her hand across her eyes. "You can't go, Andrew."

"But I have to—"

Suddenly she seemed to rear back as if she were going to hurl herself at him. "I am so sick of hearing that," she said, all tenderness gone from her voice, the words hissing through her teeth. "Where *are* you in all this? What do *you* want to do? You've read Josh's letters. Is *that* what you want?"

"No."

"Then what are you doing?"

They looked at each other across the darkness.

"Mom," he said, his voice soft, "what do you want me to do?"

"I want you to live. I want you to be a man."

"But I am—"

"Not if you go off to war just because your father or some colonel or your friends expect you to."

"Then what about Josh? What are you saying about him?"

"He did what he was told," she said, "like the good boy that he was." She lowered her face and buried it in her hands. "And you know what they did to him?" She lifted her head and looked into Andrew's eyes. "I saw him when they brought him home. Your father wouldn't look, but I had to. You know what they did to him?"

Andrew slowly shook his head as he looked into her eyes, dark and wide, and wished she would stop, knowing she would not until she was done.

"They shot away half his face. The whole side of your brother's face was just bits of bone and flesh—"

"Mom—"

"No, Andrew, you will hear this. You don't get to choose. Not about this. What was done to Josh wasn't about duty and honor. It was about sending boys to hell and then killing them, and I didn't raise you for that. Maybe your father did, but not me."

And then he watched her collapse in front of him even as she got to her feet, the muscles in her face rising up and then sinking down into an implosion of grief as she stood and went out the door.

They were silent over breakfast. It was so different, thought Andrew, from the only funeral he'd ever known, when his grandmother died six years ago, the room filled with talk of her and things she'd done and said and meant to them, all her passions and funny little quirks. But this felt like something else as he looked across the table at his parents bent over their plates, picking at their food. This was death before its time with the sense of loss and something stolen combining to overwhelm memory and gratitude for what time there was. In their place was an empty, desolate silence, a downward look, a fork soft and tentative against the plate, even the cup laid in its saucer as if given up and left behind.

His mother cleared the table.

"I'll do the dishes, Mom," and then her looking at him, startled at first, then a nod, her cheeks pulled back in a smile full of pain.

He stood at the sink and looked out as his mother had done for so many years, and he felt for the first time what drew her to it, the sight of the lawn stretching to the stone wall on the far side, the elms rising into the sky, the warm water running over his fingers, the contours of a dish in his hand, everything about it simple and real and peaceful and calming in a way he never would have guessed.

He dried his hands and put on his jacket. "I'm going for a walk."

"It starts at ten," his father said.

"I'll be here."

He walked across campus past the gym to the acres of playing fields beyond, climbing the little slope to the bleachers overlooking the varsity lacrosse field. He stood at the edge, his toes against the white line in the grass, then walked to the center of the field and down to the goal at the far end to rest his hand on the crossbar and run his fingers through the netting. Then he went on across the adjoining fields to the line of trees at the far side where he turned and looked at the buildings in the distance, the white steeple of the chapel showing above the trees. It all seemed larger than this in his memory, taking longer to walk from one end to the other, everything rising higher into the air. And then it came to him that perhaps he was never really here, that nothing he remembered ever happened, that this afternoon boys would run across these fields with no memory of him or his brother, as if they never existed at all. Joshua had made his choice and now he was dead and what difference did any of it make? He had won the senior prize for best all-around athlete and the prize for leadership and character and what did it matter now?

Andrew walked home with the wind in his face and as he stepped inside the apartment he heard them in the bedroom down the hall, their voices low, the words few and widely spaced. He stepped into his room and closed the door softly behind.

The chapel was nearly full when they arrived. The entire faculty was there and most of the staff and many students as well, drawn by curiosity about a recent graduate home dead from the war. The casket lay at the front, draped in a flag and flanked by four Marines in dress blue uniforms. Anne couldn't take her eyes off the box as she walked down the aisle, in her mind the outline of his face, the feel of his skin.

They sat in the pew reserved for them in front. The raised platform beyond the casket was lined with flowers provided by the school, and as she looked across the bank of brightly colored blooms, so full of life, an ache came into her heart. She looked at the Marines, stiff, eyes fixed straight ahead, and realized they had him even now, standing guard against her taking back the boy inside the man. Why did I consent to this? she thought. When was it decided?

A sad little Bach prelude flowed from the organ, then a pause at the end, the void slowly filling with the rustle of people behind them, the soft clearing of throats.

Andrew stared at the Marines, uniforms crisp perfection against their bodies, faces rigidly composed, unmoving and unmoved. Then he turned his head and looked past his mother to his father sitting erect, his face pale and drawn, and wondered how did he feel at this moment, realizing he had no idea, having never seen so much as a tear in his father's eye, or anything else that might reveal the inner reaches of his heart.

His mother put her hand on top of his, and at her touch he felt himself about to cry until he pushed out a breath to slow its coming, then clamped his jaw and looked away.

Sitting at the end of the pew, William was barely aware of what was happening around him because he could not stop looking at Jack sitting in a high-backed chair against the wall behind the pulpit, hands folded in front of him as he looked out over the crowd. William was transfixed, unable to take his eyes off the thin red line of blood he saw running down the left side of his face. He thought to call out or go to him, it seeming that Jack didn't know, but he couldn't move, only his mind capable of motion, and only within itself. Their eyes met and Jack made a sad little nod to which William shook his head, raising a hand to the side of his face to get him to touch the spot and discover the wound. But Jack only looked back with a pained and puzzled expression.

The music stopped and Jack stepped to the pulpit and William waited for the crowd to react to the sight of blood flowing down his face, now dripping onto the front of his jacket, but there was only a hush settling over the great hall as the headmaster began to speak of Joshua Carson and his life, William not hearing the words or those of the men who followed, teachers and coaches and a young classmate in uniform. There was only the blood and the face and the eyes looking out past what they did not see.

They sat on folding chairs arranged in a back corner of the school cemetery behind Butler Hall. William looked up and saw the sun reflect from windows in his classroom on the second floor and realized he'd have to find another room to avoid the view. He saw Jack at the far end of the row, the blood gone now from his face. He wasn't sure just when it disappeared, or if it had even been there at all.

Andrew watched his mother as she stared at the proceedings through a steady stream of tears that hadn't stopped since a young corporal spoke in the chapel and his voice caught in his throat and Andrew felt her suddenly look away. She held a handkerchief against her lips, occasionally wiping the lower edge of her eyes and then bringing it back to its resting place just below her nose. Her arm was across her middle, the hand tucked beneath the other arm, as if holding herself against spilling out onto the ground.

There were words being spoken, carried close on a breeze and then away, but whether near or far, Andrew couldn't make them out. The edge of the flag lifted gently from the casket, then drifted down. Then there was a sharp command from one of the Marines and a sudden volley of gunshots startled him and he looked to see his father cover his mother's hand with his own, and he was just beginning to draw some comfort from the sight when the command and the volley came again and then again. He closed his eyes as the mournful strains of Taps played out over the heads of the people gathered there, steeling himself to hold back tears as his mother began to sob beside him, unrestrained, beyond caring anymore, falling apart in front of them all. And then she grew quiet and still as the four Marines approached the casket and each took a corner of the flag, stepping one toward another, snapping it tight and folding it down to a small triangle resting in a sergeant's white-gloved hands. Andrew watched his mother look down at a spot in the grass as the sergeant walked slowly up to her, and then saw her head lift just a little at the sight of the brightly polished shoes coming to rest in front of her and then the Marine bending down to hold out the flag.

She stared at it for a moment, then looked down at her hands frozen in her lap.

She did not move.

Andrew's eyes went back and forth between the outstretched hands holding the flag and his mother's downturned face.

"Ma'am," said the sergeant. "This is for you. From a grateful nation."

Still she did not move, unable to look up or lift her hands.

William thought to take the flag himself, and was about to reach for it when he saw the tiny crimson spot on the white glove nearest him, shiny and fresh as if it had just dropped from the sergeant's eye, a solitary tear except for the color. He looked up into the smooth shaven face, the skin taut across the bones, and could see no sign of any wound that might issue a drop of blood.

William blinked and turned his head away, then without looking up, reached out and took the flag.

"Thank you, Sergeant," he said, resting it on his lap.

Andrew could hear his mother crying behind the closed bedroom door. His father stood in the hall, hands in his pockets, glancing

190

at Andrew and then at the door before he followed her inside. Andrew stared at the door, his father's voice low and soft coming from the other side.

He went to his room and took off his jacket and tie and lay down on the bed, his hands behind his head. He looked up at the bunk above him just as his brother had done so many nights with his own small voice drifting down through the dark. And then he let the tears pour out of him, feeling suddenly alone, first brotherless and now strangely orphaned by the war.

In the middle of the night William lay in bed and stared into the dark, unable to explain what he saw, was it real, this ubiquity of blood.

Andrew left for school the next day. His mother drove him to the station after breakfast and walked him to the bus where they faced each other beside the open door. He looked at her, feeling too far away to find a way back. She took him in her arms and held him for a moment and he felt his eyes begin to fill as she stepped back and raised her fingers to her lips.

"You remember what I said," she said, holding his gaze in her own, her eyes darkly circled with grief and lack of sleep. "You remember."

And he nodded and turned and climbed up into the bus.

When Andrew arrived at the station he called Ruth for a ride, but there was no answer and so he took a cab into town and dropped his suitcase at the dorm. Then he went outside and walked down to the river. In the short time he'd been gone the snow had almost melted away and spring was coming on. He sat on the dock, his bare feet dangling in the cold water. The sun was going down and across the western sky stretched a long thin line of dusty pink above the hills. He stared at a leaf drifting slowly by and followed it until it disappeared from view.

Nothing is the same, he thought. Not a single thing.

TWO

1

"Tell me you don't hate me," said William, lying beside her in the bed, the room dark, the dormitory quiet overhead. From the day they got the news, he waited for the shift that would signal her departure. When he came home, he listened for her, feeling for the absence, expecting her to be gone. Sometimes he checked the closet to see if her clothes were still there.

"Tell me you understand why I would."

"But I don't."

"Because you're part of it," she said. "I've seen you, with the boys, all of them, how you treat them, how you shape the kind of men they'll be."

She rolled over and looked at him.

"I remember the day you stood there and screamed at Andrew to hit that boy."

"I didn't scream."

"Yes, you did. I was way up in the bleachers and I heard every word. And it was brutal what he did and he wouldn't have done it if you hadn't told him to."

"He has to grow up, Anne."

"Is that what you call it?"

"He has to be ready."

"For what?"

"For the world. As it is."

"And you don't think preparing boys this way is what *makes* the world what it is?"

He was silent.

"I'd really like an answer to that," she said.

Still he was silent.

"Silence you're good at," she said, sitting up and swinging her legs over the edge of the bed. She stared out the window.

"I always thought your not talking about the war was your own business," she said. "Or just between us. But I was wrong. It's much bigger than that."

She sighed. "One son in the ground and another set to go. Is this what you had in mind? Is this what you got them ready for? Is this the plan? And was there some point when you were going to tell them what they were in for?"

She looked at him, waiting for the argument, the reasoned refutation, but there was only the look on his face in the dim light, his cheeks slack beneath a pale sadness in his eyes that had been there ever since the funeral.

"I need to think about that," he said, looking at the wall.

"You do that."

Andrew rapped softly on the glass and when the door opened he looked down for a moment and then up into Petersen's smile.

"Come on in."

They sat in the quiet of the office, Petersen idly handling a pencil on his desk and Andrew fidgeting in the chair, looking out the window, scanning the bookshelves, staring at his hands in his lap—anything to avoid looking into the man's face. It occurred to him to leave, that he'd made a mistake, but he couldn't see how to get from the chair to the door.

"I notice you keep leaving my office in a hurry."

"I know."

"So what brings you back again?"

"I need to talk to someone. Someone I can trust."

Petersen nodded. "Trust me to what? Not tell anyone?"

"That's part of it."

"And the rest?"

"I'm not sure."

There was a silence, and then, "We buried my brother a few days ago."

Petersen sat back in the chair.

"I am very sorry."

Andrew nodded, not looking up.

"Were you surprised?" said Petersen.

"No."

"Well," said Petersen, "the answer is yes. I won't betray you. Unless you're planning to kill people or blow things up."

Andrew shook his head.

"Good," said Petersen. "So. Can I trust you?"

Andrew looked at him, startled.

"Is that an unfair question?" said Peterson.

Andrew shook his head and cleared his throat. "You can trust me now."

"But not before."

"No."

"Why is that?"

"When you asked me why I was taking your class, what I said wasn't true. I was sent to spy on you."

Petersen was quiet for a long time, looking away, gently pressing his fingers to his lips.

"By whom?"

"I'd rather not say."

"That's okay. I can guess. And what did you find?"

"Things aren't the way I thought."

"About the war."

"Yes. And I don't know what to do."

Petersen sighed. "Well, you're a brave young man. I'll give you that."

"I don't think so."

"Why not?"

"Because if I were, I'd know what to do and just do it."

"Oh," said Petersen, drawing out the word, "but it takes courage to let things fall apart and then stick around to see what happens."

"You think so."

"I know so."

Andrew looked at Petersen leaning forward, chin resting on his hand, his face content as if watching a river go by.

"Are you a pacifist?" said Andrew.

"Depends on what you mean."

"That you wouldn't fight no matter what."

Petersen was quiet for a moment.

"That's a tough question. It turns on an absolute, and I have a problem with those."

"But what do you think?"

"I like to think I'd refuse unless I was convinced it was the only way."

"And would you?"

"Would I what?"

"Refuse."

"You mean, would I have the courage?" Petersen shook his head. "I wouldn't know that until I got there."

"And you haven't."

"No. I was too young for Korea and too old for Vietnam. So you see, it's all academic in my case."

"Not for me."

"No, not for you," said Peterson. "So how about you? Where do you stand on the subject of war?"

"I don't know."

"Well, you'd better hurry up, I guess. Time's running out."

Andrew was silent, feeling Petersen's gaze on his face through narrow squinted eyes.

"What, Andrew?"

"I was remembering something. There was this guy who showed up drunk in ROTC class last fall. He came weaving down the aisle to his chair and sat down hard and the Colonel said something like what's the matter with you and have you been drinking? The guy nodded and said yeah he had, and when the Colonel yelled at him to get the hell out, he just stood up and said something like, 'while I'm at it I might as well get the hell out of your fucking Army.'

"And then the Colonel got all red and he went right up to the guy, right in his face and he said," Andrew shook his head, "I'll never forget this part. He said, 'Well, son, I'll tell you exactly what'll happen when you do. I will personally forward your name to your draft board, and college deferment or no, you *will* be reclassified 1-A and you *will* serve in Vietnam in a combat capacity. I promise you that.' And then he walked back to the front of the room and picked up a piece of chalk and started teaching right where he left off."

"What happened then?"

"I remember the guy looking around the room, with a smirk on his face but not like he really meant it. And then he just walked out the door and never came back. I don't know what happened to him."

"So, here you are."

Andrew looked into Petersen's eyes. "What do you think I should do?"

"It doesn't matter what I think."

"It does to me. You must have some idea."

"I do. But you're the one who'll have to live with it, not me." He leaned forward. "I will say this, though. Whatever you do, do it because that's what you've decided to do, knowing why and aware of all the good reasons not to. For that, I might respect you no matter what you did. Because in that moment, you'd be living as a moral actor making choices based on what you believe to be right. What you must not do is simply go along or talk yourself into the lie that you have no choice, because then you give up the most important thing that makes you a human being. And when you do that, you not only lose yourself, you become truly dangerous."

They looked at each other across the long silence that filled the room.

"I'm sorry I spied on you," said Andrew. "And that I lied to you."

"I know."

In William's U.S. history class, they were long past the Civil War. But still he found himself dipping back, interrupting his own lecture on some early twentieth century topic to insert a phrase or a sentence that had no relevance at all that anyone could see. Discussing a Supreme Court case, he was drawing an angle on the blackboard by way of pointing from one idea to another, when he wrote the word 'Spotsylvania' in a scribble they could barely read.

"The bloody angle," he said, still moving his lips in the silence that followed, then taking in a sudden remembered breath, waving his fingers in little circles just below his face as he gave his head a little shake.

"The rifle fire," he said, "was so intense it cut down a tree," holding up his hands to indicate the girth, "two feet thick. Some men were hit by so many bullets at once their bodies simply came apart in the air." As he spoke, students in the front row noticed the color rising in his face and a line of sweat above his eyes.

And then he picked up where he'd left off, visibly shaken to those close enough to see, and strangely distracted inside himself.

It went on this way for weeks.

He was in the middle of describing the Pullman Strike when suddenly he started talking about Union soldiers the night before the battle of Cold Harbor, pinning slips of paper on their uniforms with names and addresses scribbled in pencil, knowing that someone would find their bodies and want to know who they were.

And then he explained the reality of the bullet.

"You see," he said, "when a man is shot, he doesn't just grab his arm or leg to cover the hole and go on fighting or whatever he was doing. Especially when it's a .53 caliber."

He was looking over their heads and out the window to the cemetery across the road.

"It had a slow muzzle velocity that made it lumber through the air. So instead of passing neatly through whatever living tissue it encountered, it *bulled* its way in," he said, making a punching motion with his fist, "crushing and shattering everything in its path, taking out whole sections of bone, all but cutting arms and legs in two."

He paused, still looking out the window, before going on, his voice soft and low.

"The surgeons found just a gaping hole and had no choice but to amputate what was left, having nothing to connect it to."

He shook his head.

"It's not like the movies at all, you see," he muttered, looking at the floor, a finger on his lips.

In moments like these he didn't look at them or respond to hands going up or notice the clearing of throats or even Peter Hay whispering in the back of the room.

His account of the battle of the Wilderness occurred midway through questioning a student about Teddy Roosevelt's policy of busting trusts. He walked across the room while the student was still talking and stood at a window looking out, his face just inches from the glass, the students turning in their chairs, staring at the back of his head.

"The woods caught fire," he said. "Too many sparks from too many guns, everyone blinded by the smoke, attacking in the wrong direction, shooting the wrong people. And the wounded," his voice trailing off so only the boys nearby could hear, "the wounded couldn't move, couldn't get out of the way of the fire coming slowly through the woods all night long. Burning them alive, just as slowly."

When he told them about the pigs—wandering in the night over the rain swept battlefield at Shiloh, the sky full of thunder and lightning as they fed upon the corpses—his lips moved around the words but he made no sound, himself the only audience as he watched it happening before him.

By the middle of May, unnoticed by him, a few students had snuck in to witness the rare and bizarre spectacle of what some believed was a teacher losing his mind.

Andrew attended his last classes of the semester. On Wednesday afternoons he put on his uniform and went to drill but left it to his officers to carry on in what had clearly become his growing absence. The Colonel was sympathetic, resting a hand on his shoulder as he spoke to him.

"If you were searching for a reason to go, you've surely found it now. I know you'll make us proud."

His roommates, however, sensed a distance that inserted itself like the thin end of a wedge pushing inward day by day to widen the space between them. They rushed to comfort him when he returned from Joshua's funeral, offering to go for drives in the country or swims in the river, asking him if he was okay or needed to talk. But something in his quiet refusal signaled a separation that soon grew into alienation, a subtle yet unmistakable betrayal of the assumption of solidarity and shared fate that had bound them together in spite of their differences. He was no longer one of them, but they could not yet see who or what he had joined with in their place.

Anne found William standing at the edge of a line of trees beside the cemetery, looking away toward the grassy field running down to the woods below. His body was still except for his hands raised in front of his waist, the movements fine and subtle as if keeping his balance.

She watched him stare across the field, until she saw the movement of his lips forming words, with no one there, and then she looked about to see if anyone was watching before walking across the road and into the trees.

He did not hear her coming, unaware of the school behind him, the boys hurrying to class. He felt only the saddle beneath him, the reins held loosely in his hands as he looked out over the thousands of dead and wounded, the movement of those still living making the ground seem to crawl, his horse backing away from the stench carried on a breeze from the other side.

He did not feel the hand on his arm or hear the voice in his ear.

He felt only the agitation of wanting to leave and yet strangely unable to move, his skin clammy and chilled. The horse dipped its head and pawed the ground, and then suddenly William was standing on the ground, everything that had been before him now gone, including the memory, leaving only the desire to flee and the sweat and the chill and the trembling in his hands.

His eyes darted back and forth as he looked at her, unable to speak, his face pinched around the effort to make his mind focus on a thought or even just a word. He dropped his hands to his sides and looked at the trees and the cemetery and Butler Hall, as if triangulating distance and direction to figure where he was.

"What are you doing here?" he said.

She looked at him, saying nothing as he made a brittle little smile, then looked at his watch, "I'm late for class," and turned and walked away across the road.

On his way to Adams Hall for coffee and a look at the *New York Times*, it first appeared to William as a dark spot on the slate walk that caught his attention like a stain in the middle of a clean shirt. When he drew near, he saw it was wet and then red and he stopped and stood over it, knowing what it was. Boys passed him by in little knots of energy, their voices dropping to an earnest whisper, then swelling into laughter when they achieved a safer distance. He didn't notice, being so intent on the puddle at his feet. A breeze moved across his face, causing him to lift his head in the direction of its sweet scent, and then he looked back down at the dry grey stone.

He took a cup of coffee in the faculty lounge and stared at the front page of the *Times*. Jack came out of his office and as they talked about final exams and the nearness of graduation, William couldn't help but feel comforted by Jack's hand on his shoulder, and when he looked up at the spot where the steel plate sat just beneath the skin, he felt a sadness that made him turn his eyes to the window.

When William walked out into the spring air, Peter Hay's was the first face he saw. The boy smiled and he smiled in return and was lifting his hand in a little salute when out of the corner of his eye he saw the blood running down the index finger toward the thumb. He quickly dropped his hand so the boy wouldn't see and took his handkerchief from his pocket to wrap the finger, but the entire hand was now covered in blood, the handkerchief turning red.

"Hi, Mr. Carson."

William mumbled hello, not comprehending how the boy could not see. He hurried by, holding his hand. There was no pain, no wound that he could see, but no matter how much he wiped away there was still more, the pores themselves seeming to have opened to let it out.

He cut across the grass toward home, it being all he could do to keep himself from breaking into a run. He took the back stairs two at a time and once through the door, he tore at his clothes, littering the floor as he hurried down the hall to the bathroom, tight little cries coming from his throat. He glanced in the bathroom mirror and then turned and stood still in front of it, unable to take his eyes away from the spattering of blood across his face.

Stepping through the back door and putting the groceries on the kitchen counter, Anne was surprised to hear the shower running so late in the afternoon when William would normally be coaching lacrosse. She put away the groceries and then, still hearing the sound of water, went down the hall and stood outside the bathroom door. In the stillness beneath the water's steady rush into the air, a lightness crept into her belly, a precursor of alarm, and she turned the knob and pushed the door open in front of her.

The air was full of steam, the floor wet with reflected spray from the tub where he sat, knees drawn up beneath his chin and arms wrapped around his shins. The hot water flowed down over his back and head, red from the scalding. He didn't move. Quickly she reached in and turned the water off, kneeling down beside the tub.

"Will," she said, "what's the matter?"

He stared over his knees, his arms tightening their grip on his legs, holding on.

"What happened?" she said. And then he turned and looked at her, his eyes full of tears, the skin on his face scrubbed raw.

They were silent as she patted a towel over his skin, the color of sunburn. His eyes were dry as he looked down and away. She felt an unfamiliar tenderness in his flesh beneath her fingers, a yielding she could barely recall, and as she passed in front of him she noticed a sadness in his eyes so deep it startled her into a stillness that left them both suspended in the steamy air, the towel hanging down onto the floor.

She made a pot of tea and when he dressed they sat together on the couch. He held the mug in both hands and stared out over the brim.

"Tell me what happened."

"I don't know," he said. "Except that," lifting a hand and staring at it, pink from the scrubbing, then looking her, "there was all this blood."

"Where?"

"On my hands."

"You cut yourself."

He shook his head.

"What did you do to your face?"

He touched his cheek.

"I don't know."

They lay in the dark, unable to sleep.

Softly, he cleared his throat.

"The question you asked me the other night," he said. "About the boys. What I was preparing them for. The answer is yes."

He lay awake, unable to empty his mind of the memory of blood and trying to account for the minutes or hours it took to come home and what happened after. He tried to reconstruct the day but he couldn't remember which it was or what he did or was supposed to do. He got out of bed and went to his study where he stood over the desk and looked down at the calendar, but one day seemed like all the rest.

He went across the hall into the boys' old room, standing in the dark and looking at the bunk beds against the wall. He stepped in closer and laid his hand on the wood and heard their small, young voices drift up through the dark.

He went back to bed.

In the middle of the night, as boys in the rooms above turned over in their dreaming, he fell, reluctantly, into sleep.

And dreamed the dream.

Suddenly he sat up in the bed and looked about the room, his face straining to locate the direction of a sound. Then he was up and down the hall, his bare feet slapping on the floor as he ran out the back door, his chest tight with fear as he fled across the terrace and down the slope to the lawn. Back and forth he ran across the cool grass, grazing trees as he passed them by, falling to the ground, scrambling to his feet, running in circles past bombed out houses, the burning truck, the old woman rotting in the street. Until suddenly it is no longer a dream, cobblestones beneath his feet and bullets whining through the air in search of him, seeking him out, tearing off the little finger, nicking an ear and the tender spot inside his thigh, while all around him men appear like targets in a penny arcade and he just as quickly shoots them down. His ears fill with the sound of his own breathing as he bolts up the stairs, the blue door slamming against the wall as he flings it open and runs down into the cellar and through the darkened tunnel, the smell of earth all around him as he mounts the stairs, up and up, his lungs straining from the effort, sweat pouring down his face, and on down the hall, the end receding before him, pulling farther away with every step

until suddenly everything comes to a stop and the corner rushes up
to meet him and he circles round and they are face to face at last,
crying out, so startled to see each other across the narrow distance,
their rifles raised instinctively. He is as young as William, his face
streaked with dirt, his uniform torn below the knee, his head bare,
hair shaved down to stubble, making him look younger still, almost
tender, like a boy sent off to camp.

"Put down the gun!"

"*Nicht schiessen!*"   [Don't shoot me!]

"Put it down!"

"*Ich spreche kein Englisch!*"   [I don't speak English!]

"Surrender! Now!"

"*Was soll ich machen?*"   [What do you want me to do?]

"Put the gun down or I'll kill you so help me!"

"*Bitte. Ich habe niemanden umgebracht.*"

                                        [Please. I've killed no one.]

"Speak English, god damn it, or shut the fuck up!"

"*Ich heisse Dieter.*"   [My name is Dieter.]

"Stop the bullshit and put it down!"

motioning his rifle toward the floor

"*Das kann ich nicht, sonsst schiessen sie mich!*"

                                        [I can't. You will shoot me!]

the boy's eyes darting back and forth and then slowly he is pointing
the rifle down, his face trembling as he stares into William's eyes

"*Ich bin erst seit einem monat im dienst.*"

                                        [I was drafted just a month ago.]

"Shut up!"

"*Mein gewehr ist überhaupt nicht gelade. Meine munition is
verschossen.*"   [*The rifle's not even loaded.*
                                        I used up all my cartridges.]

"Put the rifle on the floor!"

"*Bitte nicht schiessen. Wir sitzen im selben boot. Bitte!*"

                                        [Don't shoot me. I am just like
                                        you. Please!]

the boy turning his face away, eyes narrowed to a squint as he drops
the rifle, raising his hands as if warding off a blow

The time for what happens now, no time at all. Something in the boy's face is how William would remember it, and yet never able to put a name to exactly what it was, so small, so fleeting, and yet making all the difference. An expression, a softness, a vulnerability perhaps, seen in the face and the stain where the boy had wet his pants, combining to lay claim to being merely human and not one of those who'd killed William's friends one after another. Not the enemy, the cell within the body of the beast. Perhaps it was that, and the fear that never went away and the great fatigue that suddenly came over him, the longing to go home, to be rid of this, to be rid of him, to be rid of it all. And the longing and the weariness and the loss flowing through him and twisting and hardening into the simple desire to kill merely because he could, to silence the voice, deny the claim, feel the power and release in the instant of annihilation. Whatever it was wrapped around his heart and then down his arm and into the finger embracing the trigger, and before he knew a single other thing, before so much as a word or a thought had crossed his mind, the room filled with the dry, merciless explosion that seemed to erupt from the end of his arm and the boy's head snapping back as the bullet tore through his throat and the blood shot out from him, spattering across William's face, the warm drops cooling against his skin. The boy fell to the floor and William staggered back, stunned at the sight of him writhing, his throat filling as he drowned in blood. And then William heard the boy begin to cry, weeping at his own death coming over him, and he turned, his mind suddenly filled with horror, and ran back around the corner and down the hall to the stairs beyond.

A wild man running in circles on the lawn beneath a vault of starlit sky, dorm windows ablaze with light, boys leaning out to see what was the matter, and in the glow cast across the grass, the woman running toward him, her nightgown flowing out behind, which the boys would remember years later as something ghostly and unreal.

She ran up to him, but he only looked at her as if she were someone else, his eyes focused in front of her face, screaming "No!"

as he thrust out his arms and knocked her to the ground. And then he was off again, screaming and waving his arms as he ran through the dark. She got to her feet and suddenly saw the figure of a man leap over the low stone wall by the road and plant himself in William's path, not moving as William lunged on, gaining speed as he charged toward him, and when he was all but upon him the man dropping to the ground to make a tight little mound that caught William below the knees and sent him flying forward, tumbling and rolling across the grass. And then the man rose to throw himself on top of him, wrapping his arms around William to hold him down as he screamed and kicked and waved his arms in the air.

Anne knelt down beside him, looking into his eyes wild and full of tears, and then his face softening around the slowing of his breath, the earth beneath him, looking up into the sky and opening his throat as he began to cry.

Jack let go and sat back on grass.

"I'm so sorry," said William, his voice frantic, just above a whisper, his hands rubbing back and forth across his face, "I'm so sorry, so sorry . . ."

"It's all right," said Anne leaning in close, but as he said the words over and over again, she realized he was not speaking to her.

Anne sat William on the couch and laid a blanket over him while he looked at her, tears still coming from his eyes, then bowing his head as she stroked her fingers through his hair.

She walked with Jack to the door.

"I couldn't sleep," he said. "I was out for a walk."

"I'm glad you were."

"Are you going to be all right?"

She paused, looking past him at the dark trunks of the elms and a star low in the sky.

"I don't know," she said. "But you don't have to stay. He won't hurt me."

"But he knocked you down."

"I don't think it was me."

"If you're sure," he said.

"I am. Thank you."

"All right," he said. "Goodnight then."

"Goodnight."

She put a kettle to heat on the stove and sat beside him on the couch.

"It's all right," she said. "You're home now." She looked into his eyes. "Do you know where you are?"

He nodded, eyes wide, saying nothing.

"Was it the dream?"

He didn't move, looking at her, back and forth from one eye to the other.

"You went around the corner," she said, and he looked away, his head moving slowly up and down, and then his face collapsing as he looked at her and away, struggling to form the words.

"It's not a dream."

She looked at him, her face suddenly smooth.

"You mean it really happened."

She could barely make out a nod in the faint movement of his head.

She waited in the silence.

"It was a soldier," he said, "around the corner."

"What was he doing?"

"Just standing there, pointing his rifle at me. Scared I was going to kill him. Just like me."

He took in a breath, held it for a moment, then let it go.

"He was the first man I ever killed."

"In North Africa."

"No. France."

Her face took on a puzzled look. "But you were in North Africa and Italy before—"

"You don't understand," he said.

"No."

"The others were different."

He wiped a corner of the blanket across his eyes.

"I killed them all. But in a way, I think you could say I didn't really mean it. It was just there to be done. And I was afraid they'd kill me if I didn't. But this one . . . this one," he looked at her, "I took his life. You know what I'm saying? I *took* it. On purpose. I didn't have to. And I could feel how much he wanted me not to. He told me. I'm sure of it now, even though he was talking German." He shook his head. "But I did it anyway. Because I wanted to. Because I wanted to kill *him*. This one. And I can't even remember why."

"He had a gun—"

He shook his head. "I was the dangerous one."

His voice dropped to a whisper. "It was a murder," he said and then he began to tremble at the word spoken aloud for the first time, hanging in the air between them as tears rolled down his face.

She looked into his eyes, her own beginning to blur, murmuring, "no, no," as she reached across the distance between them to stroke his head, "don't think that—"

"But it was—"

"No," she said, softly shushing him. "It was all murder, don't you see? Throwing boys in together to kill each other and then leaving them to carry the burden all by themselves."

"I had no mercy," he said, the sobs coming from him as he buried his face in the soft folds of her lap.

"No, Billy," she said, rocking him back and forth, "war has no mercy, not for him, not for you, not for Josh," and then leaning forward, her face resting on his back as they rocked together, the sounds of their grief filling the air and drifting upward toward the boys who lay in their darkened rooms, listening to the strange sounds coming up from down below.

2

Slowly, by degrees delicious to them both, Andrew settled in, became more practiced and at ease, forgetting himself from time to time as he wandered in the magical terrain where sex and love commingle.

He carried the words inside until releasing them was the only way to stop hearing them in his mind.

"I love you," he said.

They were out back of her apartment and she was attaching a DUMP THE HUMP sticker to the bumper of her car. She'd been going on about Lyndon Johnson deciding not to run for re-election and the prospect of Robert Kennedy or Eugene McCarthy replacing him on the ticket instead of Hubert Humphrey. For days she talked about the Democratic Convention coming up in Chicago in August, and the chance to bring the war home and lay it at the government's feet. He saw the look on her face when she talked about Kennedy, calling him 'Bobby,' her eyes wide and full of light.

She looked up and he wondered if she heard.

"I said I love you."

She looked at him.

"I know," she said. "I also know what you want me to say."

"And?"

"Those are dangerous words for me."

"Why?"

"Because coming from a guy it sounds like something he's giving you. But it keeps turning out to be more about him than me."

"You think I'm like that."

"No," she said. "But that's just it. It never *seems* like that until it's too late."

He looked down at the ground, then up at the bumper.

"So, you don't love me, too."

"That's not what I said."

"So, maybe you do."

"Maybe," she said, and he looked up to see a little smile.

When Allen Ginsberg came to campus for a poetry reading, Ruth insisted they go early so they could get seats up front and look up into the man's darkly bearded face as he read his notorious "Howl" to the audience of young college students, most of whom had little idea of who he was except for being weird and far out and saying things they had never heard spoken at a public event. Like *cock* and *cunt* and *snatches* and *balling* and *fucking up the ass*, the last one making some of them squirm in their seats.

But Andrew was taken right away by something the other students seemed to miss as they waited to be shocked

the best minds of my generation destroyed by

madness,

wondering what kind of madness that would be, if it was anything like living in a world that was falling apart

who passed through universities with radiant cool eyes

hallucinating Arkansas and Blake-light tragedy

among the scholars of war,

and suddenly he thought of his father teaching the history of the Civil War, looking up from a stack of ungraded papers on his desk in his little study at home, the light reflecting off his glasses, the faint look of annoyance at the interruption passing quickly across his face, as if disturbed out of sleep. This is where Andrew often saw his father in his mind, or standing along the sideline of the lacrosse field, leaning on the attack stick he always carried when a game was in play, something to occupy his hands while his mind raced ahead to what was coming next. Or turning around in his chapel seat and looking up to the balcony to find his father's face, chancing on the moment when their eyes would meet with what Andrew thought to be a little smile, a nod of recognition known only to them, crossing the distance and carrying with it the comfort of a father content with who his son was turning out to be

> *Moloch! Solitude! Filth! Ugliness! Ashcans and unobtainable*
> *dollars! Children screaming under the*
> *stairways! Boys sobbing in armies! Old men*
> *weeping in the parks!*

and now he saw his father in the middle of the night, standing in the hall, his mother whispering in his ear to wake him up and steer him back to bed

> *Moloch the incomprehensible prison! Moloch the*
> *crossbone soulless jailhouse and Congress of*
> *sorrows! Moloch whose buildings are judgment!*
> *Moloch the vast stone of war!*

and in the dark of a moonless night, opening the bathroom door on his way back to bed and suddenly his father appearing before him looking straight into his face and yet something in his manner saying he was not awake, was not there just inches from his son

> *Moloch whose mind is pure machinery! Moloch whose*
> *blood is running money! Moloch whose fingers*
> *are ten armies!*

Andrew afraid, gripping Ruth's hand, not knowing who or what is blocking his path, watching his father turn without a sound and walk back down the hall, looking up at the wild man poet on the platform, taking out a handkerchief to wipe the perspiration from his face, the audience on its feet in thunderous applause, not knowing what else to do.

Walking back to Ruth's apartment, memories of his father and thoughts of the war are impossible to separate in his mind, unable to imagine telling his father that he would not do what was expected, the dread certainty of being disowned if he will not go to war.

"You don't know that," said Ruth, sitting across from him at the kitchen table. "He's lost a son. He may have changed."

"I know my dad. He took the flag, for Christ's sake."

"Maybe he was just trying to save the situation."

"No," he said. "It wasn't that. He wanted it. And he'll want mine when the time comes."

"Do you really think so? You think he doesn't love you more than that?"

"Sure he does. But some things matter more. He loved Josh, too."

"What could matter more?"

"I don't know," he said. "I just know it isn't me. He never lets on. He's too perfect for that. Not a hair out of place. Shoes shined, even at lacrosse practice, always a crease in his pants. He's always right and always in control. He could argue the Pope out of religion. All he cares about is that I measure up. He was proud when I told him I'd joined the Army. My mom freaked out, but he was proud, like I did it just for him."

"But he's your father, Andrew. He has to come around sooner or later."

"To what? A deserter? A draft dodger? A traitor?"

She watched him turn the corner of the placemat into a tight little roll. She put her hand on top of his.

"When I was little," he said, "I was snooping in his bureau one afternoon and I found this little box all covered in leather with his name in gold letters. Inside was a medal. I didn't know then it was a Silver Star, which you only get for extraordinary valor in combat. I took it out and was looking at it when all of a sudden he was in the room and I'll never forget the look on his face like I'd discovered a big secret I wasn't supposed to know."

"What'd he do?"

"Nothing. He just looked at me, but like he wasn't seeing me. Then he took it away and told me to stay out of his things. I didn't, though. The secret was about him and I wanted to know what it was. And then one day when I looked in the drawer it wasn't there anymore and I never saw it again."

He looked at her. "I'd almost rather go than have to deal with him."

"No," she said, "you wouldn't."

216

He walked into the woods east of the college, climbing through maples and oaks to stands of pine more than a hundred years old. He stopped in a clearing, looking up to a commotion in the sky, a band of crows pursuing a hawk, diving near, squawking, harassing, until finally it rode a current of air to a great height and flew slowly away.

Andrew went on through the woods until he came to a great white pine, its twin trunks rising amidst a maze of dead branches until the green emerged high above where it found the light among the crowns of other trees. He sat down beneath it, leaning back, his hands resting on the bed of needles, and then he thought of Joshua and began to cry. He'd been this way ever since the funeral, always on the edge of tears, never knowing when he'd feel the wave rising in his chest and his eyes going soft. It took almost nothing at all, just the memory of his brother's voice or a smell that reminded him of home.

He grew quiet and looked off among the trees, the forest floor covered with fern and princess pine, and then into his mind drifted his father's face, hard and smooth and unforgiving, staring across a distance that seemed impossible to bridge.

He looked up through the branches at the sky and closed his eyes, listening for his brother's voice, the wind moving through the trees, cooling his face. Then he stood and looked up along the trunk of the old pine, shaking his head.

"It doesn't matter. It doesn't matter at all."

He turned and walked out of the woods.

He told Ruth over supper. She'd been looking at him for a long time as he played with his food.

"You've decided," she said.

He nodded.

She laid down her fork and rested her chin on her fist.

"I'm not going," he said.

Her lips drew back in a smile, then sank back down.

"How'd you come to that?"

He sighed and looked out the window at the lights of the town.

"I was up in the woods and I kept waiting for Josh to tell me what to do." He made a little smile. "But he didn't. And then I realized he already had, the last time he wrote to me. And besides, it's up to me, just like it was for him."

He looked at her, his eyes rimmed with tears.

"He was a really good brother to me. The best. And then it dawned on me that it doesn't make any difference how good he was. He's dead, all the same. He always did what he was supposed to do. Not all the time, you know. He fooled around. But he never went up against Dad. He studied hard, he played hard. He joined the Marines."

He wiped his sleeve across his eyes and when he spoke, he spat out the words, slow and measured.

"And you know what? It makes no fucking difference at all. He's *dead*. He's just so much shit on the pile for all anybody knows."

"Except you."

"Right," he said, a sob struggling from his throat. "And you know what they did to him? My mom told me. The whole side of his face was shot to hell," tears rolling down his cheeks, "he didn't have a face anymore. My brother didn't have a face. And for what?"

His eyes were wide as he stared at her, waiting for her to say something, but she only shook her head and wiped her own tears away.

"So," he said, "that's how."

The door to Petersen's office was standing open when he arrived. He was sitting back in his chair, his feet propped up on the desk, a book open in his lap, the light reflecting off his glasses when he looked up and smiled and beckoned Andrew to come inside.

Andrew sat down and cleared his throat.

"I've decided not to go."

Petersen was quiet for a moment, looking at Andrew.

"You're sure about this."

"Yes."

"It's a brave thing to do."

Andrew shrugged and looked down.

"Do you have a plan?"

"I have to write my parents. They're planning on coming up."

"And after that?"

"I don't know."

"You might want to think about that. The government's not likely to just let you go. They have thousands of guys like you to deal with, but they'll still find time for you."

"The Colonel will make sure of that."

Petersen reached for a pen. "I'd rather you not tell anyone about this," he said, writing on a pad and tearing off the top sheet and handing it to Andrew. "These are phone numbers of anti-war groups in Boston. The day may come when you need them."

Andrew looked down at the paper, folding it in half and then again.

"Thank you," he said, standing and stepping toward the door.

"Godspeed," said Petersen.

Andrew made a little start and smiled.

"What?" said Petersen.

"I didn't think Marxists believed in God."

Petersen smiled. "Surprise, surprise."

William refused to leave the apartment, remembering the sight of the open windows full of light and boys leaning out to watch Anne and Jack leading him back inside.

"Everybody knows," he said, shaking his head and staring down into a cup of coffee.

On the second day, Jack came by.

"Cliff is taking your classes," he said, sitting on the couch. "He says to tell you not to worry."

"Does he know what happened?"

"No. But neither do I, really. Can you tell me?"

William watched him push a lock of hair from his forehead and could see from the angle of light the squared off indentation in his skull.

"Something about Josh?"

"In a way." He looked at him. "The war. Our war."

Jack nodded.

"I've had nightmares ever since," said William. "A nightmare. It's been the same one every time. Only I could never remember what it was, until the other night. And it turns out it wasn't a dream after all."

"We all have those," said Jack.

"This was different."

"How so?"

"I killed a man."

"Nothing different in that."

"Except he wasn't armed."

A little murmur from Jack's throat. "You have any idea how many times I was tempted to do that?"

"Yes," said William, "but you didn't."

"No, but I might've."

"But you didn't."

"And you think," said Jack, "that makes me somehow . . . better."

"And you don't?"

"No, I do not. I think it makes me lucky."

"I appreciate what you're trying to do," said William, "but—"

"And what is that?"

"Make me feel better."

"Oh, no," said Jack, "that's not it at all. I don't think you'll ever feel better. Not much anyway. The fact is, you're going to have to find a way to live with this. We all do. It doesn't matter what degree of bad it is, it doesn't go away. We're stuck with it."

"I don't know what to do."

"For starters, get poor Cliff out of your classroom."

"But they all know."

"Well," said Jack, "they know something. Or think they do. But the next thing they're going to know will be the next thing you do. And that is up to you."

William stood inside his office and faced the door as he tried to slow the beating of his heart. Then he watched his hand reach down and turn the knob and open the door.

As he walked into the classroom the boys grew quiet, watching his progress toward the desk and lectern. He looked up and noticed two boys he didn't recognize sitting in the back row. He fixed his eyes on them and they began to fidget in their chairs.

"Are you lost?" he said.

They smiled sheepishly and looked from one to the other.

"Close the door on your way out," he said, turning to the board and taking a piece of chalk from the tray. A scuffling from behind, the door softly closing.

He wrote 'Supreme Court' on the board, watching the chalk trail out the white line, arriving at the 't' and letting the line continue down until it reached halfway to the bottom of the board to form something like the trunk of a tree. He stared at it for a moment, then turned the short stub of chalk on its side and used it to widen the trunk and give it texture, then sent it upward to fill in the branches. He was at it for quite awhile until stopped by the sound of a throat clearing behind him.

He let his hand drop slowly from the board and looked out at the boys sitting in their rows of chairs.

"Is there a question?"

Kaplan, short and bespectacled in the front row, raised his hand. "What is that, sir?"

William cocked his head. "You don't know?"

Kaplan looked at the boy next to him, then back at William. "It looks like a tree."

"Good, Mr. Kaplan. I was beginning to worry. And what sort of tree do you think it is?"

"I don't know."

William turned and looked at the board, then back at Kaplan. "Well, neither do I."

It was late at night and the boys on the floors above had gone to bed. William and Anne sat outside on the steps beneath a sliver of moon hanging in the sky above the lawn. He looked into the upper branches of the elms arching out into the air and imagined a woman's hair thrown forward over her head. They were silent for a long time, their bodies close but not touching, his cigarette glowing in the dark.

"I am so sorry," he whispered.

"I know," she said.

He looked at her. "You do?"

"Oh," she said. "You're apologizing to me."

"Who else?"

"I was thinking about that young man. I think you were talking to him the other night."

He drew on the cigarette and blew the smoke into the air.

"I was awake, you know. Out there," motioning with his hand toward the lawn, the burning end of the cigarette making a little spiral in the air. "I wasn't dreaming. It was absolutely real, except that it wasn't."

He looked at the sky above the horizon and suddenly imagined Joshua lying beneath that same shade of blue, his eyes open, staring upward, seeing nothing.

William woke to the sound of someone weeping, which he soon realized to be himself. His skin was clammy against the cloth of his pajamas.

"It's all right," came Anne's voice, "it's—" and then stopping herself before she could say that it was only a dream. They were quiet as he rolled onto his back and stared up at the ceiling.

"He was so young," he said.

"So were you."

He looked at her. "He was somebody's Joshua."

He looked out the window.

"You know that letter of his," he said, "the one about being so scared. I could have written that."

"Then why so little sympathy for him?"

He was quiet for a moment, staring out the window. "I guess because I thought why should it be any different?"

"So you pass it on," she said. "His turn."

"Yes." He turned to her. "I can't stand that you think I had something to do with Josh being killed. It makes me sick inside."

She looked at him in the darkness, suddenly wanting to tell him that it wasn't what she meant, but she could see in the gaze passing between them that it was too late for that.

"But you did," she said. "And so did I. We made a man of him, and that's what got him killed. I could have fought against it, but I kept telling myself I didn't have the right, it was up to men to decide such things. I mean, what does a woman know about war?

"Then again," she said, "what men know that might keep younger men from going, they never tell." She looked at him, his face still in the darkness, his eyes full of pain. "I guess I knew as much about war as Josh before he went away."

"More," he said. "You knew more."

He sat up on the side of the bed and didn't move for a long time.

"What," she said.

"I don't know exactly. I was thinking about Josh. He was missing for months, but when they found him, he'd been dead only a little while."

"I've thought about that, too."

"So what was he doing out there all that time?"

"Maybe he was lost," she said.

"Maybe." He looked at her.

"You think he was trying to get home," she said.

He nodded, then picked up a corner of the bed sheet and pressed it into his eyes.

"Do you think forgiveness is possible?" he said.

"I don't know."

On the morning of Memorial Day, from down the hill at the far end of Main Street came the distant sound of marching bands assembling and getting themselves in tune.

"We have to talk about Andrew," she said.

"You think he shouldn't go."

She nodded.

"You think he should desert or refuse the draft—"

"Whatever it takes—"

"Become a fugitive. Go to prison. Be seen as a coward."

She looked at him.

"If you tell him not to go," she said, "he won't."

William shook his head. "He has to decide that for himself."

"No," she said. "That isn't fair. It's too much to ask. He has the weight of you and Josh and the whole world bearing down on him, telling him to do his duty and show what a man he is and how much he loves his country. Nothing is simply up to him."

She waited for the argument, but nothing came.

"You remember when I slapped you," she said, "and what you said afterward about war and being in hell?"

"Yes."

"If that's what you really meant," she said, "then how can you send your own son to hell? What would make you do that?"

He looked at her. "But if every parent did what you're suggesting—"

"If they did," she said, "then we wouldn't go to war and we'd have to find another way. Besides, we're not every parent. This is about you and me and Andrew."

He went to the window. Across the lawn and down the hill came the sound of bands setting themselves in motion, first the driving beat of the drums and then the honking blare of brass and clarinets joining in, the notes clashing in an earnest muddle of sound.

"What if I hadn't gone?" he said. "What if I had stayed home?"

"What do you mean?"

"I mean how would you have felt about that? Would you have been proud of me? Would you have visited me in prison? Would you have waited for me?"

"That was different."

"Was it? How? Was that a better war than this one? Is that the issue, how good or bad the war is?" He looked at her. "But you've never said anything about this particular war. You don't want Andrew in any war, isn't that it?"

She nodded.

"Then why me in that one? Why the hesitation now? Why not, 'Of course I would've stood by you if you'd refused to go.'"

"Did you think of not going?"

"Sure I did," he said, "but not so anybody would know. I couldn't imagine not going because I couldn't imagine living with you ashamed of me, or my mom and dad and all my friends."

"I wouldn't have been ashamed—"

"I think you would." He looked at her shaking her head.

"Tell me," he said, "when you saw me in uniform before I went overseas, that last day at home, how did you feel?"

"I was afraid. And worried."

"But weren't you also proud? Just a little? Tell the truth."

She looked at him for a moment.

"Yes," she said, "I was. We all were. It's what I was supposed to feel. The patriotic wife. And maybe that's all it takes. Feeling what we're supposed to feel."

As the head of the parade reached the far corner of the campus she imagined the ranks of children, boy scouts and girl scouts, marching behind the veterans, the steady cadence of the drums keeping everyone in step.

William sat by the grave, his hand resting on the mound of unsettled earth, and suddenly wished he'd stayed in the room when Anne insisted on opening the box. She never spoke of what she saw and now he wanted to know.

It seems so small, he thought, this little mound. He closed his eyes and imagined him down below, what was left of him decomposing in the dark, and it occurred to him that Joshua would forever barely be a man, never a father or a husband or a teacher or a lawyer or whatever he'd have gone on to be, his entire life nothing more than preparation for a brief and brutal sojourn in hell. What could possibly be the point of that? *Could* that have been the point of all those years, just to send him off to that? And yet, someone had to go, didn't they? Offered up, even sacrificed? Like the Aztecs appeasing the gods by cutting out a young heart and lifting it, still beating, into the air.

He looked up and saw the young man, startled to find him outside the dream, standing in a grove of trees at the edge of the cemetery, his face young and smooth, the uniform rumpled and soiled. They stared at each other, not moving.

"You want to know why," said William, "but I don't know. Except that I was scared and tired and sick of it all. Sick of you, sick of everyone I cared about being killed."

"*The same for me.*"

"I truly wish I hadn't done it."

"*Then why?*"

"It was all I could think to do."

"*A failure of imagination, then.*"

William looked down at the stone, the dates bracketing a life, the difference amounting to a scant twenty-two. He looked up at the trees, the wind moving through the branches.

"Can you forgive me?" he said.

But the young man just looked at him and then was gone.

Andrew decided to tell the Colonel because it seemed the honorable thing to do.

"Are you out of your mind?" said the Colonel, standing up behind his desk. "You're the top ranked cadet in the corps. We *chose* you. Do you have any idea how that will look? How it will reflect on us? On me?"

"Yes, sir, I think I do. I am sorry."

"You're sorry. But you're going to do it anyway."

Andrew squinted and blinked his eyes, as if leaning into a stiff wind.

"Yes."

"Well," said the Colonel, "at least you had the balls to tell me yourself. But you're going to need them where you're going."

Andrew swallowed. It was all he could do to keep from running out the door.

"You ought to be ashamed of yourself," said the Colonel. "And with your brother and all."

Andrew looked at him, steeling himself against the rage coming across the desk.

"Actually, sir, I think he'd want me not to go."

"He would, would he."

Andrew watched the Colonel lean forward, hands balled into fists against the desk, the color rising in his face.

"You know, Colonel, I used to think it was the VC who killed my brother. But I had it only partly right."

"Get out."

"He'd still be here if it wasn't for men like you—"

"I said, get out!"

And then Andrew turned and walked away.

Andrew woke to a pounding and thrashing coming from the other room. He listened as the sound was joined by deep, sobbing groans, then threw back the covers and hurried to the living room where he found Ruth kneeling in front of the couch, her body heaving forward as she slammed her fists into the cushions.

"God damn motherfuckers!" she screamed, and he looked down at the morning paper on the floor beside her and the banner headline, *Kennedy Assassinated in Los Angeles Hotel.*

"It's not enough they kill King," she said, her hair falling over her face as she flailed against the couch, "they have to kill Bobby, too," driving each word home with a punch as if she were beating something to death, waiting for it to still beneath her fists, unable to resist, until finally she sat back on her heels, panting as she looked up at him through swollen eyes. And then she let herself cry, her body shuddering with the effort. He sat down on the floor beside her.

"We are so fucked," she said. "We deserve to die."

Andrew was lifting the last box of books to carry downstairs to Ruth's car when Joe walked through the door. They stood for a moment looking at each other across the room. It was the first time he'd been back to the dorm since speaking with the Colonel.

"Is it your brother?" said Joe. "Is he the reason?" folding his arms across his chest and rocking back and forth on the balls of his feet.

"No."

"Then why?"

Andrew took a step forward. "I have to go."

"I don't fucking care," said Joe. "I want to know when you turned into a pussy who betrays his friends."

"I didn't."

"The hell you didn't. You're leaving us to do your fighting for you."

"It's not my fight."

"Then who's is it?"

"I don't know. The Vietnamese, maybe. I just know it isn't mine."

"Not even when your country says it is."

Andrew felt his arms let down beneath the weight of the box and he put it on the floor.

"I don't know what my country says. And even if I did, I don't know if it would matter."

"It did to your brother."

"Maybe it shouldn't have."

"So he died for nothing? Is that what you're saying?"

Andrew bent down and picked up the box. "I guess I am. Yes. That's what I'm saying. Josh died for nothing. You want to read his letters? You want to know what you're getting into?"

Joe looked at him, his face hard, and took a step back. "I know what I'm getting into."

A silence settled in around them as they looked at each other, Joe working the muscles in his jaw.

"So," said Andrew, "do I have to fight you to get out of here?"

Joe looked down and shook his head as he stepped aside.

For days Ruth stayed in the apartment, sleeping until mid-morning and then moping about dressed in a bathrobe and a ragged pair of slippers. She didn't wash her hair or brush her teeth and had no interest in sex. She drank beer in the afternoon and smoked cigarettes and sat up into the night until she couldn't stay awake any more.

"Don't you have something to do?" she said.

He looked at her standing in the doorway to the bedroom. He said nothing.

"Did you write your parents?"

"This morning."

"So, go do something else."

"I am."

She glared at him. "What, I'm your project now?"

He nodded.

"I don't need to be anyone's project."

"Neither did I."

"The hell you didn't."

"Then so do you."

She walked across the room and stood in front of him. "You're pissing me off."

"I don't care."

"You should."

He followed her into the kitchen.

"Look," he said, "if I can deal with my brother and the Army, you can deal with this."

"Maybe I don't want to," she said sitting at the table, looking out the window.

He stood in the doorway and watched her light a cigarette.

"Are you mad at *me?*"

"I'm mad at men," she said.

"Why?"

"Because they're the assholes doing all this shit and always have been."

"I guess that would include me."

"If the shoe fits."

He looked at her in silence, fear pooling in his stomach.

"I'm going for a walk."

"Good idea," she said, still looking out the window. "Make it a long one."

He went to the river and sat on the dock, looking out over the water, fighting the sense of dread coming over him, suddenly unsure of her and so, sure of nothing, unable to understand the depth of her mood and the free floating rage coming at him.

He stayed by the river until the sun went down, not wanting to go back to the apartment, but then with nowhere else to go.

"I'm sorry," she said, looking up from the couch.

He leaned back against the wall and let out a sigh.

"I don't know how to help you."

"I don't think you can."

"Why did this hit you so hard?"

"I don't know," she said, shaking her head. "I was just thinking about that when you walked in. Maybe it's growing up in a family where the possibility of something better is what kept us going. They never gave up, my parents. They marched for civil rights and they marched for peace and when I got older, they took me along."

He sat down beside her, drawn to the sound of her voice, low and full of sadness.

"But I saw something they didn't," she said. "I thought we could make the system work. If we just got the right people in power, there was a chance. They didn't believe in that, of course. They said elections are just a way for the system to reproduce itself. Smoke and mirrors. Wrong going in, wrong coming out.

"So I had a kind of secret life, like I was having an affair and I couldn't tell them because they'd say I was too young and didn't know what I was doing. I didn't think they'd understand things like how I wanted to cry when I heard 'America the Beautiful'."

"Me, too," he said.

"Hard, isn't it."

"It didn't used to be."

"Well, anyway," she said, "when Jack Kennedy was elected, I finally got up the nerve to tell them what I thought. Democracy works, I said. But they just shook their heads and said no, it just looks that way sometimes.

"And then he was murdered and I remember my dad giving me that 'see what I mean?' look, but I wasn't having any of that because I needed to believe something was possible short of revolution. Besides, I was eighteen and what'd they know."

"So now you think maybe they were right."

She nodded. "And I don't know what to do. I've always known what to do, and now I don't. I don't know how to make it stop."

"What do you want to do?"

"Bring it to its knees."

"Bring what—"

"The government. What's running the war."

"I think you'll need some help for that," he said.

She looked at him with the possibility of a smile flashing across her face, as close as she'd gotten in days.

"I wish it was August," she said. "But for now I've just got to get out of here."

Then she looked at him, her eyes suddenly clear. "Ever been to Mexico?"

"No."

"You'd like it. You want to go? You have to go somewhere. You can't stay here. Not anymore. They're going to come after you."

"I don't have much money."

"I've got some. Besides, we can live on almost nothing down there."

He looked at her, saying nothing.

"What've you got to lose?" she said. "You're an outlaw. We can be outlaws together." She looked into his eyes. "What's the matter?"

"I can't just disappear."

"Sure you can. Besides, you'd better, at least for awhile. You can't go home. That's the first place they'll look."

"I haven't done anything yet. It's not against the law to turn down a commission."

"But it is to dodge the draft."

"They haven't drafted me yet."

"And what happens when they do?"

"I don't know."

"So," she said, "let's you and I get in the car and drive down to Mexico before we have to find out."

The next morning, checking his mail for the last time, Andrew stood in front of the open box and stared down at the return address on the letter in his hand, then slid it in his pocket.

"I have ten days to report for induction," he said.

She rolled her eyes. "Those little fuckers don't waste any time."

"Not when they're mad."

"Well, that's ten days before you're overdue someplace. Which is plenty of time to get where we're going."

"Then what?"

"I don't know." She looked at him. "You worried?"

"It's like I'm crossing a line."

"No 'like' about it," she said. "You most definitely are."

"I won't have a country anymore. Or a family or a place to go."

"That isn't true," she said. "They just want you to think it is."

William couldn't get Andrew out of his mind. He kept seeing his face, a boy's face, asleep in his bed or looking up to ask another of the endless stream of questions children ask—why not and how does it work and why is it so—the lips soft around the words. He saw the young German soldier only at the cemetery, which drew him there. He did not find him at first as he stood above Joshua's grave or knelt down to touch the stone, but only later when he happened to look up and saw him standing in the little grove of trees, silent, not moving, arms at his sides, watching.

At lacrosse practice William watched the boys run up and down the field, their bodies strong, swift, precise in their movement. Other boys, he thought, lesser boys than these, will gather in the stands on Saturday afternoon to watch the chosen few, the young hyper-men. They will compare themselves and come up short, having to be content to cheer them on and share at a distance in the glory of the manhood they embody.

But then it occurred to him that it wouldn't always be that way, how the war would serve as a great equalizer among them. Which is why, he thought, it is so popular among men who know nothing of it except for the chance to be counted as real men without having to try out or make the team. Democratic, open to all, everyone the same in the face of their own mortality and expendability.

He watched the boys and remembered the afternoon when he screamed at Andrew and the sight of him colliding with the other boy to send him flying through the air and rolling across the ground. The one left standing, he thought, and the one knocked down indistinguishable in the mass, whether hurling death in every direction or marching down the road or strewn across the field or along the shallow ditch.

He paced up and down the sidelines, watching Peter Hay in the goal, whooping and beating his stick on the ground when his teammates scored at the far end of the field. And then he thought of the evening before the funeral, having a smoke outside with Andrew, the question and his reply, that there was nothing he could say that would prepare him for what lay ahead, and suddenly he stopped, staring at the boys on the field and realizing the only thing he was preparing them for was to do as they were told, to offer themselves up to something they would not understand until it was too late.

I am not turning them into men, he thought, but into things, objects that merely look and move and sound like men.

In the evening, Anne and William went to see a new movie, *The Graduate*, with Dustin Hoffman and Anne Bancroft, and for awhile it felt good to them both to laugh together, until they reached the end, the young lovers sitting in the back of the bus, their faces sober and weary, the future uncertain before them.

They were quiet driving home, Anne thinking of Dustin Hoffman's character, Benjamin, standing at the back of the church, waving the cross like a broadsword to cover their retreat from the enraged congregation of adults, even using it to bar the door. She looked at William, his face barely illumined in the glow of lights on the dashboard, his lips seeming to move, but without a sound.

"What?" she said.

He turned into the driveway and switched off the car, looking down at the keys in his hands.

"I should go see him."

She stopped breathing.

"He hasn't accepted his commission yet. There's still time."

He waited for her to say something, but there was only the ticking of the engine cooling in the night air and when he looked at her he had to lean down so the light from the streetlamp caught her face, and only then did he see the tears below her eyes squeezed shut.

"I'll go tomorrow," he said, and she nodded, not opening her eyes.

Andrew and Ruth cleaned out the refrigerator and packed up the car. He wrote a second letter to his parents and mailed it on the way out of town. As they crossed the bridge and headed south he looked back at the boat house and the dock by the river and felt himself leaving behind everything that held him safe and sure, except for the woman who sat beside him and drove the car, carrying him to a place he'd never been and from which he wondered how and when he would ever return.

"He's not here," said William, standing in the phone booth in Andrew's dorm. "All his things are gone—"

"He sent us a letter—"

"And I talked to his roommates—what letter?" he said. "From Andrew? What did he say?"

"He's refusing his commission."

"I know," he said, "they told me." He paused. "Did he say why?"

"He think's it's wrong."

"Read me the letter."

She put down the phone and after a silence, picked it up and began to read.

I've tried everything I can think of to make this come out some other way, but I keep coming back to the same thing, and with graduation so close, I have to tell you. I can't go to Vietnam, which means I can't accept my commission. There are lots of reasons, which I'll explain someday, but for now the best I can say is I've been going through a lot, not just about Josh, but stuff that happened before, and I don't see things the way I used to. Josh wrote me once that he didn't know why we were over there, and the more I've thought about it, the less sense it makes to me, too. I don't know that any war makes sense. I used to think so, if it was for a good cause, but I don't know anymore if any cause is good enough. I can't see why Josh had to die,

her voice tightening around the words,

I can't see why he had to kill that little boy,

reading on, her voice thick in her throat,

I don't want to die and I don't want to kill people and if I go that's what will happen, so I can't. I know that puts me in a lot of trouble. They'll try to draft me and then they'll come after me when I don't show up. I don't want to go to jail and I don't want to run away. I don't want any of it, but it wants me, so I have to choose. I'm sorry. I know I'm letting you down.

"Is that it?"

"Yes."

"Nothing about where he's going?"

"No. His roommates don't know?"

"No, or at least they're not saying. They're pretty mad at him. Apparently he's involved with a woman, but they don't know her name."

"He's worried, you know," she said.

"He should be."

"I mean about you."

"Me?"

"Of what you'll think of him. He's apologizing to you, not to me. It was the same with Josh. He thinks you won't forgive him."

Joe and Steve came down the stairs, turning their heads to look at William before going out the door, their faces showing only the flat expression of a soldier who has disappeared inside his uniform.

"I've got to find him," he said.

"Where will you look?"

"I don't know."

Before leaving town he went to see the Colonel, who leaned back in his chair as he spoke, his fingers touching tip to tip, making a little tent in the air as he studied William standing just inside the door.

"Go see Petersen in the history department. He'll know where your boy is."

And then the Colonel sat forward, taking a pen in his hand and beginning to write.

William found Petersen in his office, the door standing open to encourage a breeze through the window. He was surprised by how young he seemed, but then, as he stood in the doorway and saw the face turn toward him, the eyes earnest and clear behind the spectacles, it made perfect sense that it should be someone like this, intense and lean, who should be involved in Andrew's transformation.

Petersen looked at him, his face alert.

"Can I help you?"

"I'm William Carson. Andrew's father."

"Come in," said Petersen, rising to his feet and reaching out his hand, "sit down."

They shook hands and Petersen closed the door.

"Do you know where he is?"

"No."

"But you do know what he's done."

"Yes."

"Do you know why?"

"I think you should ask Andrew that."

"I can't," said William. "I don't know where he is. All his things are gone from his room. Whatever the Colonel knew, he won't tell me. So it comes down to you."

"Your son came to me in confidence." Petersen watched William's face grow hard and still, except for a little flutter in the fine muscles around his eyes.

"I need to know what happened. Please."

Petersen looked at him for a moment, then drew himself up in the chair.

"He sat in on my course because the Colonel asked him to spy on me to check on my politics. As far as I can tell, he started seeing things differently around the time his brother turned up missing. He came to class very upset. After that, apparently he spent most of his time in the library reading about the war, and the more he read the more disturbed he was. That's all I know. Except, of course, for your other son, which I was deeply sorry to hear about."

"Andrew thinks the war is wrong—"

"Yes, but I think it goes deeper than that. It's war itself that he doubts."

William nodded. "I'm told there's a woman he might be with, but I don't know her name. Can you help me?"

"I have to ask what you plan to do when you find him."

Petersen stared at the downturned face before him, the fist relaxing against the desk. And then he saw him lift his head to look at him, his eyes rimmed with tears, the effort to clear his throat showing on his face. "Please."

Petersen looked at him for a moment, then dropped his eyes to the shiny surface of the desk.

"Her name is Ruth," he said. "Ruth Koszinski."

3

As they drove south and then west, Andrew watched people in other cars, unable to keep himself from gripping the door handle whenever a car passed by too close or too fast, anticipating the siren, the sensation of being thrown against the car, hands pulled behind his back. She reminded him he had a week before he'd be missed at the induction center, which calmed him for awhile, but only just.

To settle his mind, she rolled a joint, not bothering to stop the car as she steered with one hand and manipulated the paper in the other, a feat that left him looking from her hand to her face to the highway ahead and back to her hand again.

"How do you do that?"

"Practice."

They took turns driving and didn't stop to rest until they reached Michigan and a college friend of Ruth's who lived in Ann Arbor. They took showers and slept on a fold-out couch in the little apartment on the edge of campus, then stayed up late on the fringes of a conversation carried by a steady stream of people drifting in and out.

They were mostly graduate students radically against the war and bent on going to Chicago in August, full of excited talk about student strikes in France bringing down the government, the insurrection at Columbia, the Poor People's March on Washington, a passing joke about Andy Warhol being shot by Valerie Solanis, author of the infamous SCUM Manifesto, and then the war and Kennedy and stopping Humphrey, and the thousands deserting the Army or refusing the draft, and protestors breaking into draft boards and pouring pig's blood over records, and Yale Chaplin, William Sloan Coffin and the venerable baby care doctor, Benjamin Spock, indicted on federal charges of encouraging young men to refuse the draft.

In the morning they drove south into Indiana, turning west at Indianapolis and angling downward through Illinois and into Missouri. They didn't stop except for bathroom breaks and meals, wanting to save money but, even more, feeling on the run from something they had silently agreed not to talk about. There was about them an urgency of flight at the end of which Andrew imagined the border of Mexico, lined with walls and barbed wire and bristling with guards whose only goal was to prevent him from crossing safely to the other side.

"Don't worry," she said. "The feds don't care who leaves. The tricky part is getting back in."

They were halfway through Missouri and it was nearly midnight. Andrew had just finished his shift behind the wheel.

"Tricky how?" he said.

"Them not finding out who you are. But they can't check everyone." She looked at him. "Go to sleep."

"I don't think I can."

She stared ahead at the road, then leaned over and turned on the radio, surprised to hear Buffalo Springfield coming from somewhere way out here in what seemed to her the broad flat middle of nowhere, the conservative heartland of a country in the middle of a war,

> *There's something happening here*
> *What it is ain't exactly clear*
> *There's a man with a gun over there*
> *Telling me I got to beware*

she took the small package from the glove compartment and rolled him a joint

> *it's time we stop, hey, what's that sound*

Andrew sitting back in the seat

> *everybody look what's going down*

drawing the smoke in deep

> *there's battle lines being drawn*

closing his eyes
a thousand people in the street
a gentle wave coming over his mind
it starts when you're always afraid
imagining himself
you step out of line
high above the earth
the man come and take you away
looking down on the watery blue ball
stop, children
receding in the darkness of space
what's that sound
until it shrank to no more than a dot
everybody look what's going down
falling away in his mind to drift among the stars.

Just past the billboard proclaiming "Welcome to Oklahoma," Ruth broke into song, "Ohhhhhhhhhh Ok—lahoma where the wind comes rushing down the plain . . ." Andrew joining in as best he could, not remembering the words but drawn to the spirit of the thing. He soon realized she didn't know the words, either, and was making most of it up, interspersed with long passages that consisted primarily of her nodding and humming with great enthusiasm, but none of it seeming to matter as she rolled her eyes and tossed her head and laughed and for just a little while he stopped thinking about his father and the war and the Colonel, even Joshua. When night came, they turned on the radio and he lay his head in her lap and felt through her thigh the vibration of the engine and the car against the road.

Andrew was driving and Ruth was asleep when they crossed into Texas, and before long he noticed the stares coming from drivers of pickup trucks passing by, slowing as they drew abreast to eye the anti-war stickers on the car and the woman sleeping in the back.

He looked straight ahead, unable to miss the rifles prominently displayed in gun racks across rear windows.

Ruth yawned and leaned forward between the seats, her hand on the back of his neck.

"They don't seem glad to see us," he said.

"No."

"How long does it take to get across Texas?"

"Too long," she said. "Not used to feeling so unsafe, are you."

"Not like this."

"I haven't felt safe since puberty."

"You don't act like it."

"Yes I do. What you see isn't me *being* safe, it's me *trying* to be safe."

"You think a gun'd help?"

"I've thought of it. But I decided all it does is make you unsafe on a higher level."

"You think they feel unsafe?"

"Well," she said, "I figure the bigger the gun, the more there is to be afraid of." She cocked her head and looked at him. "That's actually my theory of international relations," she said, climbing into the front seat. "It's all about their balls. They worry about 'em all the time. They can't stand to look foolish or weak or admit they're wrong. That's why they do such stupid things. Like war. They can't get their minds off their puny little nuts."

She looked at him. "Tell me I'm wrong," she said, sweeping her hand toward the windshield.

"Now this here is LBJ country," she said, her voice taking on a southern drawl, "where men are men. And that little pecker can't wait to get back down here where he belongs. He'd run home tomorrow if he could do it without leaving his balls behind in Washington. But he'd have to admit he can't control what's gonna happen over there in Vietnam," her voice rising like a tent preacher hitting her stride, "and then they'd call him a spineless coward, a man without honor, an unmanly man, a man who sits down to pee!"

Andrew laughed and grabbed his crotch with a look of mock alarm, sending the car swerving back and forth in the lane.

"And so," she said, her voice dropping to a hush over the sound of the engine, "those arrogant little shits keep on making war because they're afraid not to."

She looked at Andrew staring straight ahead, the smile gone from his face.

"You think I'm wrong," she said.

"No."

"What, then?"

Andrew was silent for awhile as they drove on, staying in the right lane, watching pickup trucks go by.

"I was just wondering," he said at last, "if my dad sent my brother off because he was afraid not to."

Ruth moved closer and rested her hand on his thigh as she turned her head to follow his gaze down the road.

"I feel like I'm running away," he said.

"You are."

"I wasn't raised for that."

"By your father."

He nodded.

"And now you're worried about what he'll think."

He nodded again.

"That you're a coward."

Andrew was silent, his eyes fixed on the road.

"A man who sits down to pee."

Still he was silent.

"Well," she said, "there is that. Except for one little thing."

"What?"

"Accepting the risk of being seen as a coward. Which most men wouldn't have the guts to do."

They found a small hotel in Laredo with a view overlooking the muddy Rio Grande and Mexico beyond. The desk clerk spun the register and handed a pen to Andrew who looked down at the blank line below the last entry and felt his mouth go dry and his mind a blank. The clerk leaned his paunch against the counter, his thinning hair matted against his skull in the stifling heat.

"You take your time, son," he said in a low and friendly voice. "It'll come to you." And then with a little smile he walked to the far end of the counter and busied himself with a small stack of mail.

Ruth snorted and poked Andrew in the side with her elbow.

"What should I write?" he said from the corner of his mouth.

"How about your name."

"Yeah, but, you know . . . "

"Then my name."

"Okay," he said, slowly spelling out the words, 'Andrew & Ruth Koszinski.'

"Just don't get any ideas," she said.

The clerk returned and handed him a key. "Okay, Mr. and Mrs . . . " he stared down at the name, then said, "*Koszinski?*" accenting the first syllable. "What kind of name is that?"

"Polish," she said.

"Is that like Russian?"

"No," she said. "It's the opposite of Russian."

"Opposite."

"Right."

The clerk looked at the name and then at her. Then he made a little shrug with his face and went back to the mail.

"Opposite of Russian?" Andrew whispered as they climbed the stairs.

"I had to think of something," she said, "you want to be fingered as a commie in Texas?"

The room was small but had a balcony over the river. He leaned on the railing and looked across at Nuevo Laredo on the Mexico side.

"It looks just like here," he said.

"I know," she said. "The border's like that. You have to get inside a ways before it really feels like Mexico."

244

They took a shower and made love on the narrow bed, the sounds of distant music and evening traffic coming through the window.

Afterward he lay on his back, a hand behind his head.

"What are you thinking about?" she said.

"You ask me that a lot."

"That's because I want to know. You want me to stop?"

"Would it matter?"

"Probably not."

"Okay, then. History."

"You were thinking about history."

"I was."

"You make love with me and then you think about history."

"Sometimes. Sorry."

"Oh, no. You're my kind of guy. As long as you tell me about it."

"Actually, I was thinking about something Petersen asked me about my dad. I told him he was in the war and Petersen asked if he ever talked about it."

"Has he?"

"No. Never. He teaches history and has nothing to say about the one piece of it he was actually part of."

"Did you ever ask him?"

"Lots of times. Last time I was home. But all he'd say was there was no way to prepare me, that I have to find out for myself."

"Like your brother."

"That's what I said, which really pissed him off."

"What do you think he's so afraid of?"

"My dad? He's not afraid of anything."

"Sure sounds like something."

"But why wouldn't he tell us?"

They crossed the border in the morning, passing through the narrow, noisy streets of Nuevo Laredo before picking up the highway south to Monterrey. The land was flat and arid and as Ruth slipped the car into fourth gear she leaned out the window and gave a long, whooping yell into the desert air, her eyes squinting, hair blowing in the wind. Andrew smiled as he laid his head against his hand, the hot, dry air blowing across his face, and smelled the scent of another country and for a moment felt the troubles of his own dropping away behind.

Past Monterrey they turned southwest toward San Luis Potosi. The sun was down and they were following an old bus through the darkness, the desert stretching out on either side of the highway, a great bowl of stars overhead. The bus stopped and a man stepped down onto the road. He was dressed in loose pants and sandals and a broad-brimmed hat pulled down over his eyes. In an easy motion, he raised his hand to adjust the hat. And then with a sputtering roar the bus pulled away, smoke belching from the tailpipe, and without looking back, the man walked off the road and disappeared into the dark.

"Where's he going?" said Andrew.

"Home, I guess."

"But there's nothing there. No lights or anything."

"It must be out there somewhere."

Before going home William stopped at the registrar's office and got Ruth's campus address. He stood on the porch, ringing the bell again and again without an answer. Then an old woman appeared around the side of the house, a rake in her hand, and told him she was gone, her and the young man, a nice young man, she said, smiling in the shade of her hat.

He drove home. For weeks they lived in a state of carefully contained panic.

He called the local draft board and was told the letter went out weeks ago, the voice on the other end of the line self-satisfied and smug.

"He was supposed to show up for induction two days ago," he said, putting down the phone.

"Do you think he did?"

"No."

He watched her gaze into the middle distance and then she blinked and looked at him.

"Her parents," she said. "What about them?"

"I don't know. I never thought of her as someone's daughter."

He called the college and got her permanent home address and a phone number in New York City. A man answered.

"I'm William Carson. Is this Mr. Koszinski?"

"Yes."

"Do you know who I am?"

"I do," the voice measured and cautious.

"Andrew's disappeared."

"I'm not surprised."

"Do you know where he is?"

"With Ruth."

"And where is she?"

"I'm reluctant to say."

"Why?"

"Because I know why he's disappeared and I'm concerned about what you might do when you find him."

"I don't see how that's any concern of yours," said William.

The line was silent and then he heard a little sigh.

"Well, sir, you have me there. But then again, nor are the whereabouts of my daughter any concern of yours. Goodbye."

"No—" said William, but it was too late, the dull click in his ear. He called back, but there was no answer.

The next morning he took the train to New York, arriving early in the afternoon. He found the address, an old brownstone on a quiet street on the west side of Greenwich Village. He climbed the stairs and rang the bell. For a moment no one seemed at home, but then a woman's face looked down from an upstairs window, her hand holding the curtain to the side. She stepped back and was gone and then with a click of the lock the door swung open.

She looked at him standing on the stoop. She was tall and broad in the hips, her face big-boned and smooth. She was wearing a loose blouse above a long, deep purple cotton skirt. She had sandals on her feet and her hair was drawn back behind her head.

"I'm guessing you're Andrew's father."

"Yes."

"I'm Simone. Ben isn't here."

"Then I can speak with you."

"I'd rather we all talk together. He'll be back in a bit. Why don't you come in and wait."

She led him through the downstairs hall to a living room that looked out over a small enclosed garden.

"Would you like some tea or coffee?"

He shook his head.

"I'm going to get some coffee. Make yourself comfortable."

He looked about the room. He'd never been inside a Manhattan dwelling and was amazed to find such warmth and comfort in the midst of what he'd always imagined to be a harsh and unwelcoming place. An entire wall was taken up by floor-to-ceiling bookshelves. The remaining walls were covered with photographs and paintings, some of them originals as he could tell when he got close enough to see the brush strokes. A couch sat in the middle of the room with end tables piled high with books arranged around dark metal lamps with Tiffany shades. Copies of the *New Yorker* and the *New York Times* lay on the coffee table.

"Ben teaches philosophy at Columbia," she said, standing in the doorway to the dining room. "I understand you're also a teacher."

"Yes."

A kettle whistled from the kitchen.

Ben Koszinski came through the front door just as she returned carrying a mug of coffee. He stood in the doorway, a small stack of books in his hands, his eyes fixed on William turned around on the couch to look at him over his shoulder. He was shorter and rounder than Simone and had a full beard trimmed close to his face.

"This is Andrew's father," she said. "You want some coffee?"

"No, thanks," he said, not taking his eyes from William. He laid the books on a little table in the hall and stepped into the room.

"What have I missed?"

"Nothing, really," she said. "He got here a little while ago. We were waiting for you."

He crossed the room and sat in a stuffed chair facing the couch.

"So," she said, "where did you two leave off?"

"The whereabouts of my son," said William.

"I don't think we can help you with that," said Ben.

"Why not?"

"Because he's taken a stand against war and we support him in that and we don't want to betray him."

"I'm not asking you to."

"Are you sure?" said Ben. "Your son doesn't seem to be."

"You've spoken with him?"

"No. But we have with Ruth."

"And what did she say?"

Ben narrowed his eyes. "You really want to know?"

"Yes."

"All right then. She said you're a hard man who expects his sons to do their duty."

The color rose in William's face and the air suddenly felt thick and close.

"I didn't come here to talk about me. I want to find my son. Do you know where he is?"

The Koszinskis looked at each other, then back at him.

"We do," said Simone.

"And?"

"What will you do when you find him?" she said.

"Bring him home."

"And what then?"

"I don't know."

"That's what worries us," said Ben.

"But he's not your son."

"No," said Simone, "he's not. And please believe me when I say this isn't easy for us. We were up most of the night talking about it. He's not our son and he is yours. But he's not just your son anymore. He's a man who's made a difficult and dangerous choice. When he did that he made himself part of something larger than anyone's family."

"What are you so worried about?" said William.

"Our fear is that you might try to persuade him to change his mind, which would make you a danger to him."

"I haven't said I'd try to change his mind."

"You haven't said you won't."

"That's between Andrew and me."

"Yes," said Simone, "it is. And whether we reveal his whereabouts is between him and us."

"I don't know if you're aware of this," said Ben, "but apparently his commanding officer plans to make an example of him. Which probably means when they catch him they'll offer him a deal. That he serve in the military rather than go to prison."

"But he's already decided that."

"In a way, yes," said Ben, "but they can make it more complicated for him. And trickier. They can tell him they won't put him in combat, for example. No prison. No disgrace. So long as he gives in and takes the oath and wears the uniform."

"Then he'd be all right," said William.

There was a long silence as the Koszinskis looked across the room at each other.

"Yes," said Ben, "if you believe what they say—"

"And," said Simone, "if you're not against war itself." She looked at him for a moment. "And there is the danger."

"Who gave you the right to decide?" said William.

"We could ask the same of you," said Ben.

"I'm his father."

"So? Does being his father give you the right to hand him over? The way you did his brother?"

Simone winced with a little gasp. "Ben," she said, "don't."

William stood up on legs that trembled beneath him. "You don't know . . . " he said, his face suddenly flushed, hands moving awkwardly in the air as he made his way toward the door.

Outside on the stoop he stood for a moment and looked down at the street. Birds called out but seemed faint and far away. Somewhere in the distance a car honked its horn and for a long moment, he could not remember the way home.

On the first day of July, just before lunch, the front bell rang and Anne opened the door to a man who introduced himself as Robert Semple, an agent of the FBI. He reminded her of the Marine officers, except for the difference in uniform, his being a dull brown suit. But the rest was familiar, the short hair closely shaved around the neck and ears, the crisp efficiency of motion, the economy of words. She stared for a moment at the badge in the palm of his hand, unable to focus at first, and then, when he moved to take it away, reaching out and stopping him to give her time for the details to register in her mind, J. Edgar Hoover's Federal Bureau of Investigation coming into her home in search of Andrew, as if he'd robbed a bank or kidnapped a child or betrayed his country.

She called William from his study.

"Do you know where your son is?"

"No," said William.

"Are you sure?"

"Yes," said Anne.

Semple cleared his throat. "It's important that we find him before he gets into more trouble than he's already in. Do you know the name . . . " flipping through a small notebook, "Ruth Koszinski?"

Anne looked at William, her eyes large.

"We have reason to believe she's dangerous, both to your son and to the United States."

"What do you mean?" said Anne.

"I mean she's involved in the anti-war movement and has contacts with radicals in certain organizations that the attorney general has deemed a threat to the security of the United States. She could make things much worse for him. May I sit down?"

Anne nodded and Semple got a chair from against the wall.

"Your son achieved an enviable record in college. And then he seems to have lost his way, which probably coincided with meeting Koszinski. He can be charged with draft evasion, which is a felony. But if he agrees to cooperate with the government and serve in the Army, that might be the end of it. I'm not a U.S. attorney, of course, and I can't promise anything, and he would not be allowed to serve as an officer."

"Is there anything else?" said William.

Semple looked up at him.

"Then you don't know where he is."

"I wish we did," said William.

"Will you let me know if you hear from him?" said Semple, handing him a business card. "A lot of anti-war types think we're the bad guys, but we're not. We want to help."

Semple left. Footsteps receded down the hall. The outer door opened and closed and the silence came in around Anne and William standing in the middle of the room. And then William looked at Anne as he slowly lifted the card in front of him and tore it in half and then again.

Almost every evening, in the softening light, William walked down across the road behind Butler Hall to the little cemetery where grass now covered the wounded earth and the flowers Anne had planted were in bloom. He sat by the stone and watched the young man watching him from the small grove of trees. They looked at each other, saying nothing. Sometimes William looked away thinking he'd be gone when he looked back, but the young man was always there. Until something unexpected drew William's attention—a hawk circling high in the sky or a gang of crows squawking nearby—and he forgot for a moment, his mind clearing, and only

252

then noticed the young man gone and when he tried to remember what he looked like, discovered he could not.

On this evening, William leaned back against the stone and watched him put his hands in his pockets and hunch his shoulders, as if from cold. William looked at him for awhile and then opened his briefcase and pulled out a pad and pencil and only then did he notice the dark wet spot on the grass just beyond his hand, almost black in the fading light. He did not have to touch it to know what it was. He wiped the back of his hand across his eyes. Then he pulled up his knees and rested the pad against his thighs and began to draw.

"This is what he looked like," said William, laying it in her lap.

She held it at the edges, at first not noticing the detail in the face, the cheeks drawn and pulled inward, the eyes large and soft beneath a shock of hair hanging down. She saw only the familiar use of line, the strokes of grey shading into black creating shadow and depth, and beneath it all the distant memory of sitting beside him and looking into his face as he drew, the muscles smooth, at rest, except for the eyes, in constant motion and full of light.

She took a tissue from her pocket and blew her nose. She looked at him.

"What?" he said.

"You don't know?"

He looked at the drawing and then at her. "I kept forgetting what he looked like." He paused. "I know it isn't very good. It's been a long time."

Anne and William were lying in bed late in the night, unable to sleep for thinking about Andrew. It often happened this way, hours of silent agitation and then suddenly one of them starting in as if continuing a conversation.

"Jack said I was just going to have to find a way to live with this," he said. "He made it sound so simple."

She was quiet beside him.

"Do you think he hates me?"

"Jack?"

"Andrew."

"He may," she said, studying his face in the faint light, noticing how much softer and older he seemed to her now. "He will forgive you, sooner or later. He has to. You're his father."

"And you?"

She looked away. "I don't know," she said, shaking her head, "I really don't. Sometimes I just hate you so much. I can't help it. I know you went through awful things, but then I find myself not caring about that. Somehow it's not enough."

She sat up and leaned against the wall, her arms folded across her chest as she looked out the window.

"It's always been my worst nightmare, that one of my boys would die before me. It's not supposed to be this way. But he is dead and nothing can bring him back. Not ever."

She looked at him.

"Every time I look at you," she said, "that's what I think."

In late July there was a phone call from Simone Koszinski.

"We've decided it's only fair to tell you they're in Mexico."

"Mexico?" said William.

"Yes. And they're all right."

"Do you know where in Mexico?"

"No," she said. "The letter was mailed from California, probably by someone who carried it out of the country for them."

"But you have some idea."

"I'm sorry," she said. "I can't help you there."

"The FBI was here," he said. "They know about your daughter."

"What do you mean?"

"They know she's involved with radicals."

"I see."

"That doesn't worry you?"

"Of course it does," she said, "but no more than I worry about living in a country that believes so much in war. Our children are all in danger."

There was a silence on the line.

"I'm very sorry about the son you lost," she said, "and for what my husband said to you. He's a passionate man, especially about this, and sometimes he doesn't think about what he's saying."

"Did she say when they might come home?"

"No. But your son wants you to know that he's sorry. To you in particular."

"I see," he said. He stood by the phone, listening to the static on the line in the silence. "Well," he said at last, "thank you. Goodbye."

"Goodbye."

The next day, William went to see Jack.

"I don't want to coach the varsity anymore," he said.

Jack sat back and ran a hand through his hair.

"Why not?"

William shook his head. "I don't have it in me anymore."

Jack's voice was gentle and soft. "It'll come back. Just give it time."

"That's just it," said William. "I don't want it back."

4

San Miguel de Allende is a small colonial town clinging to a steep hillside in the mountains of central Mexico, seven thousand feet above the sea. Ruth and Andrew found a small studio apartment near the top of a street so steep they had to lean in to make the climb. Entering from the cobblestone sidewalk through a large wooden door, they came into a shaded walkway bordered by gardens and low hanging trees, a jacaranda in full bloom over the far wall, dense with purple flowers. They made their way up a narrow staircase to what the landlord described as a penthouse, perched on the roof with windows opening onto a sweeping view of the plain below and the range of mountains beyond the town. A simple couch sat beneath a bank of windows before a rough wooden table and two chairs. There was a small gas stove and refrigerator, a porcelain sink, a double bed against the wall. The floor was tiled the color of burnt umber and the ceiling was whitewashed between dark wooden beams. The room felt not quite square, one end a little wider than the other.

Andrew stood before the windows along the south wall and looked down at the street and tiled rooftops and small courtyards full of flowers and here and there a row of brightly colored laundry hanging in the high desert air. He opened the window and leaned out. Below him was a small iron balcony, its outer edge lined with red and pink flowers, and a cage holding a parrot who looked up at him and squawked in Spanish. He looked down the length of the street to a pair of donkeys standing in the shade, bundles of sticks tied to their backs.

"Can we stay here forever?" he said.

"Almost."

———

For a month, Andrew almost forgot where he was from and what he'd left behind. He settled into the slow and gentle rhythm of a place in which time was noted less by clocks—the one in their apartment having only an hour hand—than by the movement of the sun and the arrival of rain showers in late afternoon.

Each morning they woke late, sometimes making love before breakfast and then walking the narrow streets lined with adobe walls broken by rough wooden doors and windows covered with iron grills. The streets wound toward the town square with its carefully shaped bushes and a small covered bandstand. They had coffee in a restaurant and watched tourists going by, trying to pick out the Americans from the Canadians and the occasional European.

They walked across the square and down a street winding past the cathedral, along sidewalks where women sat before small pyramids of tangerines, and then on to the open market building where they were met by cool air scented with fruit and spice, and broad faced women perched at the top of high stalls, looking down across slopes of produce to the customers below. All around were the sounds of simple, sustaining routines, of prices called back and forth, the butcher's cleaver coming down, a greeting shouted out, an exchange of laughter, children's voices.

They bought enough for each day and then meandered home, sometimes holding hands as they walked in the street, the sidewalk not being wide enough for two, and hewed to the cool of the shady side. On the way was a small tortilla factory, the rhythmic squeak of the conveyor belt announcing they were near, and Ruth stood in front of the open window and held up her hand, her thumb and finger indicating the thickness of the stack, and the woman wrapped the purchase in brown paper and handed it to her.

It began to seem as if life could go on this way forever, but as July turned into August there was a growing restlessness, first in Ruth and then Andrew, each observed in the other but left unspoken.

He could tell she was thinking of Chicago, could feel the anger coalesce and burn inside of her when she spoke of Bobby Kennedy, her voice tight in her throat as if running out of air, her hand suddenly balling into a fist. Even their lovemaking, which had always been exuberant, settled into something heavier and more dense than before.

"Fuck me hard," she said one night, her eyes closed, muscles standing out along her jaw, and he didn't understand at first, startled by the words and wondering if she meant for him to hurt her, but then drawn to the rhythm of her movement beneath him, their hips pounding together as if hurling themselves against a door that would not open.

She had waited for the shift in him, knowing it would come, the longing for home and the fear of what awaited him there. She saw it in his face when they sat in the cafe overlooking the square and he looked away from people going by, his eyes drifting upward toward the rooftops and the sky.

He missed his mother, remembering the sadness in her voice coming from the dark beside his bed that night, and the next day the look on her face when they said goodbye at the bus. He wanted to go home, but no longer knew what home consisted of or how he might find any safety there. To be an outlaw was exhilarating at first, both in spite of fear and because of it, and he sometimes wondered if his brother ever felt that way in Vietnam. But he knew there would come a time when the fear would take its place and crowd out all the rest.

In the middle of August they packed the car and drove north. The Democratic Convention began on Monday and Ruth wanted to arrive by the day before. She planned to stay with Grace, her college roommate, who lived in the Old Town section of Chicago, near Lincoln Park. They entered the United States at Laredo, Andrew saying nothing except, "Yes, sir" when the border guard asked for identification, handing him his driver's license and looking about, trying to seem calm and relaxed and then hoping the man didn't see how his hand shook as he reached out to take it back. The guard walked around the car and stood looking down at the stickers on the bumper, then signaled another guard to come over and they proceeded to unpack everything on the ground beside the car.

"What are they doing?" he said.

"Looking for drugs. Or anything else that does the trick."

"Are we okay?"

"I guess," she said with a shrug. "Welcome home."

The oil pump broke just south of Joplin, Missouri, and they had to wait overnight for the garage to open and then most of the day for the repair. They reached the outskirts of Chicago late Monday night and made their way up Lake Shore Drive past the marinas on Lake Michigan on one side and the long expanse of Grant Park on the other. Along Michigan Avenue on the far side of the park they could see the brightly lit hotels, including the Hilton where delegates would stay when not at the convention in the amphitheater farther west. Andrew stared out at the lake, dark and vast like an ocean.

Turning onto LaSalle Street at the southern tip of Lincoln Park they knew right away that something was wrong. The park was full of young people dressed for a cool summer night, and ranged against them were long lines of police. Media lights played across the crowd and the trees, making the air seem chaotic and alive, voices shouting everywhere, sometimes coalescing into chants hurled at the lines of blue

Pig! Pig!

Oink! Oink!

Mother fucking fascist pig!

Pig! Pig!

Oink! Oink!

On it went until just past the intersection of LaSalle and Clark where they saw police wading into the crowd, slashing billy clubs through the air in search of heads and bones, the crowd swaying and flowing in its flight from the assault with the police in hot pursuit. Ruth and Andrew found themselves in a long line of cars unable to move as the violence swirled around them in a chorus of screams and shouts and sirens wailing, and at the center of it all, police clubbing everyone who came in their way, demonstrators and residents of the neighborhood who'd come out to watch and a gang of boys sitting on a stoop and heckling the demonstrators. A journalist photographed a boy being beaten on the sidewalk and then the police turned and smashed the camera as they beat him to the ground. Beer cans, bottles, and rocks appeared in the air overhead, a shoe bouncing off the hood of the car before landing in the street.

Ruth rocked back and forth, her hands alternately squeezing and releasing the wheel.

"Those fuckers," she said through her teeth, straining against the seat, unable to stay still.

Andrew was transfixed by the crowd moving first one way and then another as the police charged and fell back and regrouped to charge again. Then through the open window he heard an unfamiliar sound, a muffled pop, steady and rhythmic like locusts moving through a field, and only when it aligned with the sight in front of him did he realize it was the sickening crack of hardened wood descending on skulls and shoulders. He didn't move, his hand gripping the handle of the door to anchor himself in the midst of a roiling sea of violence such as he had never known, immediate and real, waves of pain and fear that seemed to swirl about them, palpable in the air, in the blood streaming down the faces of young men running past the car, in the sobs coming from the woman kneeling beside a body motionless on the ground, in the seemingly inexhaustible rage on the faces of police.

Ruth was still and quiet now beside him, slowly shaking her head, tears rolling down her face.

Andrew reached over and took her hand and they sat in the car and watched into the night.

Anne and William leaned forward on the couch, scenes from Chicago playing out across the television screen. At the commercial, he took off his glasses and rubbed his knuckles into his eyes.

"He's there," he said.

"How do you know?"

He shook his head. "That's where she would be." They looked at each other, her eyes searching his face.

"I have to find him," he said, "or at least try."

And there was nothing she could think to say, no word of doubt or resistance, so disarmed was she by the clear and simple voice.

The next morning they drove to Boston and she dropped him at the airport.

"How will you find him?"

"I don't know. I probably won't. But if he's there, at least I'll be there, too. I owe him that much."

As she looked at him, she remembered the train she met so many years ago and was reminded of the man she once knew and only realized now had all but given up.

She went home and made a sandwich for lunch and sat in the kitchen, feeling the weight of the silence in the empty apartment. Then she went down the hall to make the bed and was just inside the door when she saw it, the piece of paper on her pillow, and crossing the room she could see it was not a note, but a drawing, and her eyes filled as she looked down and recognized the unmistakable lines of her own face.

It was well past midnight when Andrew and Ruth found the apartment on a tree-lined side street leading away from Lincoln Park. Finding no one there, they waited on the steps until Ruth heard a familiar voice from a block away, the tone going back and forth between anger and jubilance. When Ruth saw Grace she called out her name and jumped off the steps and ran to throw her arms around her. Grace had close-cropped hair and wore bell-bottoms and a shirt cut off just above the waist. With her was a young man she introduced as Lenny, dressed in cut-off jeans and combat boots, his face scraggly with several days growth. They went upstairs but no one could sleep and so they sat around on the floor and shared a joint and talked.

"What's with the cops?" Ruth wanted to know.

"They don't want us here," said Lenny.

"Why the hell not?"

"Because the powers that be don't want us here. And we won't go away."

"But it's a public park." said Andrew.

"It doesn't matter," said Grace. "They put up signs closing the park at 11:00, which is what this is all about. It's total bullshit, of course, since people sleep there all the time when it's hot, and no one cares. They're just making up the law as they go along so they can get rid of us."

"And then," said Lenny, "they can go on with their messy little war. Except they can't get rid of us, which is *really* pissing them off. Which means the war is coming home at last, right where it belongs."

They slept until just past noon, eating a quick breakfast before walking to Lincoln Park beneath a clear sky, the air cool even at midday, the streets strangely normal and routine after the violence of the night before, people going in and out of shops, cars driving by.

Crossing Clark Street they saw the police ranged beneath the trees at the southern end of the park, sitting on lawn chairs, smoking cigarettes, shaking their heads in disbelief at anti-war leaflets scattered on the ground. Andrew stuck to the far side of the group as they walked by an officer who looked up from his newspaper and nodded, "See you kids at 11:00," lifting a corner of his mouth in half a smile as Lenny touched two fingers to his brow in a casual salute.

To the north, thousands of demonstrators passed the day by throwing frisbees and lying in the sun, sleeping under trees, cooking over small fires, all to the continuous sound of drumming drifting among the trees. However they occupied themselves, they were only waiting, like the police, for the coming of the night.

They walked through the crowds to the commentary of Lenny and Grace. "You got your flat out hippies," said Lenny, "who are here just for the party. But there aren't many of those. The Yippies, on the other hand, are something else."

"That's for Youth International Party," said Ruth, seeing the look on Andrew's face.

"Hippies with politics," said Grace, "and organized, they're not."

"But they do make it happen," said Lenny. "More than your middle-class types," pointing to a young woman in Bermuda shorts and a button-down shirt hanging out at the waist. "They'd be downtown working for McCarthy if they weren't here. But they can't stay away, because they know McCarthy doesn't have a chance and this is where it's at."

"We're a long way from the convention," said Ruth.

"I don't think anyone up here gives a shit about the convention," said Grace. "Humphrey and the Democrats will do whatever they want. And so will we. The real convention is right here."

"And what exactly are you trying to do?" said Andrew.

Lenny looked at him for a moment, lips slightly parted and eyes narrowed. "I guess you could say we're trying to get the beast to show itself for what it really is."

"The beast."

"Yeah. What you saw out here last night. Most people have no idea. They sat at home and watched the tv and thought what they saw was just a bunch of good cops getting carried away and bashing some kids for being 'provocative,'" his fingers quoting in the air.

"But the thing is, the cops weren't out of control. They were doing exactly what they'd been ordered to do by the lieutenants and captains watching from across the street. And they were doing what the Mayor told them to do and you can bet Lyndon Johnson made it clear to the Mayor he didn't want a bunch of *citizens* fucking up *his* convention by exercising *their* Constitutional right to assemble and speak out.

"That, my friend, is the beast. The whole thing. That wants what it wants and if you get in the way, it'll make *you* go away.

Sometimes with B-52s and sometimes bashing heads in Lincoln Park. It's all the same."

Andrew remembered the sound coming through the window of the car and suddenly there came into his mind an image of his brother

they shot away his face

broken, lying in the dark

your brother's face

something monstrous nearby, brooding and hungry

bits of bone and flesh

and he was suddenly afraid.

They took the subway to Grant Park and joined a crowd occupying a small hill just south of the Hilton, topped by a statue of a Civil War soldier holding high an American flag and sitting astride an enormous horse, its head bowed as it pawed the ground. Andrew watched two boys scale the statue and wave a Vietcong flag as they chanted *Peace now!* until the police waded up the hill through the crowd, calling out on a bullhorn to get down.

"See," said Grace, "there they go making up the law again. *Everyone* climbs statues in Chicago. It's what they're for."

But already the police had pulled one boy down and were wrestling with the other who screamed they were breaking his arm, but no one made a move to intervene as the police took him away.

Slowly the tension in the crowd smoothed away and the demonstrators went back to waiting for whatever was coming next. Andrew and Ruth wandered off to a small grove of hawthorn trees and lay down in the shade to wait for the darkness.

William checked into a hotel just before noon and went immediately to Lincoln Park. At the pond house he bought a hamburger and sat by the water and looked out at what reminded him of an army at rest—frisbees drifting through the sunlit air, a game of softball in a clearing among the trees, the slap of the ball against gloves and bats mingled with shouts and laughter, people sleeping in the shade. But over it all hung an energy he remembered well, a tense expectancy borne of the shared knowledge that this was but a temporary lull.

He finished his lunch and walked among them, noticing how they looked at him with curious expressions, eyes narrowing at the sight of a middle-aged man in chinos and a blue button-down shirt in the midst of a crowd of young people who looked as if they'd dressed themselves in whatever was handy just before they ran out the door. A few reminded him of Andrew and he quickened his step, only to be disappointed as he drew near enough to see that it wasn't him. There are thousands of them, he thought, and remembered Anne asking him how he'd ever find one amongst all this, and a wave of despair swept over him as he sat down in the shade by a statue of the Italian hero, Garibaldi.

As evening fell they made their way north to Lincoln Park. The mood in the crowd was easy at first, quiet conversations, joints and little pipes passed around against a background of rhythmic drumming from down by the water.

By 11:00 o'clock, talk turned to the police and would they bring guns and what would come of that. William walked among them, feeling the anxiety in the air and a palpable depth of anger that he did not understand.

Suddenly a commotion turned him toward a crowd rapidly moving picnic tables and trash barrels. Bright lights from across the way illuminated the hurried construction of a flimsy barricade, the scene reminding him of news reports in the spring of French students protesting in the streets of Paris. A young man planted a Vietcong flag on top of the pile before stepping back to join the rest waiting in the silence of the media lights casting long shadows across the grass.

A bullhorn switched on with a squawk and then a booming voice that reminded William of a drill sergeant's knack for seeming both calm and menacing at the same time, announcing the park was closed and they were all breaking the law and must leave immediately.

Over the heads of the crowd he saw three long lines of police, ranged one behind the other, their faces covered with gas masks and their hands holding clubs, rifles, and shotguns, all this firepower, he realized suddenly, ranged against him, and although he felt an impulse to escape he could not think of where to go, of where else it was that he belonged more than here.

Then, from all around, the shouts and chants began

  peace now!

parks belong to the people!

  fuck the pig!

oink oink!

  hell no we won't go!

up against the wall, motherfucker!

while several hundred yards to the north Andrew stood in the midst of an enormous crowd, feeling like an alien, surrounded by people unlike any he'd ever known, their faces full of anger and fear.

He listened to Ruth lobbing slogans and insults in the direction of the police, but he was silent, feeling separate from her who seemed to have merged with something larger that he barely understood. And then he sensed someone on the other side and he turned to see a man, older than himself, not so much in years as shown in the lines that marked his face, deep pools of sadness and rage in his eyes.

He was dressed in army fatigues and at first Andrew thought he was like so many others he'd seen, draping themselves in surplus costumes of war, until he saw the combat infantryman's badge on his chest and suddenly understood the premature aging in his face.

The man chanted into the air, "Peace, now!" and turned to Andrew, nodding as he pumped the words from his body, mouthing them with exaggerated motions as if teaching him to speak a foreign phrase. And suddenly Andrew was looking into the face of Joshua and something gave way in his throat as he began to say the words, softly at first, then louder as he took the hand of his brother and raised it into the air.

William watched the long lines of police standing against the chants and drumming that filled the air, punctuated by the voice through the bullhorn, ordering the crowd to leave. But there was no movement on either side until suddenly there came a distant chorus of deep thumping sounds, like mortars, he thought, and then a flock of tear gas canisters came crashing down through the branches overhead, striking the ground with a hiss and sending out waves of gas. Floodlights came on from behind the police and played across the crowd that recoiled and shrank from the enveloping cloud, until a young man wearing an oven mitt picked up a canister and threw it back at the police to cheers sent up from the crowd. And then police with converted flame throwers emerged from the line and walked steadily forward, laying down a thick blanket of gas in front of them. William flinched at the sight, struggling to clear his mind of memories of men on fire, the gas burning his eyes and skin as he turned with the enormous crowd now moving in panic toward Clark Street and the western edge of the park. There were shouts of "Walk! Don't Run!" but it was too late for many who stumbled and fell and had to be picked up by others to avoid being trampled underfoot.

Along Clark Street a phalanx of police awaited the crowd swelling along the edge of the street as it tried to bring its surging momentum to a halt, driven forward by the line of police advancing ghostlike through the cloud of gas. A sense of trapped rage welled up from the mass of people, shouting now at the silent lines of police

peace now!

seig, heil!

peace now!

seig, heil!

hell, no, we won't go!

and then, like birds passing suddenly overhead, a flurry of rocks, bottles, and firecrackers filled the air and rained down on the line of blue. As if on cue, in a single motion, the police walked, then ran across the street, billy clubs and rifle butts raised, charging into the crowd, cutting a wide swath as they clubbed everyone within reach, arms rising into the air, falling, then rising again in a harvest of blood and broken bone. The crowd surged north to escape being crushed in the vise closing in upon them, spilling into side streets running west from the park, regrouping as the mass of police thinned out behind them, turning over trash barrels and setting them afire, or lying in wait to ambush police cars by pelting them with rocks before making their escape. Then the police arrived in force, running down the tree-lined streets, unmasked faces contorted with rage as they clubbed anyone they could find, slamming people into walls and against fences, clubs swinging freely against heads and jammed into groins, knocking people to the ground and then falling on them again and again. One leapt from his moving car and pursued a demonstrator, the club swinging high above his head, while the car, the door still hanging open, came lurching to a halt on its own.

Angry residents emerged from houses and took the wounded inside. An old woman, long white hair wild about her head, stood on the sidewalk and screamed into the face of a policeman who listened for a moment, leaning forward, hands on his hips, sweat dripping from his nose, then pointed at the stairs as he ordered her back inside.

Police entered homes in search of demonstrators who'd sought refuge there, dragging them down steps to throw into waiting vans.

It went on this way far into the night, the tear gas drifting through neighborhoods and causing residents to open windows and sniff the air. Police cruised the streets, attacking stragglers, invading makeshift hospitals to arrest the injured.

William found himself suddenly alone on a darkened street, the combat having moved around the corner and away, and as he stood beneath a streetlamp, he realized he'd been trembling almost from the beginning. He tried to make it stop, but he could not, holding one hand in the other, then sitting on a stoop and wrapping his arms around his shins. But it did no good, for it wasn't merely in his muscles or his bones, but deep within his cells, this sense of the world coming apart, as if held together by nothing more than a loose weave of old string disintegrating in a flood of rage and violence and fear that he could neither contain nor understand.

William woke late and called home.

"Did you watch the news?"

"I caught something about a riot. You haven't seen him."

"No. And it wasn't a riot. It was—" rubbing his fingers across his forehead, searching for the words, "I don't know what it was. But it wasn't that."

Slowly, over the course of Wednesday morning and into the afternoon, thousands of demonstrators moved south into Grant Park. The news spread through the crowd that McCarthy had given up hope of winning the Democratic nomination, leaving the field to Humphrey. Throughout the day, talk turned to massing for a march on the amphitheater where delegates would decide the party's position on the war and the relentless bombing of North Vietnam.

Like hundreds of others, Ruth and Andrew had spent the night before in Grant Park, sleeping in the small grove of hawthorn trees near the Logan statue, secure in the belief that the police would not attack them within sight of the delegates and dignitaries whose rooms in the Hilton overlooked the park. They rose with the sun and made their way north to Grace's apartment where they ate and showered and slept until Lenny shook them awake just after noon.

They took the subway downtown and joined the rally at the bandshell on the north edge of Grant Park. The first thing they noticed was the shift in mood from the day before, now surrounded on three sides by police to the north and west and the National Guard to the south. People had come prepared, as if knowing what was about to happen, dressed in padded jackets and football, motorcycle, and World War I helmets, faces shining through thick coats of Vaseline smeared on to protect against the gas. But, as Andrew also saw, there were no weapons except for the occasional bottle or rock held loosely in someone's hand, nothing else to throw into the battle, save for the bodies themselves.

From the stage, organizers spoke of discipline and staying in line and above all, not provoking the police, while along Columbus Avenue the long blue line moved forward into the trees.

"What the fuck is this?" said Lenny. "We're not doing anything."

A murmur swept through the crowd as heads turned to watch the advancing line. Suddenly a young man appeared at the flagpole and began to lower the U.S. flag, and no sooner had it begun its descent than he was set upon by police who beat him with clubs and kicked him on the ground. The crowd started to scream, people looking about for something to throw but finding only newspapers and flowers and so throwing them into the air and watching them float harmlessly to the ground as the police withdrew, dragging the young man behind, the long silent line advancing still further through the trees.

Suddenly, a small group of men ran to the flagpole and quickly pulled down the flag, raising in its place a bright red pair of long underwear.

"Those are undercover cops," said Lenny. "They're too well fed to be one of us. Watch this."

Immediately the police waded into the crowd near the flagpole, clubbing in all directions, but missing the small group of men who'd already made their escape, taking the flag with them. The crowd responded by hurling rocks and obscenities at the police still standing silently in the shade of the line of trees until suddenly it seemed to erupt, spewing forth ranks of blue charging into the bandshell, clubbing, turning over benches, kicking people on the ground. The crowd gave way, then stiffened and began to fight back.

The police withdrew, regrouped and charged again, clubs waiving in the air before crashing down.

From the middle of the crowd, Andrew heard the sounds of combat advancing toward them, shouts and grunts and sickening blows, distant and muffled at first, then sharper and louder as they drew near. Ruth took his hand and he looked into her face and saw his own fear reflected in her eyes, and then she looked away with a gasp as he turned to see a club rising in the air over heads close enough for him to reach out and touch. The struggle was now so near he could smell and hear its presence, no longer somewhere else, buffered by the crowd. He saw a blue uniform, a thick bare forearm covered with sweat and dirt, a hand grasping the club as it came down with a dull crack on someone's skull, and for an instant he could not move, thinking it was his father wading through the crowd, breaking heads, so full of rage. And then with a shout he couldn't hear above the din, he threw himself through the air, his shoulder planted just below the man's hip and sending him sprawling into the dirt, a hand reaching down to take the club and the officer, still on his back, peddling away on his hands and feet, frantic, crab-like, trying to escape the fury all around, until a jagged line of blue appeared, slashing through the crowd to cover his retreat.

Andrew could not stop trembling even when Ruth wrapped her arms around him and he felt the long line of her body and heard the soft voice in his ear.

He thought he had abandoned war, but now realized he had not.

William spent most of the day searching for Andrew in Lincoln Park, and as darkness fell he traveled south and discovered what had happened there as he walked among the wounded and those preparing for the night ahead. He felt himself in the midst of an army on the move, the air filled with a familiar mix of urgency and fear as people armed themselves with rocks and bottles and passed around jars of Vaseline, gathering in small groups to talk in hushed tones that rose and fell in a pulse of fury and grim determination.

Beneath a long row of trees just south of the bandshell he came upon a group of men who resembled himself, middle-aged and dressed for the part, some with grey hair he could see even in the dim light, gathered around a small group of demonstrators.

"I'm just trying to understand," said one of them. "I fought in World War II. I went because that's what you do when the time comes. Your generation gets handed a war, you go fight it. If it doesn't, well, good for you."

He was looking at a young man shaking his head. "No."

"What do you mean 'no'?"

"I mean you don't go just because it's handed to you."

"The hell you don't. It's your duty to go."

"No," said the young man, "it's not. I don't kill people just because the President of the United States tells me to."

"It isn't just him. It's your *country*."

"I don't care. I won't do it. Whatever you call it, it comes out bullshit just the same."

A young woman made her way into the group.

"Lenny," she said, putting her hand on his arm, "we've gotta go. They're waiting for us at the fountain."

"Just a minute," he said, turning back to man.

"You think this is about fighting for your country," he said, "but it's not. It's about fighting for the rich and the powerful who've never been anywhere near a war. You think your war was about freedom and democracy? I'll tell you what it was about. It was about industrial powers fighting over markets, just like they did in World War I. And that's all this war is about, keeping the world safe for capitalism and profit. It's not my duty to go fight for that. Or yours, either."

"Oh, so you're a communist, is that it?"

Lenny shook his head. "It's not that simple."

"The hell it isn't," said the vet, turning away and coming face to face with William standing just behind.

"What're you looking at?"

William raised his palms in front of him. "Don't get mad at me. I was just listening."

"You one of them?"

"No."

"A vet?"

William nodded.

"Where?"

"North Africa. Italy. France."

"You seen it all, then."

"Enough," said William.

"So what do you think?" he said, jerking his thumb over his shoulder. "Is that what you fought for? What he said?"

"That's not what I thought then."

"No? And how about now?"

"I don't know."

"All I know," said the man, "is I don't know what kind of man thinks he gets to decide whether to fight or not. A bunch of cowards, if you ask me."

"Well," said William, "for cowards they sure seem ready to take a beating."

"Hunh," said the man with a shrug. "Got it coming if you ask me." And then he sighed and looked William in the eye. "So what're you doing here?"

"I'm looking for my son."

The man pulled back as if trying to bring small print into focus, then shook his head.

"Good luck, pal," he said and walked on down the path into the dark.

As night came over the city, marchers assembled on the grass along Columbus Boulevard, parallel to Michigan Avenue and separated by bridges spanning railroad tracks, blocked by National Guard troops, gas masks covering their faces. Leaders of the march began their parlay with the police, who at first seemed willing to allow the march to continue to the amphitheater. But after awhile the police said no and the crowd grew restless, feeling trapped. Suddenly, as if someone had parted a curtain to reveal what had been waiting to go on from the beginning, masses of police and troops surged forward and attacked through clouds of gas enveloping the park, clubbing their way forward, relentless and without restraint. Andrew and Ruth joined the crowd scattering in all directions before the assault, some seeking refuge at the fountain where they dipped their hands in the water to wash their faces and clear their eyes. On it went, the mass of people shifting one way and then another until suddenly an opening appeared at the Congress Street Bridge and thousands streamed across, tears pouring down their faces, some leaning over the railing to retch and vomit, struggling not to fall before the swiftly moving tide.

On the far side of the bridge the demonstrators came upon the strange sight of three ragged mule-drawn wagons. Word quickly spread of a contingent of the Southern Christian Leadership Conference's Poor People's March, led by none other than Ralph Abernathy, heir to Martin Luther King's leadership of the Civil Rights Movement. More than that, they had a permit to parade to the amphitheater, and so the crowd, now jubilant in the certainty they would be allowed to proceed, poured across the bridge to form on Michigan Avenue behind the little parade. On they came until more than 10,000 people ranged up and down the avenue.

William felt himself carried along, beyond hope of finding Andrew but compelled to be here regardless of what would come, feeling himself in the midst of some great unfolding truth giving birth to itself in this mass of people of which he was now a part, a truth he was helpless to comprehend beyond feeling its presence deep inside himself.

A tremendous cheer went up from the crowd as it began to move down the avenue beneath a dark blue sky, the stars pale against the lights of the city. Walking a block behind the front of the march, Andrew took Ruth's hand and leaned over and kissed her and joined in the swelling chant of *peace now! dump the hump!*

After two blocks the marchers came to a halt in the face of police massed on the corner of Balbo and Michigan, just above the Hilton Hotel. Grace climbed up on Lenny's shoulders for a better view.

"The wagons are gone," she called down, cupping her hands around her mouth. "I think they're splitting us up. Looks like we're going nowhere."

"So what the hell do we do now?" said Andrew.

Lenny shook his head, "Fucked again."

"I'm damned if I'm leaving," said Ruth. "I've had it with these little pricks."

"There are TV cameras on the Hilton," said Grace, then leaned forward over Lenny's head and screamed in the direction of the police, "Smile, you little fuckers, you're on *Candid Camera!*"

People laughed and she smiled down at them, softly patting the top of Lenny's head as if playing a bongo, and then, "Wait a minute," her hands suspended in the air as she stretched herself taller to get a better view, "something's happening."

Andrew looked up at her, trying to read her expression, then saw a smile spread slowly across her face. "Holy shit," she said.

"What—"

"Everybody's sitting down."

Like a wave moving up the avenue, the enormous crowd began to sit down on the street, the sidewalk, the fringes of the park. And then a new chant began, *hell no, we won't go!* filling the air with such a din, *hell no, we won't go!* again and again, that when Andrew looked up, the buildings seemed almost to tremble against the night.

A block to the north, William unconsciously began to mouth the words, then spoke them, softly at first and then as he became aware of his own voice, louder until he was tilting his head back and shouting them into the sky.

Down Balbo within sight of Michigan Avenue, the busloads of police arrived and quickly fanned out, removing badges and name tags from uniforms and sliding them into pockets as they formed ranks in the side streets running west from Michigan Avenue. The marchers had assumed the police would never attack them so close to the Hilton, but on this night they were wrong, as they quickly discovered when the police walked toward the avenue, then broke into a dead run and charged into the crowd, suddenly on every side at once, attacking from all directions and leaving the marchers with no place to go.

William couldn't take his eyes from the faces of the police as they hurled themselves into the mass of people, a look he'd seen before, many years ago, a look beyond frustration or rage, flowing from a deeper place where there dwelled the unbridled fury of annihilation that renders violence palpable, a wave moving through the air. Suddenly he saw before him the hardened ranks of the fathers making war upon the sons for daring to turn their backs on war, for refusing to accept the legacy of horror held out to them, and in that, laying bare the lie of adults dispensing wisdom and justice and telling the truth and watching over their children to keep them from harm, the age-old betrayal passed from one generation to the next. Until now, in this moment, on these streets, beneath this clear night sky concealing nothing.

The crowd heaved and tried to move around and past the onslaught and William followed the flow through an opening down a narrow street, and he was just turning a corner, screams filling the air, when he saw him running down the sidewalk, just in front of a cop pursuing him faster than his years and girth would otherwise allow, the club raised above his head, gathering momentum as it made little circles in the air, seeking out the fair head of William's remaining son. He took off after them, his feet pounding on the street. He saw Andrew reach back and take a woman's hand and in that tiny space of time, the man and the club bore down upon them, closing the gap, and as they turned to run, William knew the distance was too small to save them now. As his mind searched frantically for something to do, he suddenly saw the possibility of an aging soldier who had traded one uniform for another, and reaching down inside himself, he summoned his most commanding voice, "Soldier! Halt!"

And the blue helmet paused as if unable to help itself, the face beneath it turning to look back at the sound as Andrew and Ruth darted around a corner and were gone, the officer slowing his pace, his face puzzled, looking ahead and seeing the sidewalk empty in front of him and then turning to walk back to William.

"Son of a bitch," he said, holding his face in close to William's, looking into his eyes as he lifted the billy club into the air and brought it down and the sharp pain shooting up the side of William's head drove him to the ground, sinking to the earth and the darkness circling round, closing in, cradling him and softening the impact as he fell against the street.

Anne stayed up late into the night, the room dark as she watched the corner of Balbo and Michigan Avenue through the cameras mounted on the canopy over the main door into the Hilton. She saw the police charge into the crowd, pinning people against the wall of the Blackstone Hotel across the way, pushing them into the Hilton's plate glass windows which bowed and shattered from the weight, people tumbling inside with the police in hot pursuit.

And there was the sight she would never forget, the crowd facing off against the police, the chant defiant as it rose from them like a single voice,

The whole world is watching!

The whole world is watching!

She stared as the networks replayed again and again what would come to be known as the Massacre on Michigan Avenue.

Around three in the morning she went to bed but could not sleep. She got up at dawn and made a pot of coffee and wandered about the apartment, not knowing what to do. Just before noon the phone rang.

"It's me."

"Where are you?"

"In jail."

"Are you all right?"

"I think so. Just a headache."

"I saw what happened," she said. "It was incredible."

"I know."

"Did you find him?"

"I saw him. But he didn't see me."

"Do you think he's all right?"

"I don't know."

"Why are you in jail?"

"It's a long story. I'll tell you when I get home."

"Do you need me to come and get you out?"

"No. I'll be okay."

In the silence, each waited for the other to speak.

"You still there?" she said.

"Yes." A pause. "Anne."

"What?"

"I understand," he said.

"Understand what?"

"What you've been trying to tell me all these months. I understand it now."

Words crowded into her throat, but she couldn't let them out past the tears which he couldn't help but join with his own as he leaned into the wall, the phone cradled against his ear, head bowed down, face resting in his open hand.

That afternoon, in a hot and crowded courtroom, William pleaded guilty to a single count of disturbing the peace and paid the fine and then went home.

5

Just after Labor Day a letter arrived from Andrew, addressed to his mother and bearing a postmark from a small town in eastern Pennsylvania.

We were in Chicago and after that I knew I couldn't just run away. I have to do something that will make a difference.

I know I'm not turning out the way Dad wanted me to. You can tell him I believe I've always done what I was supposed to and I believe now that I'm supposed to do this. I've been thinking a lot about that, about duty and what people expect of me. For awhile I felt like an outlaw, like I was doing something wrong. And I thought people might suffer because I wasn't doing my duty. But then I thought of all the horrible things that have been done by men who were doing what they were told. Following orders. Isn't that what the Nazis did? And all the dead at Fredericksburg and Gettysburg and Shiloh and all those other places Dad knows so much about.

And Josh. He did his duty, too, but I don't see what good it did. So I'm thinking that saying no isn't such a bad thing after all. Maybe it's the right thing to do, if there is one.

We're coming east. I can't let you know why because I don't know what Dad will do. When it's over, I'll write again. I'm with someone. Her name is Ruth. I think you'd like her. I hope you'll get to meet her someday.

I wish it didn't have to be this way. I want you to know I remember what you said.

She showed it to William who read in silence, then laid it on the table and went outside to sit on the steps above the lawn.

"At least he doesn't seem to hate me," he said as she sat beside him.

"No."

"What is it that you said to him?"

"I told him to be a man."

Two days later Ben Koszinski called.

"I want to apologize for what I said. I went too far."

"Thank you."

William heard a sigh on the other end and looked at Anne sitting on the couch, staring up at him, her eyes wide.

"Koszinski?" she mouthed.

He nodded.

"Andrew is the main reason I called."

"I've seen him," said William.

"Where?"

"In Chicago."

"You were there?"

"Yes."

"Why?"

"Because my son is in trouble. I went to find him."

"But how did you know he'd be there?"

"I didn't."

"Did you speak to him?"

"No. There was too much going on. He was gone before he even saw me. Ben, please. If you know where he is, tell me."

There was a pause and then a muffled "Just a minute" that left William suspended over the phone, out of time, focusing on the thread connecting him to New York and to Andrew, straining to make out the muted conversation at the other end, floating above the sound, eyes closed, his head moving slowly up and down, and then the sound of Ben Koszinski coming back on the line, "Are you there?"

"Yes."

"They're in Boston. He plans to join other war resisters at a church that's offered asylum from the FBI. They know they'll be arrested, which is why they do it. To draw attention and make a statement against the war."

"When?"

"Tomorrow evening. Will you go?"

"Of course."

"You know what'll happen when they find out who he is."

"I think so."

"But you may not know how far they'll go to make an example of him and get him to change his mind. Once they've got him . . . they're very good at that sort of thing. I know. I've seen it. They'll say anything. They'll try to frighten him with prison and what can happen once he's locked inside. If that doesn't work, they'll shame him. They'll call him coward, pussy, queer, traitor. They'll use his brother against him. You don't know how effective they can be when they really want someone and have him all to themselves."

"I have some idea."

"Andrew knows what's true. But he's young and needs to hear it from you."

"Yes."

"I'll give you the address."

Late in the evening, Anne and William sat on the steps overlooking the great lawn.

"Will you go with me?" he said.

"I want to," she said, "but I don't think so. He knows how I feel. It's you he needs now. It's better if it's you."

William parked the car a few blocks from the small Unitarian church. There was a crowd outside and a television van. He walked down the sidewalk toward the church, past men in suits with FBI badges hanging from their pockets, leaning against a car and talking quietly among themselves, smoking and glancing at their watches.

As he walked into the vestibule, William saw a small crowd gathered inside, some sitting in pews, others standing nearby, huddled in earnest conversation. At the door he was met by a young man in a denim jacket, hair falling down over his shoulders, who looked William up and down.

"Can I help you?"

"I'm looking for Andrew Carson."

The young man looked at him for a moment. "And who are you?"

"I'm his father."

The man shook his head. "The best thing you can do is go home."

"Why is that?"

"Because it's hard enough as it is. He needs to focus."

"I came to help."

"He doesn't need your kind of help," the young man said, his voice rising on a sharp edge of anger that caused some in the crowd to turn and look.

"How would you know that?"

The man sniffed as he drew himself up straight.

"He's been here a couple of days. We know about you. It's fathers like you—"

"I have to see him," said William, his voice low and measured. "I'm going to start walking now, and whatever you do, well, that's up to you."

William stepped to the side only to be met by a wall of people filling in the aisle to block his path.

Outside the church, agents consulted their watches, threw down cigarettes, began walking slowly up the sidewalk.

"Let him through," said Andrew over the crowd.

A path opened down the aisle and when William saw his son appear at the other end, he stepped toward him, noticing the young woman beside him, her hand on his shoulder, and he saw the paleness in Andrew's face, his eyes narrowed like a boy in the moment of being confronted with something he had done. But there was something else that William had never seen before, just behind the fear.

284

As his father came near, Andrew was puzzled by the softness in his eyes.

"I've made up my mind, Dad."

"I know."

"Then why are you here?"

For a moment William was unable to think of what to say, and then, "I was in Chicago. That night. On Michigan Avenue. I saw you. I saw everything."

"Why were you in Chicago?"

"I came looking for you," said William, feeling the crowd around them leaning in to hear. "It has to stop. I thought it would end with me, but I was wrong. Now it has to end with Joshua," looking down, his lips moving in silence. "I don't want you to go. When you've killed for the first time, you'll know what I mean. But I don't want you to have to go through that to find out."

"But I'm not."

William shook his head, "Listen to me," his voice even and soft, the church still and quiet around them. "They'll try anything to scare you or shame you into going. But you mustn't give in. No matter what. I know I didn't teach you to be the kind of man you'll have to be now. But I was wrong. I'd go with you if I could, but they won't allow it. You'll have to find a way to imagine your mother and me there with you so you won't be alone and you won't forget who you are and what you have to do. Do you understand?"

Andrew searched his father's face, the eyes and cheeks sunk down, looking older than he remembered, and then saw him reach into his pocket.

"There's something I want you to have," said William, holding out his hand.

Andrew stared down at the little leather box and the name stamped in gold.

"But it's yours."

"I know," said his father, opening the box. "But I think it belongs to you now."

Andrew reached out and felt the weight of his father's hand, and the hand and the box and the Silver Star became one in his mind, inseparable, the body of his father.

"Take it."

Andrew lifted the medal from the box, the faded ribbon in his fingers, the star suspended in the air, and wrapped his hand around it, pressing it into his palm. And then he looked up and saw the tears rolling down his father's face and before either could say another word he was in his father's arms, and what began as a low, rumbling murmur went upward from the crowd as, behind them, the agents entered the vestibule and paused at the back of the church, their faces puzzled and unsure, thinking it was for them, the enormous sound, the whistling and the shouts, hands clapping and feet stomping against the floor, all flowing together as it swelled and rose to the high vault of the ceiling overhead and spilled over, filling the hall, rolling through the air like thunder.

With Gratitude

I am grateful to Annie Barrett, Kristin Flyntz, and Jeanne Bonaca for their loving, thoughtful readings of the manuscript at various stages in the writing, to Anne Batterson for timely infusions of courage and faith, and to Annalee Johnson for all the ways she has believed in this book and in me.

I am thankful to the following whose work informed the writing of the novel—Ken Burns, *The Civil War*; Bernard Fall, *Hell in a Very Small Place: The Siege of Dien Bien Phu*; Todd Gitlin, *The Sixties: Years of Hope, Days of Rage*; David Halberstam, *The Best and the Brightest*; Judith Lewis Herman, M.D., *Trauma and Recovery: The Aftermath of Violence—from Domestic Abuse to Political Terror*; Stanley Karnow, *Vietnam: A History*; Robert J. Lifton, M.D., *Home from the War: Learning from Vietnam Veterans*; James M. McPherson, *Battle Cry of Freedom: The Civil War Era*; John Schultz, *No One Was Killed: Documentation and Meditation: Convention Week, Chicago—August 1968*; Howard Zinn, *A People's History of the United States*; Jens Kohler for providing the German translation. Responsibility for how I have made use of their work is entirely my own.

To Nora L. Jamieson, my soul-companion on this long, eventful, and continuing journey, go my deepest gratitude and everlasting wonder at the mystery we set in motion so many years ago.

About the Author

Allan G. Johnson has worked on issues of gender, race, and social justice since receiving his PhD in sociology from the University of Michigan in 1972. His nonfiction books include *The Gender Knot: Unraveling Our Patriarchal Legacy* and *Privilege, Power, and Difference*. His work has been translated into several languages and is widely excerpted in anthologies. His first novel, *The First Thing and the Last*, a story of redemption and healing in the aftermath of domestic violence, was published in 2010. He shares his life with Nora L. Jamieson, a writer, healer, and gatherer of women. They live in the northwest hills of Connecticut.

For more on his work, visit his website at:

www.agjohnson.com

Photo by Paul Johnson

www.ingramcontent.com/pod-product-compliance
Lightning Source LLC
Chambersburg PA
CBHW051254210726
48287CB00002B/488